BEAUTY & THE BEAST
THE

FIRE AT SEA

ALSO AVAILABLE FROM TITAN BOOKS

Beauty & the Beast: Vendetta by Nancy Holder
Beauty & the Beast: Some Gave All by Nancy Holder

BEAUTY & THE BEAST

FIRE AT SEA

NANCY HOLDER

BASED ON THE SERIES CREATED BY RON KOSLOW
AND DEVELOPED BY SHERRI COOPER &
JENNIFER LEVIN

TITAN BOOKS

33614057622770

Beauty & the Beast: Fire at Sea
Print edition ISBN: 9781783292219
E-book edition ISBN: 9781783292226

Published by Titan Books
A division of Titan Publishing Group Ltd
144 Southwark St, London SE1 0UP

First edition: May 2016
10 9 8 7 6 5 4 3 2 1

A CIP catalogue record for this title is available from the British Library.

Printed and bound in the United States.

TITANBOOKS.COM

BEAUTY & THE BEAST &

FIRE AT SEA

From the moment we met
we knew our lives would never be the same.
He saved my life
and she saved mine.
We are destined.
but we know it won't be easy.
Even though we have every reason to stay apart
we'll risk it all to be together.

CHAPTER ONE

I wrote in blood…

Despite the horrendous din of Manhattan traffic on a Saturday night, Ravi Suresh was sure he detected the echo of approaching footsteps. Furtive. Quick. After him. Way too close.

And moving closer.

His chest tightened. He balled his hands in his suit pockets, centering the plastic box containing the tiny dot in his left palm. Tiny, yes, but lethal: What he had stolen from the lab was his masterpiece. He had put the finishing touches on Chip 262b, a super-weapon capable of reprogramming the launch codes of several kinds of nuclear weapons. And Anatoly Vodanyov was crazy if he thought Ravi was going to hand it over for a measly five million dollars. There was another player in town, someone who went by "Mr. Q," and he had offered *fifty* million.

That would buy Ravi a rajah's palace back in India. Hell, that would buy him half of Mumbai. He just had to get it to his new contact before Anatoly figured out that their deal was off. But someone was following him.

I have to find a place to park it until everything's arranged.

He craned his neck, peering upward at his destination—the Penzler Building, a towering edifice of glass, steel, and brick. Down below in the crush of nighttime humanity, he was too far away to see the guests, but he assumed the balmy May weather would have lured them onto the rooftop to admire the stupendous view. He remembered the first time he had walked into the rooftop garden of Chrysalis, his employer—and for now, the legal owner of the chip. The city of New York and all its riches had lain at his feet. "Welcome to the big leagues," his new boss Steven Lawrence had told him. "Succeed with the chip, and you can write your own ticket."

It had taken him a very short time to realize that that was a lie. He was an employee. The best "ticket" he could ever hope for was an enormous salary. But he would never share in the real value of the powerful technology he and others like him—the brains of these high-tech companies—would create for their masters. He had been hired, and he could be fired. Praised like some lap dog, criticized like a child. If he displeased one of them, a single phone call could ruin his career: *Suresh is a maverick; he's hard to deal with; he's a bad risk.*

Of course Chrysalis was going to sell it for an unbelievable sum. To the US government, so it was said. Was America any better than Vodanyov? Or than Mr. Q, his new buyer? And what about the next generation of the chip, and the one after that? All that money, and only a tiny fraction of it would trickle down into his pockets.

Mr. Q was getting an incredible deal at fifty million.

He squinted, imagining he could see the hot girl who waited for him up there. Heather Chandler was a babe. A charity gathering with her family—dinner, an open bar. Safe harbor? Probably not. But for now, this was his best bet. There were security guards, and his name was on a list. Whoever it was who was following him would not be on that list.

Barely able to breathe, he hurried toward the building.

CHAPTER TWO

"Well, here we go," Vincent said softly, giving Cat's hand a warm, reassuring squeeze as they exited the burnished metal elevator and faced the open double doors. "You sure you're up for this?"

"Mother's Day will never be my favorite day, but for once it's about something else," Cat replied, then added, "almost."

Vincent studied her face. She wondered if he was listening to her heartbeat, assessing her true mood. Both of them had lived with secrets for years, and they were still learning to share their deepest selves with each other. It was such a gift to be able to let someone in, and yet, still so new. What may have once felt like an invasion of privacy was now her new normal. Someone who cared about her was using his senses to see if she was all right, just as a fully human companion would attempt to read her body language. In the time they had spent together, they had already learned a lot about how they reacted to dozens of situations, triggers. And Mother's Day was definitely a trigger.

"Mother's Day *is* tough. I miss my mom too," he confided. "But I gotta say, my relationship with her was a lot less complicated than your relationship with your mom."

She felt a pang, as she always did, but it stung a little less than usual. She missed the mom she'd thought she had, as well as the "real" Dr. Vanessa Chandler. Like daughter, like mother: Secrets had forced her mother to keep her true self hidden. "My mother's relationship with you was complicated, too."

Cat's mother had been one of the lead doctors working on the Muirfield Project, a military operation created in order to turn Vincent and the other volunteers in his unit into super-soldiers. Believing that she was protecting innocent lives including Vincent's own, Vanessa and her team had injected everyone in his company with a serum that had transformed them into mindless predators whenever their adrenaline levels increased above a certain threshold. Beasts. Her experimental subjects had massacred an entire Afghani village, torn apart innocents. The Army had ordered that all the beasts be exterminated. Cat's mom had risked her life to save Vincent, and for her interference, she'd been gunned down in cold blood years later. Vincent had been forced into hiding for over a decade, and had only recently dared to resume a normal life.

A life that included his medical career... and their marriage. Sometimes Cat could hardly believe that they'd actually managed to have the wedding that had eluded them for months. And it was the fairytale ceremony they should have had all along, shared only with the people who mattered most to them—their best friends Tess and JT, and Cat's sister, Heather—in their own magical world of the rooftop of Cat's building.

Now *their* building.

"Dr. Keller! Mrs. Keller," a voice called. "We're so glad you could make it." A dark-haired woman seated at a black-draped table in front of the ballroom offered up two nametags. "Let me give you a lanyard, Mrs. Keller," she added, indicating the raw silk black jacket Vincent had bought her for Valentine's Day. "There's no way you should stick a pin through that gorgeous fabric."

Cat was wearing a sleek black pantsuit paired with the jacket. Steely gray pearl earrings, a gray and silver cuff bracelet, and gray silk kitten heels finished off her ensemble. Beside her, Vincent was model-handsome in a beautifully cut ebony suit and gray silk shirt open at the collar. Dark brows above his deep brown eyes matched his hair, which he had grown out a little, the way it had been when they had first met. It made him look younger. He would age slowly, so much more slowly than she.

Her heart skipped a beat at the thought.

"Are you sure you're okay?" he asked.

"I'm fine. Thanks," Cat said to the woman, as she took the tags with a smile. VINCENT KELLER, MD. CATHERINE KELLER. Call her a throwback, but she loved claiming his name, at least when she was acting as a private citizen. Tonight she was a doctor's wife, not a cop.

"May I do the honors, Dr. Keller?" Cat pinned the tag on his lapel.

"If you'll allow me, Mrs. Keller." His eyes gleamed and the dimples on either side of his mouth deepened as he draped the lanyard over her head like a Hawaiian flower lei. Then he brushed his mouth against her parted lips. A tingle worked its way up from the small of her back. *Later*, she promised herself, imagining themselves at home, in their bed, wrapped in each other's arms.

Hand in hand, they swept into the glittering ballroom located on the twenty-fourth floor of the Penzler Building. This was the New York General Hospital's Mother's Day dinner dance to benefit the planned expansion of the obstetrics wing. A slowly revolving mobile of golden cupids filled the enormous space above their heads. Gold and white banners proclaimed "HEALTHY HAPPY BABIES" and cherub-and- white-orchid centerpieces topped circular ivory tablecloths dressed with gold place settings. It was a spectacular effect.

Beyond the panorama windows, Central Park gleamed in miniature and the bright lights of the big city twinkled like stars that had landed on the earth. Below, a hundred dramas were playing out. Crimes were being committed.

I'm off duty, she reminded herself. *I am not a police force of one.*

"Vincent! Cat!" Cat's sister Heather called. Dressed in a scarlet satin mermaid gown, she approached with her arms crossed awkwardly over her chest, capping her shoulders. Halting, she gave Cat a once-over. "Wow, marriage certainly agrees with you, Cat. You look fantastic."

"And may I say the same," Cat replied. "I mean, about the fantastic part."

Last year Heather's ex-fiancé, Matthew, had dumped her via a text message, and Heather had only recently waded back into the dating pool. Cat was a little worried that she and her new boyfriend Ravi were moving too fast. Heather didn't know very much about him and she didn't understand most of what he said because he usually talked about his highly scientific work. Cat had to admit that he was super good-looking, and pleasant enough. So maybe if Heather took things lightly and just enjoyed his company, things would be okay. But Heather was already making comments that it took him forever to get back to her when she texted him. Also, he had forgotten one of their dates and Heather had wound up at the movies alone. Cat kept hoping for a heart-to-heart at Il Cantuccio about him, and she wondered if Heather kept putting her off because in her own heart, she knew Ravi wasn't a good prospect.

"Vincent, glad you and your lovely wife could make it," another voice said. Dr. Grillo, head of the ER, and Dr. Adams, the director of the hospital, paused en route to the other side of the room. "The more physicians in attendance, the better."

"Attending physicians, that's a good one, sir," Vincent said, and the three doctors shared a smile. The two bigwigs moved on, and Heather grimaced like a madwoman.

"Oh, my God, *look*," she whispered, lowering her arms. Streaks of tiny red bumps washed her collarbones and upper chest.

"You have a rash," Vincent said.

Heather rolled her eyes. "*Thank* you for that diagnosis. It's my new moisturizer, Cat. I washed it off but it was too late. Ravi's due any second and I look like I have leprosy!"

"Actually, you don't," Vincent offered. "Leprosy presents more like a dark brown—"

"Didn't you bring a wrap?" Cat asked.

"No." Heather's voice rose. "I was going to be late and I just jumped into a cab and…" She trailed off. "I can't let him see me like this!"

"Here." Cat snaked off her beloved new jacket and held it out to Heather. Then she grabbed it back and held it against her chest. "I won't catch her rash, will I?" she asked Vincent.

"Well, it depends," Vincent began, as Heather yanked it away from Cat and slipped it on.

"Hey," Cat protested.

"Thanks," Heather said. It shouldn't go with the dress, but on Heather, the combination was spectacular.

"Ravi at three o'clock," Vincent announced.

Heather turned her head. Her eyes widened. "Wow, just in time."

Ravi Suresh, PhD, was a lanky twenty-something from India, with lush blue-black hair that he wore in a topknot, deep-set hazel eyes, a sharp, angled jaw, and an accent that made women swoon. He saw Heather and gave her what was at best a half-hearted wave. Heather returned it with a bright, anxious smile, which was on no level reciprocated. Cat took note. Ravi was usually very warm and open, but tonight he trudged toward Heather with zero enthusiasm, his mouth set in a line and his brow furrowed. Maybe he'd had a rough day at work. He worked for Chrysalis, a high-tech firm, and even though he was one of their irreplaceable geniuses—according to Heather—Cat knew the pressure on him to produce results was enormous.

"Oh, hi, Ravi," Heather said shrilly, smoothing the black jacket in place.

"Good evening, Heather." His smile almost made it to his eyes as he pecked her on the cheek.

Heather shifted her weight. "This is my sister, Cat, and my brother-in-law Vincent Keller. Vincent is a doctor and Cat is a police detective."

Ravi's blossoming smile faded. He blinked. "Oh, really?"

"Yes. Really," Heather said.

Cat reminded herself that a lot of people were uncomfortable around cops. It was one of the drawbacks of the job. Still, it didn't endear him any more to her. She looked around. "Shall we find some seats? It looks like they're going to start serving dinner."

"Oh, boy, speeches," Vincent murmured.

"There's a nice table." Heather took Ravi's hand. Her sister was almost as nervous as Ravi, but in Heather's case, Cat knew why. For the Chandler women, Mother's Day was nearly as emotionally trying as their mother's birthday. Cat had been their mom's person, yes, but Vanessa had never seemed to have enough time for Heather. Cat had tried to fill that void, often crossing the line between big sister and surrogate mother during their growing-up years. Special days like this unleashed so many emotions in both the sisters that they rarely celebrated them. But in support of the cause, generous Heather had purchased two tickets.

The four sat near a floor-to-ceiling window. There were

other place settings at the table, but those seats had yet to be filled. Ravi lifted his water glass and gulped down the contents. Beads of sweat glistened on his forehead.

"Are you feeling all right?" Vincent asked him, and Ravi jerked as if he'd been shot.

"Fine. Very," he replied. "Just a hard day at work." He glanced around the room again. "I could use a drink."

"Oh, the bar's outside," Heather piped up. "I could—"

"Yes." Ravi pushed back his chair and stood. "Would you like something, Heather?"

"I'll go with you." Carefully holding the jacket shut, Heather rose. "Cat? Vincent?"

"I'm fine." Cat smiled at her sister.

"Me too," Vincent said.

With Heather leading the way, the younger couple disappeared into the crush. Cat turned to Vincent, who was frowning.

"Something's up with that guy," he said.

"I think so too."

"Great minds think alike. His heartbeat doubled when he heard that you're a cop."

"It freaked him out," she agreed. "But it freaks a lot of people out."

"Yeah, I get that." He shrugged. "Still…"

"Yes."

They both picked up their water glasses at the same time. Sipped at the same time. Put them back down in unison.

"Nothing came up on him on my background check," Cat reminded him. If Heather ever found out that Cat had vetted her date, she'd be furious.

"Just because you didn't find anything doesn't mean that there's nothing there."

"Yeah." But she was good at uncovering information others missed. Look at Vincent—she'd been the one to figure out that he wasn't dead, despite every official record under the sun asserting otherwise. "Let's keep an eye on him."

"Agreed."

She sighed. "Heather left a bride magazine on the breakfast bar this morning when she came over to get the keys."

"That's no good. Rubber chicken at five o'clock," Vincent announced. A waiter was heading their way with a plate in each hand.

"Ravi could be okay." She sat back slightly so the waiter could serve her. A mixed salad in a miniscule golden bowl. "But I don't think he's the one."

"Not the one," Vincent echoed. "Maybe I should pay him a little visit. Beast out and scare him off."

Cat smiled faintly. He'd never do it, but it was sweet to see how protective he was of her little sister.

"I'd do it, too," he said.

"I know." She grinned and covered his hand with hers. Then she made a face. "Oh, my God. You don't think he *gave* her that rash, do you?"

"Are these seats taken?" A quartet of newcomers approached their table—two couples attired in finery. Cat shook her head and made a welcoming gesture.

"Please," she said. "Those four are still up for grabs. I'm Catherine Keller. And this is my husband, Vincent."

"ER," Vincent said, half-rising to shake hands.

As they made their introductions, her anxiety about Heather receded into the background. She was here with her wonderful soul mate, the man for whom she had been destined. They had risked everything to be together, and they had triumphed. Together, they could handle anything. And they would.

"It didn't look like an STD," Vincent said under his breath.

The woman who had been about to sit down froze. "I beg your pardon?"

"Just shop talk," Cat said mildly. "My, this tomato looks tasty."

"He's probably dumping her right now," Vincent said. "Texting her while they're standing on line." Then he smiled at the newcomers. "No one here has an STD."

CHAPTER THREE

Tess Vargas flashed her biggest fake smile at her brother as she stood shoulder-to-shoulder beside JT Forbes and held out her hands for the drop. "I'm telling you, Jamie. We've got this," she said.

Her brother chewed the inside of his cheek, his "tell" that he was not quite committed to his decision. "You screw this up and you're dead."

No, you're *dead,* Tess thought. Despite the fact that her brother was a hardened NYC cop just like the other four, Jamie's wife ruled the roost. And the tawny little chihuahua struggling in her brother's arms was officially Connie's dog, not Jamie's.

"We won't screw up," Tess insisted. "It's one tiny dog."

"This is not just a dog. This is Princess Mochi," her brother shot back, nuzzling the dog's tiny face. She bared her fangs and snapped at him, and he jerked back his head.

"Um, I think she may be peeing on you," JT drawled.

Her brother swore under his breath and straightened his arms. Princess Mochi dangled above JT's marble floor. She yipped. Her teeth flashed and her bulbous dark eyes seemed to go red in the subdued lighting. Princess Mochi, right. Princess of Hell.

Tess took the dog from her brother and set her gently on the floor. Princess Mochi spun around and around in a circle like a windup toy and took off like a shot. Her tiny nails clicked on the stone.

"She just wants to inspect her new territory," Tess ventured. "You should take off. You're delaying the inevitable."

"No, seriously, I can't wait to go to Disney World with twelve of my closest in-laws," her brother grumped. "Did I mention that Connie's brother is on anti-psychotic medication?"

"Antidepressants," Tess corrected. "Give it a chance. You'll have fun."

"And her uncle spits wherever he feels like it and calls me Chachi?"

"That's better than dumbass, which is what I call you," Tess said. She pointed to the door. "Go. Get your ears on."

"If *anything* happens to Princess Mochi…" He wagged a finger at her. "I'm not kidding, Tess."

Like a mosquito, the chihuahua buzzed into Tess's line of vision. Whirring beside JT's sofa, she uttered chuffing noises and assumed a squat.

"No!" JT thundered, darting toward her. "No, bad dog!"

"She is not a bad dog. There are no bad dogs," Jamie said. "You need to tell her what you want."

"Oh, I'll tell her, believe me," JT said between clenched teeth.

"No hitting! Hit her and I will shoot you," Jamie said.

"Who beat whom at the shooting range?" JT reminded him. At a recent birthday party, JT had gotten pissed off at the way Tess's brothers were dissing her and scored well enough on a paper target to qualify for sergeant.

"Okay, we're done here." Tess flattened her hands on her brother's chest, turned him around, and pushed him toward the door.

"No hitting the dog," her brother said.

"None. Ever. JT would never hurt a fly."

"You have her feeding schedule. Her food. She needs two walks a day."

"Yes. Yes, yes, yes. *And if I didn't owe you for covering for me when I forgot Cousin Sal's birthday, someone else would be walking her. Like at a boarding facility.*

At the door, her brother turned back around. "Don't forget to brush her teeth before bedtime."

Brush her teeth? Oh, my God.

"No problem." She opened the door.

"Ouch! She bit me!" JT howled.

"You're upsetting her with this long, drawn-out goodbye," Tess told her brother.

"I love you, Mochi," Jamie sing-sang in a lovey-dovey voice. "Be good for Aunt Tess and Uncle JT!"

She firmly put him outside like a garbage can and shut the door in his face. Then she fell against it and sighed before heading across the room to assess the damage. Clutching Mochi against his chest, JT was staring in horror at his right arm.

Two tiny pinpricks stared back at him and Tess. Mentally she rolled her eyes. She loved JT, but she did not love his hypochondria. "Let me get the antiseptic."

"And the rabies shot," he grumped. "Remind me again why we're doing this."

"It's nothing. Like I told my brother, we've got it." She retrieved the first aid kit from behind the bar. And a bottle of Scotch.

"How long are we doing this?" JT asked.

"A week. We can do anything for a week."

"Hah. Trying holding your breath for seven days. Please hurry with a bandage. I'm bleeding all over the floor."

A flutter of nausea caught Tess off guard. It was one of many flutters she had experienced lately. *No, I can't be,* she thought, and an image of the unopened pregnancy test kit that she had bought yesterday flashed through her mind. The kind with the little stick you peed on, and then if a cross appeared in the little circle, it was positive.

"And for your information, I *would* hurt a fly. I've been known to beat up bad guys. I am very fierce."

"Yes, JT, you are fierce. And brave."

Much braver than Tess.

No way was she peeing on that stick.

CHAPTER FOUR

Something tells me that he's not nervous because he's going to propose, Heather thought, as she and Ravi *finally* snagged his gin and tonic and her appletini at the charity dinner's rooftop bar. The line was a mile long. Her rash was on fire. Ravi was looking everywhere except at her and while she'd had a lot of *bad* experiences with guys, that translated into a lot of experience, period, and she knew a brushoff when she saw one. She may as well face the truth now. Ravi just was not that into her.

Then suddenly he brightened, set his drink down on the edge of a burnished planter containing a miniature Italian cypress, and enfolded her in an embrace. She inhaled his spicy cologne with her sharp intake of breath and allowed herself to melt against him. So much for the brushoff and *hello* cuddling.

"Heather," he breathed. "Forgive me for seeming so preoccupied."

"You had a rough day at work." Her joyous words were muffled against his neck.

"That's no excuse for ignoring such a beautiful woman." He nibbled on her ear and gathered her up even closer. "I need to learn how to turn off."

On. You need to turn on. "I can help with that," she said huskily. Her mind traveled to where her body was already going, and she caught her lower lip between her teeth in sudden panic. Wait. How could she get naked with him? With this hideous rash?

"Um," she said. His hands were following the curves of her chest, and the fingertips of his right hand were dipping into the pocket of her jacket. They came back out as if he had realized he'd made a wrong turn.

Then he kissed her with such intense passion that her head swam. Just as she was getting into it, he released her. "We're out in public," he reminded her. "We should get back to the table, to your sister and her husband. You didn't mention that she was a cop."

"Why? Does it bother you?" Poor Cat; back in her dating years, she'd gotten dumped a lot because of her badge.

"In my country, police officers are rough. And corrupt." He smiled. "I'm sure your sister is very different."

Not as different as my brother-in-law, Heather thought impishly, sipping her appletini. They laced their fingers and headed back to the table. She wasn't certain her feet were connecting with the ground.

Maybe she could hide the rash with a good dollop of foundation.

Cat and Vincent were both gazing at the two of them intently; Heather couldn't help a rosy smile. Maybe Ravi was the one. Maybe all the elaborate wedding plans she had made first for herself and Matthew and then for Vincent and Cat wouldn't go to waste after all. Heather Suresh. Heather Chandler-Suresh. It had a nice ring to it.

A platinum ring. With a marquise-cut diamond.

"Chicken's getting cold," Vincent said with his mouth full. His tone was stern.

"It looks delicious." Heather gave her attention to Ravi

as he pulled out her chair for her. She sat back down as he pushed it back in.

"Oh, my phone just vibrated," Ravi said, patting the pocket of his beautifully cut black trousers. "I must have a text. Excuse me." He fished out a cell phone—not his usual one—and studied the display. His face fell. "Heather, I'm so sorry, but I have to go."

"Oh?" She frowned at him. "Is there something wrong?"

He grimaced and put the phone back in his pocket. "It's work. They need me to come back. An emergency. You know how it is."

Heather did, actually, and while it sucked that this was happening, she did understand. When he brushed his lips against her cheek, she flashed him an unconcerned smile.

"I'll make it up to you, I promise," he said.

"I know. Well, g'nite." She glanced over at Cat and Vincent, who were regarding him stonily. They looked like disapproving parents, and a little frisson of defensiveness played her spine like a xylophone.

"It was very nice to meet you both," Ravi said, and then he walked away. Heather watched him go, holding her breath and willing him to look back one last time at her. She had almost given up hope when he did turn, smiled, and mimicked holding a phone to his ear.

I'll call you.

She wiggled her fingers at him and took another sip of her drink. Then she set it down and folded her hands on the table.

"People *do* get called into work, you know," she ventured.

"No one texted him," Vincent said in an undervoice. "He didn't get a message."

"How...?" Heather began, but she knew: Vincent had used his beast sense. His hearing was better than, like, a dog's.

She finished her appletini in one gulp and picked up her wine glass just as a waiter filled it. White. Fine. She guzzled it down. Then she noticed the strangers at the table. "Good evening," she said dully. She scooted back her chair and slid her arms out of the jacket. Her hands were shaking.

"I'm going home." She rose and held the jacket out to her sister. "I'll be by tomorrow before you fly out."

"Heather, wait." The jacket bundled in her arms, Cat began to get up. Every instinct within Heather ignited full blast to let her sister comfort her. But if Cat did, Heather would start crying.

Heather shook her head. "No, it's okay, Cat. I-I'm just not in the mood for chicken, you know? It's just... oh, my God, do you know how much I spent on this dress?"

She winced at the bemused expressions on the faces of the other people at their table. She would not cry in front of strangers. She would save it for her couch and her half-gallon of Moose Tracks. And lots of Netflix.

As she moved away from the table, she heard Vincent say, "That is not an STD."

CHAPTER FIVE

Though he had a to-do list he should attend to, Vincent could barely keep his eyes off Catherine. As usual. She was so beautiful. In her stockinged feet and fluffy white bathrobe, she folded the jacket she had lent Heather with a sad little sigh. The *Sea Majesty*'s baggage service van was due in fifteen minutes and the jacket was the last thing left to put in her suitcase before she attached the TSA-approved lock.

Vincent had already completed his packing and was making last-minute notes for the charge nurse on his rotation at the hospital. Catherine had begun an email to Tess outlining her progress on a number of cases, and she'd vowed to finish it before she crawled in bed. He admired her work ethic and her dedication. They had both committed their lives to protecting others; it was no wonder they wrestled so hard with Homeland Security's insistence that they continue working cases involving innocents who had been experimented on, as well as other beasts. If there still were any other beasts or victims of experimentation.

Hopefully we're done with both.

He was tired at a bone-deep level. They'd been going

full-out for so long; this fifteen-day cruise to the Hawaiian Islands was a belated honeymoon, and he fully intended to relax, recharge, and devote all his time and attention to making sure Catherine did the same. He hadn't imagined that marriage would make him love her any more, but he couldn't deny that the bond between them had been strengthened the moment they had spoken their vows and exchanged rings. He felt connected to her in a way he could never hope to explain. They were each still individuals, yes, but there was an incredible *oneness* that he had never experienced before. It was magical, mystical.

Truly, they had been destined.

The buzzer sounded and Catherine pressed the intercom. It was the luggage service, a nice touch: their suitcases would be flown ahead to Los Angeles and transported to the *Sea Majesty*. Everything would be waiting for them in their stateroom when they came on board. One less thing to worry about.

Catherine buzzed the driver in and Vincent helped organize the luggage in the elevator. Catherine, Heather, and Tess had gone shopping last week for some "special items" that had been declared top secret.

I can't wait to see them. On her, he thought happily. As the elevator doors shut, he gathered Catherine in his arms. She nestled against him.

Then her cell phone trilled.

"You're on vacation," he reminded her.

"It's Heather." She took the call. He could hear every word, but tried not to. "Yes, of course," Catherine said. "Sure. Now? Okay."

She hung up. "She's coming over now. She's so upset," she said by way of explanation. "So she's just housesitting one night early."

"No problem." He was determined not to get sulky. He

could afford to be generous. He would have fifteen glorious days—and nights—on a cruise ship with his wife. It was kind of Heather to watch the apartment for them; it was a nice break for her as she currently had a roommate. A win-win.

"You're the best," Catherine said, and kissed his cheek. And then his mouth. And then his chest.

Plenty is never enough…

They moved to the couch. She was still kissing various parts of his body when Heather unlocked the front door and let loose with a shocked little squeal.

"I didn't see anything, I didn't," she cried, covering her eyes as she half-ran down the hall to where her bedroom used to be. "But next time, get a room for real, okay?"

The Kellers burst into giggles. Vincent scooped Cat up into his arms and carried her into their bedroom.

And locked the door.

Bathroom.
Pregnancy test.
Bathroom.
Pregnancy test.

Tess huffed and sat up in bed. Beside her, JT stirred but didn't waken. But across the room, Her Royal Highness lifted her head from her puffy pink velour monogrammed dog bed—"PM"—and destroyed Tess's eardrums with a piercing yip.

"What? What?" JT yelled, slamming into Tess as he attempted to scramble off the mattress. Tess grabbed hold of him.

"Easy. It's just the dog," Tess said.

Princess Mochi did not move as she yipped again. Tess's ears hurt. She pushed back the covers and put her feet on the floor.

"What do you want? Breakfast in bed?" Tess asked.

"Maybe she has to go out," JT said, fluffing up his pillow and lying back down. "You wake her, you walk her."

"We did not agree to that," Tess said. "And I didn't wake her up." Except maybe she had. And the dog had already had one accident on JT's floor.

And if she walked the dog, she wouldn't be able to take the test. A plus.

"Fine." She rose, threw on underwear, jeans, a bra, a T-shirt, and some flip-flops, pocketed her phone, and grabbed the pencil-thin pink rhinestone leash. Princess Mochi descended from her little pink cloud and sat beside Tess. Tess couldn't deny that she looked pretty cute—she was so teeny—and she chuckled as she attached the leash to Mochi's matching rhinestone collar. She picked up her phone—a habit that had become a necessity when she'd been promoted to precinct captain. Police business was now her business twenty-four seven. It was kind of like dog duty, actually.

Out the door they went, JT making a moaning sound in farewell. Tess checked her phone. Cat had texted *On our way!* with a picture of the two of them waving at her. Cat had a big fake hibiscus blossom tucked behind her ear. Sweet. She was so, so happy for her best friend. Cat and Vincent had been through hell and back and the bond between them was unbreakable. Not even dog-sitting could tear them apart. There was the whole he'll-live-longer situation to deal with, plus they were talking adoption for having kids, but they had a love that would conquer all. Even a chihuahua.

Mochi's entire pee output consisted of a teaspoon, but Tess decided to walk around the block anyway to make sure, and to clear her head. Speaking of crap, she had a lousy case to deal with when she got into work: The son of some friends of Chief Ward had been caught in a drug sting and they were calling in some kind of favor to get him off the hook. Tess was not a naïve rookie, but it galled her that she was expected to extend a courtesy to people she didn't know. For four years, she had broken laws to cover for Cat and Vincent, and her solid faith in the power of black-and-white, by-the-book police work had suffered many blows. She loved truth, justice, and the American way, to put it in JT terms. She felt so satisfied when the system worked. Proper detective procedure leading to a clean collar resulted in a fair verdict at trial. Period.

They're probably rich, Tess thought. *And he's some spoiled prep school kid who was doing this for kicks. And I'm supposed to put myself on the line because he burned his fingers.*

"Can I pet your doggie?"

A little girl in pink-and-white striped leggings and a fuzzy lavender top decorated with a winged fairy in a tutu tiptoed toward Mochi. She looked so cute that Tess couldn't help a smile.

"Better just look," Tess advised. "She's a biter."

But to her surprise, Mochi sat back on her haunches and silently looked up at the little girl with her big brown marble eyes. Tess tensed, about to warn the girl to steer clear again when the girl approached Mochi from the side and stroked her back. Mochi didn't move a muscle.

"It scares them when you pet their faces," the girl said. "So you do it here. Nicely pet, nicely pet," she said in a sparkle-fairy voice.

"Good to know," Tess replied.

"What's her name?" the girl asked.

"Princess Mochi."

The girl nodded. "That's a good name. That's what I would name her." She gave Mochi another couple of strokes. "I have to go." She gazed wistfully at the pup as she straightened. Mochi made a kind of distressed panting noise. "I wish I could have a dog."

"You probably will, someday," Tess said. *But be careful what you wish for.*

The girl kissed her own fingertips and then tapped Mochi on the head very lightly. Mochi licked her fingertips and hopped up on her hind legs like a scrawny petite bear cub. Tess gently tugged on the leash and Mochi came back to earth.

"Bye, bye, Princess Mochi," the little girl said.

"*Yip,*" Mochi replied.

The little girl waved at Tess and headed toward a four-story brownstone. Tess waved back.

Trying to go after her new admirer, Princess Mochi tugged on the leash. At the same time, Tess got a text from JT. *Hold on, coming to join you.* She smiled. That was sweet of him. Honestly, he hadn't wanted to dog-sit in the first place. He was only doing it for her.

But what if I'm pregnant? she thought. *What if we're having a kid?* Maybe it wouldn't be so bad, if the kid was like that little girl.

She called him. "Hi, don't bother. I'm on my way back."

"But you just left."

"A walk with a chihuahua is a short ride."

The tugging grew harder. Then Mochi erupted into a barrage of shrieks and barks. Tess looked up—straight into the face of a hulking, mean-looking mutt. Filthy, no collar, all teeth.

"Back off!" she shouted as Mochi launched herself at the dog. He growled and lunged and Tess hoisted Mochi into the air above her head. Mochi struggled and yodeled, nipping at Tess's wrists. "Get! Get!" Tess yelled.

Preparing to spring, the wild dog moved back on his haunches. Tess's mind sprang forward, weighing her options—either kicking at it or retreating. She saw stitches at urgent care at the end of either decision.

In a frenzy of pipsqueak barking, Mochi peed on her head. Tess roared in fury.

The dog backed off, turning tail and disappearing into an alley. Tess did the same, heading back to JT's place. Mochi had not shut up. Of course not a single New Yorker batted an eye.

JT was standing at the door when she marched up and thrust the crazed dog into his arms. Fuming, Tess stripped off her clothes and did not pass go. She stomped into the shower and washed her hair.

When she got out, wrapped in a towel, JT said, "Are you sure your brother gave us the right food? She just threw up."

"What?"

"Yeah. In your shoe." He pointed across the room. "Oh, whoops. Which she is now eating."

"*What?*" Tess ran barefoot to where Mochi was attacking her best black leather pump. The right shoe, in fact, of her *only* pair of black leather pumps. "No, stop! You filthy little *beast!*"

"Tess, look out!" JT cried.

Too late.

Tess stepped in Princess Mochi's vomit, slid, and landed hard on her butt. *Ow, ow, ow. Ass! Elbow!* She swore under her breath as the dog leaped out of reach, dragging Tess's shoe along with her.

I am never having children. Never, ever, ever, Tess vowed, as JT rushed to help her up.

But what if she was?

CHAPTER SIX

Still dressed in her sushi pajamas and drinking coffee, Heather looked around the empty living room of Cat and Vincent's apartment, which was flooded with daylight, and felt sorry for herself. There was nothing for her from her temporary employment agency and Cat and Vincent were off to Hawaii. Their itinerary was held in place on the refrigerator with a red heart magnet that she had bought them for Valentine's Day. She couldn't help her envy. They deserved to be happy. No one had been through more than they had. But it was hard to be left behind.

Ravi had phoned six times now, and texted at least a dozen. She was sorely tempted to call him back. But a woman had to keep her pride. Still, what if there was a reason he had lied to her face and ditched her at the charity dinner last night? A *good* reason?

Another text came in: *Heather, please take my call. Urgent!!!!*

"Yeah, what, are you horny?" she asked the phone.

The phone rang. Ashamed of herself for being so weak, she took it.

"Heather." He was breathless, as if he'd been running. "Please answer your door."

"My door?" She looked at Vincent and Cat's door. "Where are you?"

"At your apartment. I need to see you."

Yes, he's horny, she thought dismally. "Well, I'm not there," she snapped. "I slept somewhere else." Let him chew on that.

"Did you change your clothes?"

She frowned. "Huh?"

"Please, see me. Please. Oh, my God."

He was frightened. She blurted, "I'm at my sister's. I'm housesitting."

"Let me come over."

"I don't think so." She cut off the call. Looked at the phone. Almost called him back. *What the heck?*

She poured another cup of coffee and picked up the phone again. He'd been a butthead last night, and now this... this *weirdness.* Was he in trouble? That was *his* problem. She wasn't like Cat, throwing herself into oncoming traffic to save a slow pigeon. Wait, that wasn't fair. Cat wasn't like that. Heather's ex-therapist had suggested that Cat devoted herself to saving others because she had been unable to save their mom.

"And only three hundred and sixty-four more days until *next* Mother's Day, Dr. Freud," Heather said aloud.

Sunlight glinted on the phone. Heather kept her distance from it as if it were a rattlesnake. She drummed her fingers on the breakfast bar, sipped more coffee, and opened up the pantry. Wow. You could tell when people were trying to do too much when their spices were all jumbled up like this. Anise was lying on its side. Marjoram's cap wasn't even on all the way.

"Basil, cinnamon..." She stopped herself. Alphabetizing someone else's spices was too OCD even for her.

Laundry. If she knew her sister, Cat had made the bed with fresh sheets before they'd left for the airport. Heather checked the hamper and voila, there was the used set. Heather could wash them for her. She got out the laundry basket, the soap, and the fabric softener. It felt good to have something to do, a plan. Something other than wondering what was wrong with Ravi Suresh.

She added her pajamas and took what she'd intended to be a quick shower before she used up the hot water to do the wash, but in the middle of conditioning her hair, she'd indulged in a pity-party—she and Matthew had planned a honeymoon in Italy, and here she was instead in the city, housesitting, with another Mr. Wrong messing with her heart—

Was that the phone?

Who cares?

The shower sluiced away her tears. She toweled off and slid into jeans and a short-sleeved purple-and-black patterned top. Where on earth was she going to wear that mermaid dress again?

"There will be other obstetrics charity dinners," she promised herself aloud. She put on some makeup and twisted her hair into curls. Not that anybody was going to see her today. But still.

He sounded frightened.

Resolutely, she picked up the laundry basket and went back down the hall and into the kitchen. She picked up her phone. He *had* called back.

Boom, boom, boom.

That was the apartment's front door. The sound so startled her that she nearly dropped the basket.

Her heart thudding, she set down the laundry and peeked through the door's little peephole. She was shocked to see Ravi looking back at her, his tan face distorted by the fisheye lens. Oh God, how had he found Cat's apartment? Maybe he used a secret search protocol? Hijacked the GPS coordinates from her phone? JT would surely know…

Boom, boom, boom.

Heather jerked back from the door as he pounded on it with his fist. How did he get into the building's street entrance? Had she been dating a stalker maniac?

"Heather, please open the door," he said, loud enough for all the neighbors on the floor to hear.

A flush heated her cheeks. This was so embarrassing. Also, kind of flattering, but still.

"*Please.*"

No way was she going to let him in but her concern about the racket he was making—and her curiosity—got the better of her. She peered through the peephole again. There was pained desperation in his dark eyes. It looked like he was crying. The sight made her heart clench. Then familiar tender feelings welled up. Was he really sorry for what he'd done, how he had treated her? Did he want to make it up to her? Did he love her after all?

"Ravi, calm down," she said to him through the door. "I'm going to open it but I'm keeping it on the chain. You're scaring me."

When she turned the knob he pushed hard, making the door rush inward and the chain snap taut with a *thunk*.

"Heather, you've got to let me in." He pressed his face in the gap, his eyes pleading, his cheeks streaked with tears. He *had* been crying. Over her. "They almost caught me."

Not crying over her?

He sounded crazed and that scared her even more.

"Who? Ravi, what are you talking about?"

"I think they're in the…" He snapped his gaze to the right. "Oh, no…"

A hand appeared above his head and thick, stubby fingers gripped his topknot. Each finger had a blue-dark tattoo above the first knuckle. Ravi's eyes squeezed shut as the hand wedged his forehead, cheeks, and chin back into the narrow gap between the door and its frame.

"Open door," said a man's voice from the hall. He sounded like a Russian bad guy in a cartoon.

Heather couldn't move.

Ravi's head jerked a couple inches to the side and she saw the muzzle of a pistol pressed against his temple.

"Open door or I blow his brains out now."

She couldn't close the door—Ravi's face was blocking it, as was the toe of a shoe that was definitely not his. Ravi was a narrow Italian loafer kind of guy; the shoe in the door was a steel-toed boot.

She tried to unfasten the chain. It was impossible with the door ajar.

"I can't!" she cried. "Oh, my God, what do you want? Are you robbing us? I'll give you my purse!"

Get Cat, she thought, but Cat was gone. *Call the police.* But her cell phone was on the breakfast bar.

"One," the man said. "Two…"

"Wait, wait. I can't get the chain loose unless you move back," she said.

"No tricks," the man said. "I kill him then I kill you. Through door."

Where are Cat's neighbors? she thought. If she screamed— *If I scream, they'll shoot Ravi.*

It was more of a stumble than a decision when she stepped backwards, almost landing on her ass in the laundry basket. The chain went slack as Ravi and the boot were withdrawn.

For a fraction of a second Heather considered throwing her body against the door, but she wasn't sure she could actually close it with the counterweight of two bodies on the other side. So she whirled and raced for her cell phone. She got just three steps before she heard the chain splinter off the jamb and the door slam back against the wall behind her.

"You stop!" said the voice. "You stop now."

She turned. A thickset man in a dark blue windbreaker

and jeans bull-rushed Ravi into the apartment. He had a very tight crew cut, sandy brown hair almost shaved to the skin. Though he was shorter than Ravi, he easily controlled him with one hand in his hair and the other holding the pistol jammed against the side of his head. Eyes huge, Ravi was silently pleading with her. To do what?

As Heather staggered in reverse on weak knees, a third person entered the apartment. A blonde woman, late twenties. Tall, slender, dressed in fashion-forward black leather pants and a form-fitting black jacket, with a cross-body sleek metallic-gray messenger bag and heeled boots. Her blood-red nails and perfect manicure looked jarringly out of place wrapped around the grips of the ugly black handgun. The woman closed the door and locked it.

"What-what do you want?" Heather's words came out in a shrill prepubescent squeak.

"What is belong to us," the man said, shoving Ravi forward past her, forcing him to his knees in front of the sofa.

The woman waved the muzzle of her gun in Heather's face and then pointed it at a chair beside the dining table. Heather half-fell down into the chair.

"Put hands on lap," the blonde said. "Keep them there. Do not move."

The woman put her gun in the messenger bag—Heather lurched but realized the man could still shoot her—and grabbed up a pair of lavender latex gloves. She quickly pulled them on with a *thwack*. Then she trained her pistol on Ravi as the man also donned gloves.

Heather's pulse pounded in her head. There was only one reason for latex gloves: They didn't want to leave fingerprints behind. That was not good. So not good.

The room spun as the woman zip-tied Heather's hands to the back of the chair. For a second Heather was sure she was going to faint. Or throw up. She had to keep it together. If there was one thing she had learned from all of Cat's years as a cop, it was that you couldn't lose it. The people who gave up were the ones who wound up dead.

Plus all the other ones who did other wrong stuff…

Ravi looked over his shoulder at her with mournful puppy-dog eyes as his hands and feet were likewise bound with wide, white plastic straps. "I'm so sorry, Heather," he said in a choked voice. "I didn't mean to get you involved in this."

"But you did, didn't you?" she snapped back.

The short man laughed, apparently amused by her surprise and anger, and the depths of Ravi's betrayal.

The blonde's full mouth compressed into a thin, red-lipsticked line. *Disapproval?* Heather wondered. Yes, definitely disapproval. Perhaps a little nervous? Yes, almost twitchy. She looked like she could have been a model in her younger years. She had the figure and the face for it. Big blue eyes with a slight slant to them. High cheekbones. But there was nothing feminine or alluring about the way she handled the square-ended automatic. She knew what she was doing, and she had done it before.

"You will give it to us now," the man said to Ravi. "And we will forgive small inconwenience."

Yes, he was Russian and so was the woman. Heather looked at the kneeling Ravi and the man looming over him with a gun. How could someone so smart be so stupid to get caught up with the Russian mob?

"If you make us wait," the man went on, "give us trouble, it will be painful for you and her."

"Where is chip?" the woman asked. Unlike the man, her tone was not twistedly playful; it was businesslike and cold.

"I don't have it," Ravi said.

The woman glanced at the Russian man. "Where *is*?" she asked.

"I hid it."

The pistol in the man's hand arced down in a gray blur. Ravi let out a groan as his head snapped sideways from the impact. Heather could see blood trickling through his hair and onto the back of his shirt collar.

"Stop!" she cried. "What is going on?"

"You making me angry," the man said, once again twisting a hand in Ravi's hair. Ravi gasped.

"I parked it."

The pistol rose up again. Heather cringed. But before it came down Ravi blurted out, "I put it in the pocket of her black jacket at the party we went to last night. The left-hand pocket when she wasn't looking."

"*What*?" Heather cried.

"Where is jacket?" the woman said to Heather.

"It wasn't *my* jacket…" The admission just seemed to pop out of her mouth. She bit her lip. She didn't want Cat involved in this mess. She was on her honeymoon. Too late now.

"Who has jacket then?" the woman said.

Her sister and Vincent were en route to the other side of the country. Soon they would be on the other side of the world. For the moment at least they were out of reach, safe from harm. She wasn't. She realized if she didn't manage to survive she wouldn't be able to warn them about the danger they were in.

"It's my sister's," she confessed.

"Where is it?" the man said.

"She took it with her. I just borrowed it because, well… I have this awful rash and…" She looked down at her front. Her top had been yanked down when her hands were tied behind her back and the rash was visible. "See? I'm telling you the truth."

"Is STD," the man said, grimacing.

"I don't have—"

"Where is jacket?" the man said, cutting her off. He

stepped forward with gun raised to hit her as he had Ravi. The blonde moved between them and blocked his path. He could have stepped around her but he didn't try.

"Where is sister?" the woman said, turning back and staring hard into Heather's eyes.

"She bought the jacket for her trip. She's gone. This is her apartment. I'm housesitting until she comes back."

"This *her* apartment?" the man said, shaking his head.

He said something in Russian to the woman. To Heather it sounded like "Mush-bow-cratch-noz." Then he headed for the kitchen and the cute, fifties-style refrigerator. The door was decorated with magnets and family photos and a copy of Cat and Vincent's travel itinerary. The man found the itinerary and pulled it down, sending the heart-shaped magnet skittering across the floor. "Cruise to Hawaii?" he said, shaking the paper at her accusingly.

Heather didn't know how much to say, but she had to say something. "It's their honeymoon."

"Did you touch pocket of jacket?" the woman asked. "Put one thing in pocket? Take one thing out of pocket?"

"No, I didn't know anything was in there." She looked at Ravi and added, "He didn't tell me... anything."

"She didn't know," Ravi piped up. "She doesn't know about the deal..."

The man turned towards her and with obvious pleasure said, "Your boyfriend is liar and thief. And he is greedy. Five million of dollars not enough for him. And now he get five million of nothing. Chip very small, smaller than stamp, maybe in so small plastic case. You didn't find?"

"I didn't touch the pocket. It wasn't my jacket. It was new."

"Okay," the man said, "we search apartment. You don't move."

The two Russians left the room. Heather couldn't budge with her wrists attached to the chair back. Ravi, on the other hand, could have gotten to his feet and hopped to the front door, but apparently he wasn't brave enough to try.

They were left alone while the Russians ransacked Cat and Vincent's bedroom. She cringed when she heard glass breaking and presumably emptied drawers hitting the floor.

"I'm so sorry," Ravi said, trying to catch her gaze.

Heather looked away. Ravi was posed like a man about to be executed; she was tied to a chair. Tears rolled down her cheeks. She was a terrible judge of men. Always looking for Sir Lancelot and seeing him where he wasn't. This was the second guy who had put her life in jeopardy because he was a selfish bastard. Darius Bishop being the first.

As expected, the man and woman came back from the bedroom empty-handed.

"Jacket not here," the man said to her.

"My sister took it, I told you. To Hawaii with her."

"Look, you know where the chip is now," Ravi said. "You don't have to hurt us. We're telling you the truth."

"We know only where you *say* it is," the woman said.

"If chip where you say, we don't need you," the man said. "If sister has, we only need her." With that he quickly grabbed a fluffy pillow from the sofa with his free hand and jammed Ravi's head face down on the sofa cushion with it. The other hand held his pistol.

The blonde reached out to stop her partner, then let her arm drop as if she knew trying to restrain him was useless. A sadness flitted through her eyes; it was only there for an instant, but Heather saw it clearly. It made her look ten years older. Without a word she stepped into Heather's line of sight, blocking her view of the sofa.

"No, please!" Ravi cried into the cushion.

Muffled by a silencer, two gunshots fired.

Heather jolted on the chair at each one. Ears ringing, she began to shake uncontrollably. The plastic ties cut deeply into her wrists. It had happened so fast.

So fast.

Oh, my God, Ravi, she thought.

The smell of gun smoke and spilled blood filled the apartment and she gagged, on the verge of throwing up. She was sure they were going to kill her too. Leave the bodies for Cat and Vincent to find in a couple of weeks. Fearfully she looked up at the blonde woman. On her face was an expression of disgust. Heather could see how tightly she was holding the gun, so tight her knuckles were white from the strain. So as not to chip a nail, the woman took off the safety with the ball of her thumb. Heather wanted to pray, but she was so frightened she couldn't remember a single line of anything remotely religious. The harder she tried the farther away the words slipped.

The woman kept the pistol along the outside of her thigh, aimed at the floor as she turned to face the man. She said something in Russian in a tone that was unnervingly calm.

Blinking away her tears, Heather saw the man's face. It was bright red. Was he embarrassed? Ashamed? Or was it fury he was holding back? She tried not to look at the couch, but she couldn't help it. Ravi was no longer pressed face first into the cushion. He was slumped on his side on the floor in front of it, still bound hand and foot. He wasn't moving. The sofa cushion and seat back were soaked in glistening crimson, as was the underside of the pillow.

"He cheat my uncle," the man protested, speaking in English, as if he wanted Heather to understand why he had shot Ravi. "He have to pay."

"There is five million dollars on table. He could have copy of chip. From company Chrysalis," the woman argued.

The man shrugged, but his face turned redder.

She looked hard at Heather. "You know his work? You can get?"

Heather couldn't speak. She could only quake. The blonde stared down at Ravi and spoke in Russian again.

"Who cares?" the man said in English. "Cut him up in bathtub. Take him down to street in three suitcases." He smirked at Heather. "What, too messy? Take too long?" He pointed his gun at her. "We do the same to you."

The woman snapped at the man. She sounded like she hated him. The two went back and forth in Russian as Heather kept working to keep from losing it. Were they arguing about killing her? She was a witness. They knew she didn't have the chip. Her sister did.

"What's on roof?"

It took a moment for Heather to realize the woman was talking to her. "A little garden. Laundry." She didn't tell them that Vincent and Cat had gotten married up there. Flashes of memory sparked through her mind's eye of all the preparations for their impromptu wedding. How much fun it had been, and how joyful. She didn't want these people up there. *Ever.* She began to pant, and forced herself to take a deep, slow breath.

"Fence is on edge of roof?" the woman asked.

Heather shook her head, not following. "No. There is no fence."

The woman said something to the man. He raised his chin and sneered at her, then stomped back down the hall toward Cat and Vincent's bedroom. The way to the roof was through their window to the fire escape. Did they know that? Was he going to inspect the roof?

The woman took a knife from the wooden block in the kitchen and cut the ties on Ravi's wrists and ankles. She put the bloody scraps in her purse. There was blood on her purple gloves now. Blood everywhere.

The man returned with the duvet off Cat and Vincent's bed. It had been a wedding-shower gift that Cat hadn't been able to return when their first wedding had been called off. There had been no card attached to it. Heather had always thought it was from someone who had known either their mom or Cat's bio-dad, but hadn't come forward.

"Soak up blood," the man said, showing Heather the duvet.

When the woman stepped behind Heather with knife in hand, Heather's heart jumped into her throat. He was taunting her, frightening her on purpose. He didn't care what she saw and heard because she wasn't going to live long enough to pass any of it along. She tried desperately to see the woman's face, but couldn't turn her head far enough. *God, she's going to cut my throat.*

Instead, the woman cut the tie on her wrists.

"Get up," the woman said.

Heather couldn't move. The woman prodded her with the bloody fingertips of her glove. Ravi's blood was on her. Heather rose, and the woman fastened a new zip-tie around her wrists. She could barely feel it.

The man spread the duvet on the floor and pushed Ravi into it. Heather stifled a cry as his ruined face appeared, then was swiftly covered as the man rolled him up.

"You take us to roof now."

Heather watched the man roughly hoist Ravi's wrapped body over his shoulder. No way was she going to show them the fire escape route Cat and Vincent used. If she could make them go the normal way, down the hall to the interior staircase, someone might open a door a crack, see them, realize she was in trouble, and call the police.

The woman opened the front door, checked the corridor in both directions, then pulled Heather out by her arm. "Which way?"

Heather passed in front of the closed doors, hoping against hope. No one looked out. She led them up the narrow flight of stairs to the roof.

Since it was daytime the fairy lights weren't lit. The little table with two chairs, checkered tablecloth, and vase looked smaller; the rooftop itself looked grungier—covered with patches and irregular seams of asphalt. Cat and Vincent had gotten married in this secret garden under the stars surrounded by the lights of New York City. Heather knew that for her it would never again be a sanctuary and a place of happiness.

The woman peered over the edge, then said something to the man. He brought his burden next to her and they both looked down. Then she took off her bloody gloves, put on fresh ones, and dug through the layers of duvet to Ravi's feet. She took off his loafers and set them to one side on top of the wall.

And Heather knew in that moment what they had planned for Ravi. Her heart virtually stopped for a few beats. Her gorge rose. She had to stop this.

He's already dead, she reminded herself. *He couldn't have survived what they did to him.*

"You stay," she told Heather. "Do not move."

Heather couldn't stop her tears. She thought of Ravi's family. Cat had told her many things about her cases over the years, and she had gleaned a few tidbits. One of the strangest things she had ever heard was that people who committed suicide by jumping often first took off their shoes.

They already shot him.

But they weren't trying to kill him. They were trying to slow down the autopsy results, delay recognition of his identity.

Buy time to find Cat.

Heather watched in horror as they manhandled the limp body into position against the wall. They both bent down, each grabbing a leg behind the knee, and then lifted in unison, shoving Ravi's body off the roof head first.

Heather knew it was a long, straight fall to the alley below. She was grateful she couldn't hear the sound of the impact over the traffic noise.

The man began folding up the blood-stained duvet.

Am I next? she thought, weeping hard. *Oh, God, is this it?*

A rush of air brushed her neck as the woman came up quickly behind her. Before she could react she felt a short, sharp pain behind her right ear, and then she felt nothing at all.

CHAPTER SEVEN

Anatoly Vodanyov listened carefully as Ilya and Svetlana reported in. The two fell over each other's sentences as each attempted to one-up the other, currying Anatoly's favor. One was his nephew and one was his protégée. Svetlana was much smarter than Ilya, but Ilya was blood. On the other hand, Svetlana had talents that extended beyond murder and mayhem.

Anatoly was watching them on an iPad that Ilya had set on a cardboard box. One of Anatoly's many holding companies had signed the lease on this warehouse years ago. He didn't even remember what was in the cardboard boxes any more.

"So then we threw him over the side," Ilya informed him.

Anatoly nodded calmly, but inside, he was furious. Had they not even considered that Suresh could have gotten them another copy of the chip? It had taken Anatoly nearly a year to recruit Suresh to betray his employer. Suresh had been his only contact there. Mischa Stepanoff, the "mutual acquaintance" who had served as Anatoly's go-between with Suresh, had died ages ago. Anatoly had made it look like a drug overdose, but it had simply been a case of ensuring there were no loose ends where the chip was involved.

But now Anatoly suspected that Mischa had been the one to introduce Ravi to Mr. Q. He would never know. And these two idiots had ensured that the chip was lost to him—unless he managed to get the tiny plastic box away from a police detective on her honeymoon.

"None of the neighbors saw her leave," he said to them.

"I propped her up between us in the car. No one could tell there was anything wrong. She looked completely fine," Svetlana assured him. Svetlana was upset. Good. At least she understood what a debacle this was. Ilya, on the other hand…

Oh, Ilya. What should he do with his sister's idiot son?

"Suresh was so stupid," Anatoly grunted in Russian as Ilya and Svetlana dragged the weeping girl over to a chair and began to attach her to it. Anatoly liked zip-ties. No knots.

"Please, please, let me go," the girl sobbed. Her makeup was smeared all over her face. She looked like Heath Ledger as the Joker. Anatoly couldn't help a smile. Good movie. But truly, had she looked like this on the drive over? He wouldn't call that fine.

"I haven't done anything. There's nothing I can do to help you," the girl blubbered.

And you're just as stupid as Suresh, if you think that, he thought.

Ilya bound her wrists together with a plastic zip-tie and anchored them in her lap, forcing her to hunch her shoulders. Soon she would be begging them to unbind her. At that point, she would find ways to be helpful. Many ways. In his mind's eye, he saw himself cutting a Joker smile into her face with a serrated hunting knife. A burst of rage coursed through his veins, but he quickly suppressed it. His fury lurked beneath the surface like a shark, always, but he was its master. He remembered what he had once said to a different American prisoner: "We Russians are like you. We laugh, we cry. But then we grow up."

That man had died weeping.

This girl would too.

"I didn't know he put anything in the jacket," she sobbed. "I barely knew him!"

She was smart enough to talk directly to him, although she couldn't see him, of course. The iPad was programmed for one view only: He could see all of them, but the reverse was not true. She also couldn't see the rat that skittered across the dirty concrete floor behind her, six inches from her feet.

In Russian, Anatoly said to Ilya, "She was there when you killed Suresh?"

"Saw the whole thing," Ilya confirmed, also in Russian. "Shouldn't we just kill her now?"

"Show me the cruise itinerary again."

Ilya held the paper up to the iPad's camera. It was spattered with Suresh's blood, but still legible. Dr. and Mrs. Keller were spending the night in Los Angeles before boarding the *Sea Majesty* for a fifteen-day cruise. There would be five straight days at sea. Day six would see them in Hilo, Hawaii.

He put the iPad on mute, pulled out his cell phone, and dialed in a number. It was answered on the first ring.

"*Da,*" a voice answered.

"An American couple is staying at this hotel," Anatoly said, reading the address off the page. "Their names are Catherine and Vincent Keller. Madame owns a black silk jacket, and in that jacket is a small plastic box that belongs to me. Get it. If you need to kill them to retrieve my possession, do it."

The voice on the other end of the phone assured Anatoly that it would be handled as discreetly as possible, and that he would be informed the moment that the mission was accomplished.

"Of course," Anatoly said, and disconnected. He turned the sound back on.

Ilya and Svetlana had finished tying up the girl. They

stood back, framing her as if inviting him to admire their handiwork. Ankles tied to the chair, wrists bound, face smeared with color, she looked like a silly clown, a silly repulsive clown. She looked like she would sink like a stone if they threw her in the Hudson.

"My sister is a cop," she said between hitching sobs. "If you don't let me go, the entire New York City police force will come looking for me. And they-they'll find me."

See? Americans were so childlike.

He cocked his head. "Do you by chance speak Russian?" he asked her directly, in English.

"What? No. No, I don't." She hesitated as if trying to decide if her lack of knowledge was good or bad. "So whatever they said to each other, I couldn't understand them. Okay? Honest. I don't know anything about any of you."

"Except that they killed your boyfriend."

"He wasn't my boyfriend. We'd just started dating. Oh, God, please, please let me go," she cried. "I don't know who you are. Your names, nothing. I can't identify you."

"You're so helpful," he said. "Listen, Heather Chandler. You may be able to save your own life. As you know, your sister has something that belongs to me. It may come to a trade, you for it. You will need to be able to speak to your sister. But you cannot do that if you are dead. And my two friends there will kill you if you try to escape. Do you understand? They will not hesitate."

"Okay." She nodded, pulling herself together with a sniffle. "Okay, I understand." She nodded like a bobblehead toy.

"So do I have your word that you will not try to escape?"

"Yes." She sounded almost eager to sign her own death certificate. Surely she must understand that he could never let her live. If her sister was foolish enough to agree to the trade, they would still kill her. More quickly, maybe, but where was the fun in that?

I must not give in to my emotions, he reminded himself. *They are a sign of weakness. Look at her, so hysterical. A disgusting display.*

"Svetlana, knock her out," he told his beautiful one in Russian. "It's tiresome, *da*? All the tears."

"Poor thing," Ilya chirruped.

Svetlana glared at Ilya, then flashed Anatoly a sour smile, pulled her gun from her jacket, and clubbed the girl over the head with it. Heather Chandler's face fell forward.

"Put her in the cell," he said to them both.

He watched as Ilya and Svetlana picked up the chair together and shuffled off to the left. Out of his line of sight, he heard the squeal of the cell door. There was a thud. A giggle. And then a clang.

Ilya and Svetlana reappeared. Ilya was grinning like a naughty little boy. Svetlana's lips were pursed in silent disapproval.

"Done," Ilya announced.

"Ilya, what did you do?" Anatoly prodded.

"Her chair tipped over when we set it down," he said. "We left it that way."

Anatoly pictured the rat. And then her face. Where there was one rat, there were others. He tried to decide if a group of rats could chew enough of her face off to kill her before he would need her to speak to her sister. *If* he needed her at all.

Better safe than sorry.

"Put her chair upright," he said. Ilya's face fell. "Ilya, do as I say."

"I'll do it," Svetlana announced.

She marched out of his visual range; while she was gone, Ilya pouted. "It was Svetlana's fault that we knocked the chair over. And she was the one who made such a mess when we killed Suresh."

Anatoly was a bit alarmed. Not a lot. But some. "There

was a mess?" This was a detail both of them had omitted.

"A lot of blood," Ilya said. "She shot him on their sofa. We didn't have much time for cleanup."

"And this was her fault."

"Head wounds are bloody."

"And she was the one who shot him."

Ilya reddened. "She'll say I did it."

Anatoly realized with a shock that his nephew was lying to him. *Ilya* had done it. Was he so stupid that he thought his uncle wouldn't see through this falsehood? Why even bother? What did he hope to gain?

Ilya was so immature. Thank God for Svetlana. A scrawny little child when he had taken her off the streets. A woman now. His woman. Or one of them, anyway. A man in his position must protect himself with redundancy. He must have backups everywhere. He could not rely on one particular hit man. Love one specific woman.

Trust one particular relative.

"Was there a blood trail to the van?" Anatoly asked. Ilya shook his head, but uncertainty blazed in the younger man's eyes. Anatoly couldn't help another attack of anger. It didn't show on his face but he dug his fingers into his palms to maintain control. Emotion was always weakness.

"Torch the car," Anatoly said. "Then junk it."

His phone rang. He muted the iPad and looked at the ID. It was the man he had called in Los Angeles.

The voice on the other end said, "We've got someone headed for the Kellers' hotel now."

Anatoly huffed. "Don't bother me with the details. Just let me know when it is done."

"*Da*, Anatoly."

Anatoly hung up. *I am surrounded by idiots.*

And idiots can be dangerous.

CHAPTER EIGHT

The moon cast ripples of silver on the easy, cresting waves of the Pacific Ocean. Sea foam bubbled onto the warm sand. It was a night straight out of the pictures from the tour brochure Catherine had downloaded.

"This was a wonderful idea," Cat said as she and Vincent strolled barefoot along the beach. Catherine's strappy sandals were dangling from Vincent's fingers and her faux hibiscus flower was nestled behind his ear. The Pacific was chillier than either of them had expected, but the evening air was balmy and smelled of honeysuckle and star jasmine. They had flown into Los Angeles the night before the cruise and were enjoying a luxurious stay at a Spanish Colonial-style hotel in a part of Los Angeles called Playa del Rey, dining on fresh swordfish and mango salsa. Two margaritas later, they were kissing under the palms, already under the sway of their romantic getaway.

"This is so perfect," she murmured as they finished one kiss and began another. "I hope everything is all right back home. Heather didn't answer my text—"

"No," Vincent said firmly. "No texting, no Wi-Fi. There's a reason you left your phone on the nightstand, remember?"

"Yes." She smiled lovingly up at him. "And he's standing right here."

"I love you," he whispered. "I can't even tell you how much."

"Then why don't you show me?" she asked huskily. "Back in our room?"

"You don't need to ask me twice."

They turned around, passing through an arch of bougainvillea illuminated by flickering torches with their arms around each other. A distant guitar played a sensuous Spanish melody.

They bypassed the elevator and climbed the stone stairway together. Each riser was decorated with a matching row of colorful tiles. Then they were at their door, which was made of wood and ornately carved.

And hanging open.

They looked at each other. No phones. No gun. She left it to Vincent to go first. If there was trouble, he could beast out.

Their single overnight bag lay on its side, and all the contents were strewn on the mattress. Cat's surprise sheer black nightgown lay on the floor. The drawers to their nightstand were open, the dresser as well. They didn't touch any of it as they moved across the room. The sliding glass door to their balcony was open too. They looked down, scanning the palms and purple jacaranda trees surrounding a tile fountain where a few guests were drinking at wrought-iron tables beneath colorful umbrellas.

Nothing.

"Do we call the front desk?" Vincent asked.

Cat knew what he was asking: *Do you think this is something we need to keep off the books?* Something beast-related? Liam, the ancient beast who had killed their ancestors Rebecca and Alastair, was dead, and as far as they knew, all Julianna's human-enhancing experiments employed to combat him had been accounted for.

Cat assessed their options. "If they're thieves, they may be hitting other rooms right now. Innocents may be at risk."

"We could take them on ourselves."

"We'd have to explain a lot. Unless we know for sure that someone is being hurt, we should let the local authorities handle it," Cat suggested.

Vincent nodded. "Then we call."

"Agreed. We call."

They both rushed back inside and Vincent picked up the room phone. He asked for the manager while Cat studied the debris field and went through a mental list of what they'd packed. Nothing appeared to be missing. Even her phone was still there, thank goodness, plugged into the wall socket behind the nightstand to charge.

In just a few moments, the manager arrived with the hotel's head of security. By then the hotel had learned that several other rooms had been tossed, and some jewelry and cash had been stolen. Cat and Vincent were escorted to another room—a palatial suite, in fact—so that the LAPD could secure their original lodgings and dust for prints. Luckily they weren't asked to surrender their belongings. Cat and Vincent agreed to the move so that they could do some private sleuthing on their own, but the other guests who had been burgled were insisting on being relocated to other hotels.

"We're so very sorry about this," the manager said anxiously. "I don't understand how it could have happened, but please be assured that we've doubled security and the police are on their way. If you discover that something *is* missing, please let us know immediately." His face was pale. "It would be a good idea to contact your credit card companies as well. Even if the thieves didn't take the physical cards, they may have cloned them."

"Thank you. I'm a detective with the NYPD. If I can be of assistance, please let me know," Cat said. She knew she had no clout in California but her cop brain compelled her to ask as many questions as he would answer. "You must have security cameras."

"Oh, yes. Of course we do."

I wish we could see the footage, Cat thought.

"And you're examining the key locks for hacking." They had been in possession of both their key cards when their room had been tossed.

"Yes. Everything is being handled."

"I suppose you have a list of all the victims and what was taken."

His smile was tight. "Please, Ms. Keller, I assure you, we have the entire situation under control."

Not really, she thought. But she kept her own counsel. He wasn't going to give her anything to work with. Maybe he was afraid they were going to sue him.

"Please just enjoy the suite with our compliments," he continued. "Of course there will be no charge. For anything."

"Have you—" she pressed, but Vincent put his arm around her and gave her a squeeze.

"Thank you," Vincent said. He walked the man to the door. The manager left and Vincent closed it quickly. He waited a few beats, then opened it again.

"Did you get the thief's scent in our room?" Cat asked him, and he nodded.

"*Their* scents. There were two of them. A man and a woman. They went through everything, as if they were looking for something to take."

Again she felt the sting of an insult. "We have nice stuff."

"This is a really high-end hotel," he reminded her. Then he flashed her a grin. "I've got my job back. Be patient and we'll amass a bunch of stuff worth stealing. Next time, they'll take *everything.*" Before she could respond, he added, "I'm going to track their route."

"I'll go with you."

He held up a hand. "No offense, Catherine, but you don't have a gun and I can move faster if I'm on my own."

She knew that was true. It frustrated her to agree to stay behind, but she acquiesced with a nod and a kiss. He blurred, increasing his speed to a point where the human eye could not detect his presence. No one would even realize he'd left their room. Her own parents had altered his DNA to the point where he was something new and different, a human-beast hybrid whose chemistry and physiology would fascinate a company like the one Ravi Suresh worked for. They'd have to be careful around him if he remained in Heather's life.

I hope Heather kicked him to the curb. I don't trust him.

She got out her sexy sheer nightgown, then shook her head. How many times had she gone to the scene of a B&E and the victims had told them how violated they'd felt? She couldn't put this nightgown on now. Besides, Vincent had already seen it. Lucky thing she had lots more sexy lingerie for the cruise.

As a cop, she was lunging at the leash to find the perps and arrest them. But as a brand new wife, she wanted to end this night on a much higher note. Maybe the hotel gift shop was still open. Finding a replacement nightgown would give her something to do, at least, and maybe the thieves had attempted to rob the shop as well. She might be able to get some information from the clerk.

She called their credit card companies and put alerts on their cards. Then she made sure she had the room key and scrawled a message to Vincent on the hotel notepad. She placed it beside the nightstand and this time she took her phone. She thought about calling Tess but just as quickly nixed the impulse. Tess was not expecting her to stay in touch. Tess and JT had given Vincent and Cat express orders not to include them on their honeymoon. It was for the two of them, not the four—or the five, if you included Heather. They weren't supposed to include anyone.

"So, Tess," Cat said to the phone without placing the call. "We're having a pretty crazy first night."

All Cat found in the gift shop was a pricey gold lamé bikini, which she decided to buy because never in a million years would Vincent expect her to own one, and it was Just. So. Hollywood.

"Did you hear about the burglaries?" she asked the clerk as she verified the purchase because of the fraud alert. "My husband and I had our room broken into."

The woman's eyes widened. "And you're the honeymooners," she said. "I'm so sorry." She leaned forward. "Mitchell Samosa's room was hit. You know, the actor."

Cat knew who he was—a really hot young star. He'd also just gotten married. In fact, he'd been married less time than Vincent and her.

"Was he here on a delayed honeymoon too?" she asked the clerk.

The woman leaned forward even closer. She looked left, then right. "No," she said in an undervoice. "But he wasn't here by himself." Cat stared at her. "Makeup girl," she whispered.

Cat was scandalized. The woman nodded, pleased to have made an impression.

"Do you think this might have been a retaliatory act?" Cat asked. The woman frowned, not following. "Do you think someone was trying to publicize his indiscretion? Tossing his room, getting it into the news that he was here with someone besides his wife?"

"That might be," the clerk said, thinking it through. "But George the security guard told me that nothing was taken. It would have been stickier if something had been. Insurance report, police. But nothing. We already put the two of them in cabs and sent them on their way. Two different ways. So much for *that*."

Cat nodded. In a perverse way, she felt a little better that her own stuff had been overlooked.

"Don't tell anyone I told you about it," the clerk requested. "I'd lose my job. So would George."

"No worries." Cat smiled. "Your secret is safe with me."

As she left the shop, the woman put the CLOSED sign up. Cat was about to take the stairs when she had the strangest sensation that she was being watched. Call it years on the job or simple intuition, but she was sure someone was lurking nearby.

The shadow of a palm tree afforded her cover as she took herself out of view. She turned on the video portion of her phone and panned it as steadily as possible as she performed a visual scan of the stairway.

"Catherine, it's me," Vincent said, and she stepped away from the palm tree.

"Any luck?"

"The thieves left together in one car. There were tire tracks. I'm sure the police will take prints. And *yes*, I took pictures of the tracks with my phone." He grinned at her. "What were you up to? You can take the cop out of New York City…"

"Just making a small purchase." She rattled her bag. "Which I will now model for you if you'd like."

He tried to peek in the bag. She gave him a little bat.

"I would like," he said.

When they got to their room, she put it on. He was about to take it off of her when an expensive bottle of champagne and a large bouquet of roses arrived—Vincent had planned ahead, but it had taken the hotel staff some time to locate their switched room—as well as an elaborate fruit and cheese basket and vouchers for massages, courtesy of the apologetic management. They filled up their two-person in-room whirlpool tub with bubble bath while Vincent popped the cork and Cat arranged a platter of delicacies and placed them within reach of the frothing bubbles.

"They could have at least taken my phone," Cat said as she slid into the churning water. "It's practically brand new."

"We shouldn't look a gift horse in the mouth," Vincent argued. "If they had taken something, we'd probably be making statements to the police instead of drinking champagne and eating strawberries naked."

"I wonder if any of the other guests who moved are shipmates of ours." She had already shared the gossip about Mitchell Samosa with him. "What a way to start a vacation, you know? It's like we're crime magnets or something." Cat popped a pineapple chunk into Vincent's mouth. He chewed appreciatively. "I'm *so* glad we shipped our bags ahead. What a mess *that* would have been."

"Luck's on our side. For people whose stuff gets manhandled."

They clinked champagne glasses and luxuriated.

CHAPTER NINE

Anatoly pinched the bridge of his nose hard to keep from launching into a barrage of Russian swear words and screaming at the top of his lungs.

"What do you mean, you didn't find it?" he said into the phone. "She packed the jacket." He had a thought. "Was she wearing it?"

"No. We had a tail on them. They had dinner and walked down by the beach. She didn't have on the jacket."

"Then it had to be in her room," he said through clenched teeth. *Unless she lost it. Or someone else got to it before we did.* Suresh had had another buyer but Anatoly had no idea who "Mr. Q" was. Could it be that this mysterious rival had already tracked down the chip? *Did Suresh tell him about the jacket?* The pieces didn't quite fit.

"We tossed her room, and several others to make it look like a random crime of opportunity. The hotel moved them. She went to the gift shop but he stayed in the room. But Anatoly, we looked through everything they had."

What if she had misplaced it? It was possible, if she was even half as stupid as her sister.

"Check the lost and found of the hotel and the restaurant.

Search the beach. Call me back in half an hour."

He disconnected and phoned Svetlana in New York. It was two a.m. there. Seven a.m. in London, where he was.

"*Da*," she said sleepily.

"Wake up the girl. Make absolutely certain that her sister packed the jacket. I don't care what you do to her. Make sure she's telling you the truth."

"*Da*, Anatoly." She sounded more awake now. Good girl. Good smart girl. "Do you want me to get Ilya?"

"*Nyet*. This you can do on your own." He was throwing her a bone, allowing her to show some initiative while at the same time giving her a break from his nephew. He hoped she appreciated it. "Call me back when you have something concrete."

He hung up.

Heather gasped as ice water hit her in the face. Her hair, face, and front were drenched and as she sputtered, a harsh white light blinded her. When she jerked against the zip-ties, needle-sharp pains sliced through the numbness in her arms and legs. She choked back a cry of agony and fought not to panic.

"Hello." The light receded and as Heather blinked, the figure holding the flashlight wobbled into focus. It was the Russian woman. Svetlana. She was wearing a sweatshirt and black leggings, and her hair was pulled back. She wore no makeup and Heather was surprised to see how young she looked. Her age, maybe. And naturally pretty. Heather was in some kind of cell, like in a prison, with vertical metal bars. She could see stacks of boxes. Something stank like sewer water. A creature chittered in the dark.

Rat, she thought, gooseflesh rising along her arms. She tried to lift her legs off the ground but they were restrained against the chair.

"Please untie me," Heather said. "This hurts so much and

I've already sworn I won't run away."

"Shut up." Svetlana aimed the flashlight in her eyes again. "Now, listen. Where is jacket? Your sister does not have. We have sent new people back to apartment. If they find, I shoot you. Through your eye. For lies."

"*What?*" Heather cried. "Are you kidding?"

Her answer was a sharp slap across her face. Her head snapped back. Yellow dots exploded behind her eyelids and she heaved, sick to her stomach. Svetlana threw more water at her. Heather was so dizzy that for a moment she thought she'd fallen sideways again.

"Do I seem joking? Where is jacket?"

"She said she was going to pack it!" Heather cried. "We were talking about it because she was worried about getting my rash, and Vincent told her it was fine. If she left it behind I'm sorry! I had it but I gave it back to her!"

"You were Suresh girlfriend. He tell you about chip."

"No!" She winced, pain and fear firing every synapse. She was shaking so hard her ribs ached as if they would crack. She didn't want to know about any of this. The less she knew, the better. If she knew too much, they'd kill her.

"Wait," she said, as Svetlana prepared to hit her again. "*Wait.* She *packed* it. Of course she doesn't have it." She heard herself. She had one more chance not to lead these people to Cat. But Cat was her only hope, her lifeline. And there was Vincent, her beast brother-in-law. He'd tear these people apart—literally—if they came after him and Cat.

"What you are saying?" Svetlana demanded. "Packing is in suitcase! Suitcase is in hotel room! Chip is not there!"

Heather nodded, trying to think straight. It felt so wrong to tell her. But she couldn't figure out what else to do.

"There was a special s-s-s-service." Terrified, cold and wet, she was stammering. "Please, can't you untie me? I'll tell you. It hurts s-so much I can't even think."

The woman frowned. "Ilya will see."

"S-so? Is he the boss of you?" Despite the horror she had witnessed, Heather had had the presence of mind to watch her captors. They didn't like each other. Each was vying for control.

Svetlana balled a fist and Heather braced herself for a lot of pain. But the punch did not come. Instead, Svetlana left her alone. What if she had gone to get a gun? What if she was going to shoot her through the eye here?

Oh, God, oh, my God. Heather went blind with panic. She jerked on the zip-ties and squeezed back hot tears.

The woman returned. She was holding a knife and as before, Svetlana cut the tie that bound her wrists together. The pain as the blood rushed back into her constricted hands and fingers was almost more than she could bear. She held her hands together, then tried to make herself rub them.

"Okay, I did for you," Svetlana snapped. "Talk."

Heather wanted to ask her to free her legs, too, but she didn't want to piss Svetlana off. But it was hard work to form words.

"They sent their luggage ahead," she said. Svetlana scowled at her. Maybe she didn't understand. Heather tried again. "The cruise ship company took their suitcases. They sent them to Los Angeles. To put on the ship."

Understanding dawned. Svetlana closed her eyes slowly as if in frustration.

Try to grab the knife, Heather told herself, staring at it. *She won't expect it. Go for it.*

But she couldn't make herself do it. She was paralyzed, both with fear and the trauma of the long hours in restraints. Her legs were still tied to the chair. And how much damage could she do with a knife? Ilya was probably somewhere around here. Svetlana would yell for him. And tell him to bring a gun.

"Okay, good, Heather Chandler," Svetlana said. She turned to go and started walking out of the cell.

The door was open all this time, Heather thought. *If I hadn't been tied up, I could have made a run for it.*

"Please, Svetlana, my legs?"

Svetlana stopped walking. She hesitated for a beat. "*Nyet,*" she replied without looking at Cat. Then she shut the cell door behind herself.

"Cat, I'm sorry," Heather whispered.

Come back for me...

"You understand what I am saying, Miguel," Anatoly said. He had removed the SIM card from his phone and inserted a fresh one to place this call. He had stacks, piles of SIM cards and throwaway phones. It was nine a.m. in London now. Why did everything move so slowly every time there was need for urgency?

"*Sí,* Anatoly. No worries. You know what I can do. I have lots of people in L.A. for this kind of thing. I've done many jobs like this before. Successfully. I'll get my people aboard and no one will know who they are."

"No one suspicious. The woman is a police detective."

"They'll melt into the ship's population. No one will realize they're my operatives. I swear it."

Anatoly tried to picture the kind of people Miguel Escalante would send. Not gangbangers, that was certain. Miguel was a wealthy, classy Angeleno. He had moved himself out of the *barrio* early in life, become educated, moved in high circles. Yet no dirtier street fighter walked the alleys of East Los Angeles.

If Anatoly were aboard the *Sea Majesty* himself, would he be able to identify Escalante's soldiers?

"Very well," Anatoly said. "Do it."

"*Por favor,* put the deposit in my offshore account."

Anatoly could feel himself relaxing. Just a little, but it was a welcome respite from all the tension. In his early years, he had questioned his suitability for this path in life. In the movies, those who operated outside the law were portrayed either as depraved monsters or heartless sociopaths. He was neither. He was a normal person, and just like any other normal person, he got nervous when business wasn't going well. Even billionaires bit their nails when the stock market tanked.

But he had more faith in the individual to whom he was speaking than anyone in his own organization, sad to say. Faith, however, was not the same as trust.

"By the way, amigo, I assume you have not been contacted by anyone else," he said slowly, "for any reason, about the *Sea Majesty*."

"No, and if I am, I will explain to him—or her—that I am unable to be of service."

Like hell you will.

Yes, faith was not the same as trust. The best strategy he could employ was to diminish the value of the chip to anyone but himself. No one else need wonder why he wanted it. Even though, of course, any good businessperson would.

"Once we hang up, I'll move them in. And I won't call until I have results," Escalante continued.

At last. Someone who is competent.

"Good." Anatoly disconnected. He clicked a button on his laptop computer and sent the money to the proper account. Done.

He took the incoming call from Svetlana.

"If we don't untie her legs, she may lose them. There is no circulation," Svetlana said. "She may die."

They both already knew she was going to die. It was just a matter of timing. "Okay. Our business may take a while. Untie her, but watch her."

"She's harmless. But of course I will."

You'd better.

Anatoly would breathe easier once that stupid little idiot was dead. Stupid people were more unpredictable than smart ones. Anyone who tried to double-cross him was pretty stupid. And no one was harmless.

No one.

CHAPTER TEN

JT groaned and turned over. He nudged Tess with his
elbow.

"You know the rule," he mumbled. "You wake her,
you walk her."

Princess Mochi yipped in agreement. Without opening
his eyes, JT grimaced. Mochi understood a few words, and
one of them was W-A-L-K. You were supposed to spell it or
say something like "that thing she likes to do" or else there
would be no peace in New York City until one of her human
minions got up, got her leash, and got going.

"Well, you woke her up." Tess was barely coherent. She
sure was sleeping a lot. When they'd gone to bed last night,
she'd looked really tired.

"I didn't wake her up," JT said. "You're the one who
used the bathroom." She sure was going a lot. Maybe she
was sick.

Tess grunted. "You got up after that to drink some orange
juice. I heard you. It was like five minutes ago."

Whoops. He hadn't realized she'd been awake. But wait,
she'd gone *again* right after that. "Yeah, but then—"

"Yip, yip, yip!" Mochi demanded.

They both sat up and slung their legs over opposite sides of the bed. Both of them had on T-shirts and underwear. It was easier that way, so they could slide on more clothes and take Her Royal Highness outside at a moment's notice.

This was a stupid argument. He was not going to bicker with Tess over who had to walk a three-pound dog.

"I'll do it," he said. "You need your beauty rest."

"What's *that* supposed to mean?" Tess snapped.

He raised his brows. Why was she taking offense when he was letting her off the hook? She didn't want to get up, he didn't want to get up. *Jeez, cranky*. Had she contracted rabies or something?

"It means nothing. It means that I'm trying to be nice to you." Her face shifted, but not in a good way. He tried again. "You just looked tired when we went to bed."

Without having sex, he added silently. Tess had declared she just couldn't do it in front of their miniscule houseguest. So did that mean he was cut off for a week?

Glowering, Tess stood and lifted her sneakers off the nightstand. She had moved all her shoes up so high a mastiff couldn't have reached them. She said, "I can't go back to sleep. I'll take her out."

JT zipped up his jeans. "Here's a thought. Why don't we both take her? And do something together like we used to?"

Tess shrugged. "Okay."

Her lack of enthusiasm wounded him. While she put on her sneakers, he crouched over the wriggling pup and attached her leash to her collar. For his trouble, Mochi tried to bite him. He gently held her muzzle.

"Grrr, grrr, grrr," Mochi said, obviously dog-speak for "thank you." So very not.

"I'm ready," Tess grumped.

We just started taking care of Princess Mochi. How are we going to last a week? God, what if Vincent and Cat have a kid and ask us to babysit? We'd probably kill each other.

JT's blood ran cold.

"Wow," Cat murmured. "It's so big."

"Enormous," Vincent agreed.

The *Sea Majesty* had been billed as "fifteen decks of aloha, elegance, and fun." It would carry nearly two thousand passengers. Back in New York, Cat had studied all the images in the downloads about their cruise, but until they'd actually arrived at the cruise lines hub at the Port of Los Angeles, located in the town of San Pedro, she hadn't had a handle on the scale of the ship. It was like a small floating city rising high above the dock, topped by a control tower as tall as three billboards. Aboard, the walls were painted in beautiful murals of coral, blue, white, and silver and washed with golden California sunlight. Wood and brass gleamed everywhere. Many of the other passengers were wearing aloha shirts and flowered dresses. Vincent had on a loose light blue silk shirt and khaki pants, and Cat was wearing a white shell top, dark blue linen walking shorts, and matching blue wedges. Her straw purse, a gift from Heather, was tiny.

"Three pools, hot tubs, a spa, a dozen restaurants, and a casino," Vincent said happily. "Are you feeling lucky?"

"Oh, yes. Every minute of every day."

Hand in hand, they joined the line of check-ins boarding the *Sea Majesty*. Hawaiian slack-key guitar music was playing and as each passenger stepped onto the ship, a woman dressed in a coral-colored sheath and a necklace of darker coral placed a lei over his or her head and said, "Aloha. Welcome to your journey to paradise." It sounded corny but Cat didn't care. She'd been looking forward to this cruise for months. Last night's bump in the road had only served to underscore just how badly she needed a vacation.

At their hotel last night, it had been too good to be true

to assume they wouldn't get a visit from LAPD before they went to bed, and sure enough, after their whirlpool soak, one Sergeant Gutierrez had taken their statements and double-checked to make sure they hadn't discovered that something was missing. When Cat had revealed that she was NYPD, he'd been a bit more forthcoming about the burglaries, even though there wasn't much to tell: They suspected that it was some local teenage rich kids who made a game out of breaking into homes and hotels in the area on a dare.

"We can't prove it yet," he continued, and he sighed. "Even if we get something ironclad, it might just go away."

Cat lifted a brow. "Let me guess. Rich kids have rich parents."

"Rich parents with publicists," he affirmed. "Those movie stars you see on the big screen? They're too busy being famous to raise their kids. The kids notice. Act up to get attention. And it still doesn't work."

Ouch. She thought about Mitchell Samosa. What if he'd already had kids of his own, who learned of his tryst because of this stunt?

Back on the *Sea Majesty*, Vincent gave her hand a squeeze. "You're off duty," he reminded her. "You're still thinking about the break-in, right?"

She flushed. "Is it that obvious?" She moved her shoulders. "There. I'm letting it go." She nodded. "It's gone." Wrinkled her nose. "Almost."

Soon there was just one passenger in front of Vincent and Cat, a man in a black business suit wearing a pair of sunglasses. He looked distinctly out of place, and reminded Cat of one of the many FBI agents she'd dealt with since her life with Vincent had begun. Curious, she watched him accept his lei but wave away the offer to have his photograph taken in front of a backdrop of curving palms framing a beautiful Hawaiian sunset.

"Ready to be aloha'ed?" Vincent asked her. His eyes glittered mischievously.

"So is that what we're calling it these days?" she replied, snuggling up against him.

Once upon a time, their secret world had consisted of lies, sneaking, and stolen moments. Now it was made of shared memories, in-jokes, and code words. They had traded the thrill of danger for the excitement of building a life together—one rooted in true love.

"I can't wait to aloha with you in our cabin," Cat whispered.

Then, as the woman in the sheath prepared to put the sweet-smelling lei over Cat's head, she looked over at Vincent and said, "Wait. I think you two need to be photographed together. I just can't imagine one without the other."

Cat glanced in surprise at Vincent and he smiled and shrugged good-naturedly, moving up beside her. The woman, whose nametag proclaimed her "DANA CUSHING, CRUISE DIRECTOR," arranged Cat's lei on her shoulders, then stood on tiptoe in an attempt to do the same to Vincent. He bent down and lowered his head.

"Is this by chance your honeymoon?" the woman asked. "You're both just *glowing*."

"Actually, yes," Cat said. "We've been married for a while, but we had trouble getting away."

The woman held up a cautioning finger. "Words like 'trouble' are not to be spoken aboard your floating paradise. We're here to melt your cares away, and cater to your every whim." She led them to the scenic backdrop. "Put your arms around her. Good. Smile at each other." She half-turned her head and waved at a man dressed in a coral flowered shirt and navy blue trousers. He stood behind a small camera attached to a tripod.

"Kimo, can you get them both in? I'm sorry. I mean, Cecilio?

We had a last-minute substitution for our photographer," she told Vincent and Cat.

"You two look great." Cecilio nodded at them and depressed a button on his camera. "Fantastic."

"Your pictures will be displayed in the Majestic Memories shop every afternoon. Pick the ones you want and they'll be added to your room charges," Dana told them.

"Thank you," Cat said. As they made way for the next guest's Kodak moment, she added under her breath, "We're going to have to watch it. It looks like paradise could get expensive."

His eyes gleamed as he gazed down at her. "No, Mrs. Keller," he said softly. "Paradise is free."

"Aloha." A man balancing a stack of colorful folders on top of a clipboard smiled at the two of them. His nametag said ROBERTO. "The Kellers, am I right?"

"You are," Vincent said. "We're in stateroom twenty-one on the Maui deck."

"Not anymore," Roberto shot back. "You've been upgraded to the honeymoon suite, compliments of the *Sea Majesty*. It's number one, Kuuipo Deck. *Kuuipo* means sweetheart in Hawaiian." He smiled and lifted the top folder off the stack. "Your passkey swipe cards, maps, and information are here. Your data is encoded onto your swipe cards, but if you lose one, please let us know right away."

"Upgraded?" Cat echoed. She slid a glance toward Vincent. "Did you do this? Champagne, roses…?"

"No." He turned to Roberto. "Do you know who informed you that this is our honeymoon?"

"No, sir." Roberto's smile never faltered. "Would you prefer not to be upgraded? The honeymoon suite is quite luxurious. It has a beautiful view. You'll see dolphins, maybe even whales. You have an in-room whirlpool bath and a Baja shower surrounded by plumeria and pikake plants, a movie and sound system, and all the furnishings are handcrafted from native Hawaiian koa wood. It's often booked as much as a year in advance. It was sheer luck that it was available at such short notice." He paused. "But if you don't want it, I'm sure we can move you back into a room on par with Maui twenty-one."

"No, no, upgrading is good. Right?" Vincent turned to Cat, and she nodded eagerly.

"Upgrading is great," Cat replied. "I'm all for it." She grinned at Vincent. "Double aloha."

"Triple."

Cat took the folder and looked inside. There were two wood-grain passkeys, one with *Catherine* embossed in gold and the other, *Vincent*. Catherine showed them to her husband. "I doubt we'll ever be apart long enough to need a separate key, but just in case…"

"Just in case," he agreed.

"I'll escort you to your suite and introduce you to your steward," Roberto said. "He'll show you around your home away from home."

Vincent laced his fingers through hers. "Let's explore paradise."

CHAPTER ELEVEN

Rubbing her temple, Tess sat at her desk, ignoring the blister from the brand-new black heels she had bought during lunch, and scanned the case file lying open on the blotter. There were a lot of charges—possession of an illegal substance with intent to distribute, possession of stolen property, illegal possession of a firearm, and *resisting arrest?*

Huh, Tess thought, raising her gaze from the document to the family seated before her. The "kid" who had been brought up on this raft of charges—the one Chief Ward wanted her to clear—was not a kid at all. He was an entitled, sulky, bad-mannered twenty-four-year-old. His parents had accompanied him into Tess's office and were perched on either side of him, both leaning forward earnestly, waiting for Tess to wave her magic wand and make it all go away. The "kid" sat sprawled with his arms crossed, pointedly sighing and staring off into space as if this was all a gigantic imposition on his time.

"Okay, see—" Tess looked at the file again "—*Scott,* I'm having a problem. These are very serious charges and from what I'm reading in the arresting officer's report, all the evidence points towards your guilt."

"No, they trumped up those charges," his mother—Mrs. Daystrom—cut in. She had been weeping when they'd walked in. The father looked no better. There were deep circles under his eyes and he kept twisting his wedding ring, a nervous tic. She had no idea how old they were but unless Mrs. Daystrom had had Scott when she was fifty, parenthood had significantly aged them both.

"He was in possession of two kilos of pure cocaine," Tess said. *You don't trump something like that up.*

"They planted that on him," Mrs. Daystrom insisted.

Tess glanced over at Scott's father. He was staring at his son as if he had no idea who he was. His heartbreak was painful to observe. She could read his thoughts on his anguished features: *Where did we go wrong?*

"Mrs. Daystrom, I know the arresting officer personally. He's a good cop. He would never plant evidence on a subject." Tess tried to be gentle.

"Then you don't know him very well," the woman said shrilly. "I know my son. He's not a drug dealer. And as for resisting arrest, I'd fight back too if I were falsely accused." She reached to take her son's hand but he slid his fists into his armpits. "It's all over the news, how the police are-are corrupt." She covered her mouth, then fidgeted with her hair. "I don't mean you personally, Captain Vargas. *Please…*"

"Unless you drop all charges right now, we're going to sue for false arrest." Those were the first words out of Mr. Daystrom's mouth, and Tess could tell they had been rehearsed. The man's cheeks were blazing red. He didn't want to say them. He had been told to say them. "And I know Chief Ward will back us up."

Ward can't possibly know the facts of this case, Tess thought. *This is such an indefensible crock. He wouldn't do that to me.* She sighed inwardly.

She looked straight at the kid, who was still avoiding eye contact. "Your parents are good, decent people. They're going to bat for you. If this goes to trial and you need a lawyer, I'm sure they would spend every dime they have defending you. And your attorney might get you let off. But if you agree to lesser charges, I may be able to get the DA to—"

"Hello, Brad," the kid's father said into his cell phone. Crap, that was Captain Ward's first name. Mr. Daystrom stared down at his lap, utterly ashamed of himself. "We're having a little trouble down here at the police station. Yes, she's here. Sure."

He raised a brow as he held out the phone to Tess. As she took it, Scott smirked. Beside him, a tear slid down his mother's face. Mrs. Daystrom knew that Scott was guilty.

"Yes, sir," Tess said into the phone.

"Vargas, how's it looking?"

"Depends," she said evasively. If she were the squirming type, she'd be squirming now. Scott's parents were studying her as if she were a bug under a microscope.

"On?" Ward asked.

"This is a serious case, Chief."

"He has no priors."

Neither did the Son of Sam. And he was a serial killer.

"Sir," she said, but she wasn't going to go into it with these people in her office.

"You should be an expert at this. You covered for your partner Detective Chandler enough times," Ward bit off.

Tess was livid. "*Chief Ward—*"

"Scott Daystrom's a good kid. Whatever happened, he just got swept up in it. I'm sure this will be an object lesson. Make it right, Vargas."

Or else. That's the part he wasn't saying. He didn't need to. She wasn't an idiot.

But she also wasn't empowered to do anything about it. A report had been filed. Evidence had been bagged and tagged.

And despite all that, I did make cases go away for Cat. He wasn't wrong about that. But nothing was ever proven. My official record as a police officer reflects that. And he wants me to get dirty for this self-absorbed moron who doesn't give a damn about what he's putting his parents through.

No way. I will make it right.

"I'm hanging up, Vargas. I don't want any more calls from Jack Daystrom. Do I make myself clear?"

"Clear," she repeated as neutrally as she could. She hung up the phone and rose. "Mr. and Mrs. Daystrom," she said, "you need to get your son a lawyer. A good one." *Which means, unfortunately, an expensive one.*

"Wait, what?" Scott blurted.

"Oh, you're awake. Nice you could join us," Tess said hotly. "You'll be staying with us tonight." She picked up her office landline phone. "Miller to my office, please." She hung back up. "He'll get you set up."

"But Brad said—"

"Brad is not the captain here," Tess interrupted. "I am."

She hoped they couldn't see that she was trembling, both with anger and, okay, call it apprehension if you didn't want to go as far as fear. Which had changed, her or the job? Everyone was making side deals, bending the rules. Breaking the *law*. That wasn't what she'd signed up for. Protect and serve, not swerve. Well, it ended now.

There was a rap on her door. It opened, and Officer Miller stood in the doorway—all six feet and four inches of him. An amateur bodybuilder, he was bald, bulgy, and very intimidating.

"Please make our guest comfortable for the evening," Tess told him.

"Hey, wait! Wait!" Scott cried. His head whipped toward his mother, expecting her to intervene as no doubt she always had. "Mom, stop her!"

"Scott!" Mrs. Daystrom got to her feet. Mr. Daystrom stood up and pulled out his cell phone again.

Tess said, "Move it, Miller."

Miller expertly whirled Scott in a half-circle, cuffed him, and marched him out of Tess's office in an efficient, professional blur. His parents stood aghast.

"Sit down, both of you," Tess ordered them. "*Now*."

To her relief, they complied. She planted her hands flat on her desk and leaned forward, staring into their glassy eyes, willing them to get what she was about to tell them.

"Mr. and Mrs. Daystrom, I've been a police officer for a long time," she began, "and I've seen it all. Please listen to me when I tell you that if your son does not face the consequences of his actions now, he'll have to later. And by then, he'll be in deeper. And there will be nothing left of the son you raised and loved. I guarantee it. He will be a criminal. And he will either die on the streets or rot in jail."

Maybe she was laying it on too thick. Thing was, in her gut she knew she was right.

Mrs. Daystrom burst into fresh tears and sank back into her chair. She couldn't hold back the dam; what had to be years of disappointment and frustration welled out of her. Mr. Daystrom went to her side and put his hands on her shoulders.

"Linda," he said, "oh, honey. Honey, stop." When he looked at Tess, she saw naked desperation and nights pacing the floor and worrying. "Please, look what this is doing to her. It's killing her. I'm calling Chief Ward again and if he doesn't fire you—"

"I'm not backing down," Tess told him. "I'm the only hope your son has."

"Are you insane?" he cried. "Fine. That does it." He got out his phone.

Then Mrs. Daystrom wrapped her hand around his

forearm. "No, Jack," she said through a torrent of tears. "She's right." She nodded at Tess. "I know you're right."

"You're letting her bully you," Mr. Daystrom said.

"Just like Scott has been bullying you both." Tess picked up a box of tissues and held it out to Mrs. Daystrom. The woman grabbed a handful and buried her face in them.

"This will ruin his life," Mr. Daystrom said. "He's not some juvenile delinquent. He's an adult."

Bingo. "Get him a lawyer and work with the system. He has to know there is one before it's too late."

She walked to her door and opened it. Scott's father's lips parted but he made no sound as he gently helped his wife to her feet. She was hunched over, carrying the weight of this family's pain on her shoulders.

"Showing remorse would be very helpful when he goes before the judge," Tess said.

Lost and frightened, the couple began to shuffle out. Tess kept her heart where it belonged—out of this case. What they had been doing to Scott was called enabling, and she would have no part of it.

As Mrs. Daystrom crossed the threshold, she looked up at Tess. She said, "When Scott was seven, he wanted a BB gun. We said he was too young and he had this terrible tantrum. He said he was going to beat Santa Claus up."

"So you got him a BB gun," Tess filled in.

"No." She wiped her eyes with the tissue. "We didn't. He cried and carried on for *days*. I couldn't wait for Christmas vacation to be over." She kept her gaze on the tissue as she folded it into squares, then into tinier ones. "It was so exhausting."

Your son is twenty-four years old, Tess thought, but she understood. She got it. Being a parent was twenty-four seven, fifty-two weeks a year. It never ended. You got tired. You gave in once. And then another time. Pretty soon capitulation was your new normal.

Or you did everything right, and your kid still grew up to be the Son of Sam.

"I'm calling Brad," Mr. Daystrom muttered, but Mrs. Daystrom shook her head.

"No, Jack. You're not."

She turned to Tess, swallowed hard, and sighed.

Tess shut the door after them. Her shoulders sagged. Her blister hurt. Her head hurt. Her heart hurt. Stupid heart.

Then her cell phone rang. It was JT. *Yay.* A ray of sunshine in a field of gloom.

"Hey," she said, "I sure hope your day is going better than—"

"Tess," JT said over her, "Princess Mochi is missing."

Before Roberto escorted Vincent and Catherine to their suite, he took them on a tour of the amenities on their deck, which contained a handful of staterooms. Vincent was astonished. There was a grotto-like pool carved from lava rock with a love seat positioned beneath a misting waterfall. Drinks could be ordered from an underwater keypad and delivered poolside. They could share couple's massages on thickly padded tables positioned beneath hanging trellises of orchids. Even now, his-and-hers custom massage oils were being blended according to a profile they both filled out. Then a waitress brought them mai tais and black lacquer platters of coconut shrimp and sushi, and Roberto announced that it was time to go to their suite.

When they got there, a short blonde man in the ship's colors of coral and navy was bent over, closely inspecting their card lock. Vincent assumed he was their steward, but when the man straightened, Roberto frowned at him and said, "May I help you?"

"I'm Lars," the man said in a heavy Scandinavian accent. "Is this the Kukui Suite?"

Roberto relaxed slightly. "No. *K-u-u-i-p-o*," he sounded out. "Kukui is one deck down."

"Oh." Lars touched his forehead. "I'm sorry. I was confused."

"That's no problem," Roberto said smoothly. "These are the Kellers. Our honeymooners."

"That's wonderful," Lars said. He shook Vincent's hand. "Much happiness to you both."

"Thank you," Vincent said.

"Off you go to Kukui, then," Robert prompted. "You wouldn't want to keep *your* guests waiting."

"No, of course not." Lars scooted away.

Roberto watched him go, his forehead mildly furrowed. Then he said to Catherine, "If you will do the honors, Mrs. Keller?"

Catherine inserted her key into the lock and the door opened to a trill of birdsong. Vincent enjoyed the ripple of happiness that showed on her face and wished they were alone so he could carry her over the threshold. Instead, he closed the door and fell into line as Roberto led the way.

"Unbelievable," Vincent murmured as the man turned and faced them. There were flowers everywhere—hanging from the ceiling, in large wooden vases and urns, surrounding several couches and chairs upholstered in Hawaiian fabrics. Between them a coffee table was loaded down with roses, a champagne bucket filled with ice and a bottle, a basket of fruit, cheese, and a row of golf-ball-sized chocolates. Catherine was gaping at it.

"That's your truffle bar," Roberto announced. "Please sample them and put your preferences on this tablet." He went to a wooden chest beneath a plasma screen TV hung between woodblock prints of sea turtles and dolphins and handed the tablet to Catherine. "Every night, you'll have a turndown service, and your steward will leave two of your favorite truffles on your pillow. This is included in your upgrade," he added smoothly.

"Which has been taken care of," Vincent underscored.

"Yes, sir." Roberto gestured to the table. "That controls the sound system, the TV, room service, movie selections..." He trailed off and held up a finger. "If you'll excuse me..."

Then he glided across the large room to a wooden door, which he opened. He peered in. "Hello?"

"Hello?" a man's voice echoed.

Roberto walked through the doorway. Vincent and Catherine followed close behind. They entered a bedroom dominated by a circular bed hung with fabric matching the woodblock prints that framed the plasma screen. On the other side of the draperies, a slight man with jelled raven-black hair and sideburns stood over one of Vincent's suitcases, which was situated on a luggage stand. Vincent tensed.

"Oh, Paul, it's you." Roberto smiled. "I thought you were going to meet us."

Paul carried a stack of Vincent's underwear to the open drawer of a wooden bureau and carefully arranged it as if he were handing the most precious objects on earth. Vincent bristled with a tiny surge of beast reaction—that was *his* underwear, thank you very much, and he and Catherine had just had all their stuff pawed through by a disinterested thief the night before—

Catherine glanced at him and raised her brows. She mouthed, *Calm down.* His eyes must be beginning to glow. He exhaled and gazed down at the floor, seeking a more zenlike state.

"I was hoping to finish unpacking for the Kellers first," Paul replied. "To surprise them." He straightened and held out his hand. "I'm Paul, your steward. I'll be taking care of you during the entire cruise. Night or day, please press the S on your tablet for me. If I'm not available, one of the other stewards will come. But most of the time, it will be me."

"Thanks," Catherine said, stepping forward. She gazed into the drawer. Paul opened the one next to it with a flourish and she murmured, "Oh. Looks like you put all my clothes away first." Her cheeks blazed. Vincent grinned, remembering the surprise items she, Tess, and Heather had shopped for. Catherine turned to Paul, managing an awkward smile. "How... thoughtful."

"Every night, I'll turn down your bed," Paul said, "unless you type in a request not to be disturbed." He moved to the nightstand, opened it, and pulled out an impressive booklet. "This explains all the commands available on your tablet. It's very simple, really." He set it down. "Let me show you the whirlpool and the shower. The bathroom suite is truly spectacular, the nicest one on the entire ship. Once we're finished, there are lovely tropical beverages and macadamia nuts waiting for you on your private lanai."

Paul and Roberto spent another fifteen minutes or so acquainting Vincent and Catherine with all the features of their suite. Vincent pulled out a small envelope from his jacket and handed it to Paul; it was the custom to tip your steward every day. He gave Roberto a small cash tip and the two left the honeymooners alone.

"Wow. Paradise is spectacular. But crowded," Vincent said as they sat on their lanai—a stone-decked patio with a two-person chaise lounge, two tables and chairs, gorgeous potted plants—orchids, plumerias, anthuriums—and an incredible seaside view of the harbor.

"And complicated." Cat put the booklet and tablet on the table and accepted a blue drink in a hurricane glass with *The Kellers* stenciled on it. "What if we think we're summoning Paul but we're actually ordering a lobster dinner?"

"Then we'll eat lobster naked in bed with butter dripping off our chins," he said, putting his arms around her.

"Speaking of naked… it was pretty freaky when we found Paul putting away our things." She cocked her head. "Your eyes began to glow."

"Yeah, it was too close after what happened at the hotel. I hardly ever beast out anymore. Unless I want to. It just caught me off guard." He kissed her. "But I'll be careful. We're going to be on a ship in the middle of the ocean. I can't lose control."

She returned his kiss. "I'm sure everything will be fine. After all, we're sailing to paradise. What could happen?"

A ship's horn sounded loud and long and they both jerked. Catherine reflexively reached for her gun—that wasn't there.

"Aloha, everyone," said a voice through their room speakers. *"We'll be casting off in ten minutes. All guests of passengers please return to shore. Ten minutes until we set sail!"*

Catherine touched her chest and Vincent chuckled. "Man, we're both so jumpy. We really need a vacation."

They left the suite and strolled to the deck, brushing shoulders with some of the other passengers. Everyone was massing at the railing to wave goodbye. The ship's horn echoed against the buildings. A trio of pre-teens was throwing rolls of toilet paper over the rail and cracking up.

Vincent gestured with his head toward a bald man in a black suit. The man was wearing wraparound sunglasses and he was not smiling.

"Odd duck at two o'clock," he said to Catherine. "I noticed him before."

"Me, too," his wife said. "What do you think?"

"He can't be FBI. He's too obvious even for them." He put a hand on her shoulder. "I'm sure it has nothing to do with us."

"Uh-mmm." She sounded dubious.

"We can't go looking for trouble. It'll find us if it wants us."

"Look there."

A lanky girl about fifteen or sixteen, dressed in black

T-shirt, skinny jeans, and flip-flops, wearing thick shiny eyeliner and dark red lipstick, had been heading toward the railing, but froze halfway there when she spotted the man in the suit. She crossed her arms over her chest and backed away.

The man came toward her.

She shook her head, her henna-red hair twisted into curls that grazed her cheeks, and mouthed a couple words that Vincent couldn't make out. Then turned around and melted into the crowd, which parted and moved around her like a buffalo stampede. The man moved through the throng, obviously dogging her. Then Vincent lost track of him, too.

"That didn't look good," Catherine said.

"I think they're together. Both wearing black. Both not fitting in."

"Both not happy about being here," she finished. "They bear watching."

"Va-ca-tion. Say it with me." However, in his heart, he agreed. Something was up with those two. Father and daughter? Some other kind of relative? Or had this been some kind of chance encounter, and some instinct had warned the girl off?

"She's too young to be traveling alone," he mused. "He's got to be in charge of her somehow."

"Yeah," Cat said slowly. "In control of her."

She had altered the meaning with her word choice. Vincent knew then and there that Catherine was going to make a project out of figuring out what was going on. That was all right. He was going to as well.

CHAPTER TWELVE

As the *Sea Majesty* cast off, a call was made to a very private phone number. At his compound in Beverly Hills, Miguel Escalante gave his wife a "wait a minute" look and took the call. She motioned with a flickering kitchen match for him to hurry. Half the birthday candles on their daughter's cake had already been lit, and Rachael's little guests were giggling and falling all over themselves as they prepared to blare out their version of "Happy Birthday." Rachael was six today.

"*Sí*," he said into the phone.

"Our people are on board. It went fine," his caller told him. "The targets don't suspect a thing."

"You're absolutely sure," Miguel said.

"*Sí*." There was a pause. Alarm bells sounded in Miguel's head.

"What?" he demanded. "Is there a problem?"

"Did you move them? There was a room change."

The bells clanged louder. Miguel's wife Barbara was smiling questioningly at him, urging him to hurry. Above the guttering trio of birthday candles, her face glowed with joy. They had only managed to have Rachael after years of infertility treatments, some of them forbidden by their Catholic religion. Barbara was spoiling their only child, but what did it matter? The man Rachael eventually married would spoil her too. Miguel would see to it.

"Describe the room change."

When his caller explained that the targets—no names were ever used, *ever*— had been moved to the honeymoon suite, the bells did not go silent, but Miguel did relax a little. He'd done lots of business in the tourism industry—cruises and tours were perfect venues for taking care of matters that would be more difficult to accomplish closer to the target's home—and he knew that upgrades such as these were commonplace. They generated enormous goodwill and extra publicity as the favored individuals blogged and used other social media to brag about their good fortune. If they booked another cruise, they would be far more likely to pick a ship from the Majestic Line, and encourage their friends to do the same.

Still, it was bothersome that any sort of deviation had occurred. Predictability always made the job easier.

"Was your partner briefed about this upgrade?"

"*Sí*. And we've made changes in our strategy to account for it. Trust me, we have the situation well in hand."

"*Bueno*. Keep me informed." He disconnected and nodded at his wife, who quickly finished lighting the candles. She blew out the match and picked up the pink cake with its spun-sugar castle. A princess cake for their princess. He joined Barbara and together they walked into the decorated party room of their Tuscan-style mansion.

"One, two, three, 'Happy...'" Barbara led off.

All the kids started singing "Happy Birthday," and Rachael grinned from ear to ear. Times like this made all the effort worth it. Miguel pushed thoughts of the assignment to the back of his head as his wife set the cake down in front of his daughter.

"Make a wish," he told Rachael.

She closed her eyes, took a deep breath, and blew. Then she opened her eyes and said, "I wished to marry you, Daddy."

Her parents chuckled, and Miguel gave her a kiss on the crown of her head. "What would we do with Mommy, then?"

Rachael looked up at him adoringly. "What you do with the other ladies, Daddy."

"Here." Through the bars, the Russian girl thrust a bottle of water and half of a commercially packaged roast beef sandwich in its torn wrapper at Heather. Heather was sitting on her chair, a preference rather than a necessity. The floor of the cell was filthy and there were rats. She had dozed on and off but she wasn't sure she had actually slept. Outside the cell, there were two metal folding chairs, a rickety white metal occasional table, and a camping lantern. Her jailers didn't have it much better than she did. Except that they could actually use a restroom. They had brought her a bucket and a roll of toilet paper.

The sandwich smelled kind of bad but Heather wolfed it down in three bites. She tipped back the water and drank so fast she began gagging.

"What, it's vodka?" Ilya asked her snidely as he sauntered over and peered at her through the bars.

Heather looked down. She was terrified of Ilya. His favorite game to play with her was Russian roulette, where he would show her that he'd put a bullet into his gun, then spin the cylinder, press the barrel against her head, and pull the trigger. She kept telling herself that it had to be some kind of trick or he wouldn't dare do it. He'd piss off their boss, whoever he was, if he killed her.

That was what she kept telling herself.

But as time dragged on and it became clear they had no plan for how to take care of her, she began to wonder if there was really a bullet in the chamber. She was beginning to lose it more often, crying silently, and he loved that. She'd force herself to stop. Then she would flex her arms and legs to keep them from stiffening up, and plot out ways to get out of the cell. All of them depended on getting a gun.

Svetlana appeared. She and Ilya spoke in Russian that grew more heated. Ilya kept glancing over at Heather. She kept her eyes fixed on the wrapper on her lap. And then she realized that there was a cash register receipt stuck to it. Surreptitiously, she peeled it off. *Marco's Cash & Carry 121 Dup...* The rest of the address and date were smeared but she might be able to make them out if she had more light. That could tell her how long she had been there, but more importantly, where she was.

She slid the receipt into her pants pocket. The conversation had escalated into an argument. Ilya wound his fist around Heather's cell door and gave it a shake. When Heather jumped, he laughed and pushed his face against the bars.

"You are scared, baby? Good, good! I make you more scared."

Svetlana pushed him away. He reached back a hand as if to smack her and she pushed him again. Yelling at him, she pulled out her phone and showed it to him. Threatening to call their boss, Heather guessed.

Face darkening, Ilya threw up his hands and stomped off. Heather swallowed hard and tried to breathe, but her chest was too tight.

"What asshead," Svetlana said, glowering in the direction of Ilya's exit, and Heather burst out with a jittery laugh.

"Yeah, no kidding." Heather wiped her face. "Thank you for the food."

Svetlana narrowed her eyes as she studied Heather through the bars. "I am not friend. I am not good person."

"Sorry," Heather said. "But I kind of think you are. You're more good than he is, anyway."

Svetlana shrugged. "He is arranged."

"If you mean 'deranged,' I agree with you." She took a breath. "I really didn't know about Ravi and the chip," she said.

Svetlana sighed. "But you know now."

"Yeah, sucks," Heather murmured. Her heart went into overdrive. *She's sad because she knows I'm screwed. She knows they're going to kill me. How can they ever let me go?*

"Sucks," Svetlana agreed. There was genuine regret in her voice.

Heather cleared her throat. She was so afraid to say the wrong thing. But she was beginning to be more afraid that her time was running out.

"So, is Ilya your brother?"

Svetlana pulled a comical grimace of horror and crossed herself. "No way. Colleague only. His uncle…" She stopped herself. "Don't ask questions."

"Okay, sorry." Heather held up her hands. "I'm just scared. I talk a lot when I'm scared."

Svetlana said, "Is good you're scared." Then she shook her head, pulled up the folding chair outside the cell, and plopped down into it. "Doesn't matter."

"Why not?" Heather extended a shaking hand toward her. "Svetlana, are you… are you going to kill me?"

Svetlana's eyes flashed with anger. She sat up straight. "You see what we did. You see we kill Ravi Suresh."

"I know *Ilya* killed him, not you. And I also think that was a mistake. You do too," Heather said, pushing. "He *could* have gotten a duplicate chip for you."

The other woman caught her lower lip between her teeth. Then she nodded.

"You feel the same way. Svetlana, it would be a mistake to kill me. My sister is a cop. NYPD."

"If I am ordered," Svetlana began, but she didn't finish her sentence. Instead she rested her elbow on her knee and cradled her forehead. Her loose blonde hair draped forward. She laughed wanly. "Look at this. Crazy mop of hair."

"I've worked in fashion," Heather said. "You know, fashion? Like *Project Runway*? You have great cheekbones. And you're tall and thin. You'd be a good model."

A harsh laugh was Svetlana's response. "I am Russian criminal, not model."

"But you could be one. They like those kinds of edgy backgrounds." When Svetlana didn't appear to understand, Heather elaborated. "They like dangerous women for models."

Svetlana sucked in her cheeks, raised her chin, made as if to raise a pistol, and cried, "Bang!" She didn't aim her fantasy gun at Heather. She aimed it in Ilya's direction. "Die, asshead!"

The two shared a smile. Then Svetlana went dark again. Heather needed to keep a bond between them. "Do you think I could have a towel or a blanket to sleep on?" she asked. "The ground is so cold."

Svetlana shrugged. "We don't have here."

"I know. But maybe the next time you go home, could you bring me back something? An old rag, something you don't care about?"

Something shifted in Svetlana's gaze. Heather couldn't quite read it, and she didn't know what it meant. But there was a change, and Heather wondered if it was good or bad.

Oh, my God, what if I don't have one more night?

"Maybe I bring," Svetlana said.

"And… if it wouldn't be too much trouble, maybe a flashlight? It's so dark in here and the rats come…"

Svetlana's gaze shifted toward the ceiling. For the first time, Heather noticed a tiny ebony square. Was it a window? Was she just one story below a street where there were people? If she opened her mouth and screamed, would anyone hear her? Could they get to her in time?

"Nice try, smart girl," Svetlana said. Then she got up and

left. The cell door lock clicked ominously behind her.

But she had left the camping lantern on. On purpose? As a gesture of kindness? Heather had often listened to Tess and Cat discussing their cases back when they were partners—on the phone or during a movie night at the apartment—and one of the most interesting things they talked about was getting a bad guy to "flip." To become a good guy, basically. To reveal information that would solve the case, incriminate his or her friends, or confess. Most of the time, people flipped to save their own skin. But sometimes they did it because their conscience was bothering them. They weren't completely bad. They were still redeemable.

Was Svetlana redeemable? Svetlana had stepped into Heather's line of vision when Ilya had killed Ravi. She'd made him back off when he'd taunted her. She'd brought Heather a sandwich. And she'd left the light on even after glancing up at what might be a dirty window.

Does she have a guilty conscience? Can I use it against her to get her to help me? Or should I try another way to flip her?

It was perfectly acceptable to lie to suspects and tell them that someone else connected to the case was spilling their guts and blaming everything on them. Cat and Tess were excellent liars themselves—look at how well they had covered up for Vincent all this time—and Heather had picked up pointers about how to lie convincingly: keep your eyes wide open, keep your story simple, and don't try too hard.

She doesn't like Ilya. Could I lie about something he told his uncle? They probably only speak to each other in Russian. What could I make up that she would believe?

"Nothing," Heather whispered. The jitters came then; she shook uncontrollably and her eyes welled with tears. Control. She had to stay in control. But it was so hard when she was frightened, dirty, hungry, and exhausted. *She* wasn't a cop. She was an event planner.

But I'm Catherine Chandler's sister, she reminded herself. *Okay, her half-sister, but I've got the half that matters. Mom was smart, brave, and sneaky, and so are we. I can do this.*

And I will *do this.*

"Bring it," she whispered. "I'm ready."

CHAPTER THIRTEEN

The *Sea Majesty* had left the Port of Los Angeles behind and made for the open water. The passengers were busily acquainting themselves with the pools, the volleyball court, the casino, and the shopping mall, which was extensive. There was a queue in the Majestic Memories shop to see the embarking photographs, which were displayed on video screens.

"There she is." Cat gave Vincent a nudge in his side. The girl she had noticed before sat on the side of the grotto pool with her legs in the water. She was wearing a black nineteen-thirties-style bathing suit and a broad-brimmed black straw hat, and she was hunched over a book.

"And there *he* is." Vincent gestured with his chin.

The guy in the black suit and sunglasses was barely visible as he studied the girl.

Cat sauntered casually over to the pool and stopped beside the girl. She allowed her shadow to fall over the girl's book. No reaction. Cat squinted at the page. *Poems of the English Romantic Period*. Homework?

"Is the water nice?" Cat asked.

The girl shifted slightly but didn't answer. Cat leaned over and stuck her hand in the pool. "Ooh, it's a little chilly."

Huffing, the girl looked up from her book. "It's perfect. You should go in." Judging by her tone of voice, she was silently adding, *And leave me alone.*

Cat slipped off her wedges, lowered herself to the cement, and put her legs in. She fanned them back and forth but didn't speak.

The girl turned a page. Then she looked over at Cat, looked again. Gave her head a quick shake.

Cat glanced at her. Without looking up, the girl said, "I thought you were Kate Middleton."

Cat was so surprised that she guffawed. The girl frowned. She said, "It was an honest mistake."

"Oh? Have you met Kate Middleton?"

This time the girl looked at her full on. "Yes, I have. Haven't you? I thought they put all the people who had met Kate Middleton on the same deck."

Oooh, touchy. Cat moved her shoulders. "Okay," she said, "I think I'm busted. Here's the deal. My husband and I noticed a man following you and we want to know if you know him."

Paling, the girl sucked in her breath. "Oh, my God," she whispered. "*No.*"

"You do know him," Cat pressed, senses going on alert.

"Where…? I mean, I have to go." She closed her book. Cat placed a hand on her forearm.

"Let me help you. Who is he? Are you traveling with him?"

"Stay away from me." The girl got to her feet and looked around. Cat began to get up too, but by then the girl had taken off—in a one-eighty away from the man.

Cat looked over at Vincent, who gave her a nod—*I'm watching*—pulled her legs out of the water, put on her wedges, and headed straight for the man. He saw her coming, turned away, and disappeared around the corner.

She edged her way through the small crowd—their deck was very exclusive—and saw him moving down a narrow passageway dotted with rows of plain metal doors. He glanced over his shoulder, spotted her, and picked up speed.

"Wait," she called, but that was all she could say. She couldn't invoke the power of her badge. She wasn't a cop here. She was just a civilian.

I'm never not a cop.

He took a right.

So did she.

He went down a flight of metal stairs, ducking beneath a sign that read NO PASSENGERS PLEASE! apparently in several different languages. She heard his footfalls clanging, then her own, as she followed him. When she reached the bottom, she saw him moving down another tight passageway. As before, she pursued, and when she was almost close enough to reach out and grab him, he whirled around and yanked on her arm.

Instinctively Cat executed an open-palm strike, slamming the heel of her hand beneath his chin. God, he was made of iron; his thick neck muscles prevented his head snapping back so much as a fraction of an inch. He deflected her uppercut to his midsection, wrapping his hand around her forearm and throwing her against the wall. Anticipating his counterattack, she had tucked in her chin and so her shoulder took the brunt of the impact. She used her own momentum to push off with a sidekick that caught his jaw, and before he could grab her ankle, she twisted around and rammed her elbow into his side and punched him in the face.

Then she let herself fall to the floor and contracted her legs into her chest, thrusting hard when he began to bend over her. But it was a feint; he had backed off. She jackknifed to her feet—and faced down the barrel of a gun.

"Fire!" she shouted without hesitation. "Fire on the ship!"

That was the magic word to utter in a crisis situation.

Not "help" or "nine-one-one" or even "call the police," unfortunately. That was because a fire could affect everyone including a random passerby who might not otherwise be inclined to get involved.

"Shut up." The man raised his gun.

"I don't think so." She kept her voice even and steady. "Fi—"

"Who do you work for?" he asked at the same time she started to yell.

"I'm NYPD. You?" she shot back.

"*You're a cop?* Where's your badge?"

"Who wants to know?"

"You know who I am." But he looked uncertain. He dabbed at his split lip and frowned at the blood. "Wait. What'd she tell you?"

"Who are you?" she said again, sensing that once he'd realized she was a cop, he abandoned the idea of shooting her.

"Terry Milano. Her bodyguard."

"No way," she blurted.

His smile was sour. "Let me guess. She told you I was some master criminal after her father's business secrets. Or some pervy pedophile."

"But you're... her *bodyguard*? Do you have credentials to prove that?"

He reached in his pocket and handed her a wallet. She checked it. He had a California driver's license identifying him as Terence Milano. She also found a permit to carry a concealed weapon.

"My best credential is inside the Neptune Suite," he said. "My boss, Forrest Daugherty. Her father. You can speak to him if you want. Or to the head of security aboard the *Sea Majesty*. His name is Brian d'Allesandro."

That was correct. From force of habit, Cat had looked up the name of the ship's security chief when she and Vincent had booked the cruise. Sometimes you came across ex-cops who had left the force. They got paid a lot more doing private security and put up with a lot less politics.

"D'Allesandro knows I'm carrying," he added. "He knows I'm working for the Daughertys."

I've been played, Cat figured. *That girl is probably laughing her head off right now.*

"Why didn't you just tell me that?" Cat asked him.

He shrugged. "Not in my job description. And if I'm not mistaken, you don't have a job aboard this vessel." He decocked his gun and put it in a pancake holster inside his jacket and held out his hand. She took it. They shook.

"What's her name?" Cat asked.

"Well, her code name used to be Six-Six-Six but she found out about it and told her father. I could tell he thought it was funny but he told me to change it. So now it's Garbo. For Greta Garbo, the actress. She was a recluse. 'I vant to be alone,'" he mimicked. "But her real name is Bethany."

He gestured for them to walk back the way they had come. It looked like all she'd given him was a split lip, but she was a little sore. Her ego required her to mask the damage, and she kept pace with him.

"Are you going to tell her father?" she asked him.

He scoffed. "What, and lose my job? She used to pull this kind of crap from time to time, but that was when she was in playgroups. I hadn't seen her for a while. She's gotten more sophisticated."

"Poor little rich kid?" she asked, looking over her shoulder at him.

"You could say that, but I never would." He wrinkled his nose. "I think you might be getting a shiner. Sorry about that."

"No problem. I've had worse."

"So you're not here on the job," he said. "Buy you a drink?"

"I'm here on my honeymoon. I'm sure my husband would love to join us."

He grinned at her. "All the good ones are married or gay."

She grinned back. "Trust me. They're not."

They walked up deckside to find Vincent standing expectantly beside Bethany Daugherty, whose arms were folded and her shoulders hunched. If looks could kill, no one within a fifty-mile radius of her would be alive. When she spotted him with Cat, she practically spit fire. She wheeled on her heel but Vincent had hold of her arm. She jerked herself out of his grasp but made no effort to flee. Maybe she realized her goose was cooked.

"So this is what happened," Cat began, but Vincent said, "Got it figured out. You okay?"

"Thankfully, yes," Cat answered. "Although Mr. Milano was compelled to pull a weapon on me."

Vincent gaped at her. Lowering her eyes, Bethany smiled.

"Oh, I almost forgot to make introductions. Terry Milano, Vincent Keller."

The two men shook hands. "Sorry I kind of beat up your wife," Milano said.

"We're cool," Vincent replied.

"So, hi, Bethany," Cat said pleasantly. "I'm Cat. Terry and I decided we should attack that truffle bar and get to know each other better."

"Sure," Milano said. "Sounds terrific."

Dear Bethany let loose with a barrage of swear words, some of which Cat had never heard before—and she was a streetwise New York City cop. Vincent chewed the inside of his cheek, equally impressed.

"There is no way I'm going anywhere with any of you," Bethany informed them.

"Fine. We'll pay your dad a visit instead," Cat said.

"He'll be too busy to talk to you. He's always too busy."

Cat didn't press. She didn't want to get Milano in trouble with his employer. And while she was used to the self-absorbed sulkiness of teenagers—after all, she'd practically raised Heather herself—she knew that bratty behavior often masked real pain. Maybe she could do something to help Bethany.

"I need to feed Sprinkles," Bethany told Milano flatly. "Let's go. I have to change."

"That's her dog," Milano explained. "They're keeping him in a kennel below decks."

"This ship sucks," Bethany grumbled. "Last time I got to keep my dog in my stateroom."

"That was Mariposa, and she was a Yorkie," Milano filled in. "Sprinkles is a little bigger."

"Still, if their suite's the biggest one on the ship, it would seem like a trivial matter to let her keep her dog with her," Cat argued. "I'd hate to be separated from my dog if I had one."

"You can come with me to see Sprinkles." Maybe Bethany knew Cat knew she was playing her in return, or maybe the girl really did want Cat to come with her. She looked straight at Cat. "Just you."

You're not armed, are you? Cat asked silently. She met Milano's gaze over Bethany's head. He gave her a quick nod— permission granted. Maybe he would follow at a more discreet distance, or maybe he would trust a cop—even an unarmed one—to take care of Bethany for one harmless stroll.

Cat kissed Vincent's cheek and said, "Catch you later. We have the late seating for dinner, right?"

"Yeah. I'll catch up on my video games."

A flicker of interest lit up Bethany's eyes. "What do you play?"

Vincent rattled off a short list of titles. Cat had grown to accept that her man had a boyish side that included making cannonballs when he jumped into swimming pools and playing video games. Lots of video games, preferably games that required two players and had a lot of explosions. Enter the necessity of a best friend, that being JT.

After a long, hard, dirty day as a cop the last thing Cat wanted to do was pretend-drive a speeding car and pretend-shoot bad guys. On the other hand, Vincent had no interest in watching TV shows about doctors, or chick-flicks "where nothing ever happens."

Enter Tess and Heather.

"You any good?" Bethany asked Vincent.

His answer was a bunch of scores and other statistics. They must have been good—Cat had no idea—because the jaded teen let her admiration show. Vincent said, "Tell you what. After you and Cat visit your dog, we can have a tournament."

"Your father is planning to have dinner with you in about an hour," Milano reminded Bethany. Her face began to re-harden into its surly mask.

"Maybe I can introduce myself, tell him we'll look after her," Vincent suggested. "We can get a bunch of stuff to eat in our room."

Bethany was all smiles now. All excitement.

So much for the first romantic night of our honeymoon, Cat thought, but Vincent's generous spirit warmed her heart. They had the rest of their lives to be together, and Bethany appeared to need someone now. Cat crossed her fingers that Mr. Daugherty would give her permission to hang out with them.

"Sounds like a plan," Cat said. "We can both go with you while you change and meet your dad."

"It's this way," Bethany said. She walked off, obviously expecting them to follow. Bemused, Cat and Vincent fell in. Milano allowed some distance between himself and the trio, although Cat didn't know why he bothered. In his austere suit, he was impossible not to notice.

They ascended a stacked stone riser dressed with tiki torches leading to a pair of curved lava doors. There were no signs indicating that this was the Neptune Suite. Cat supposed that if you needed to ask where it was, you didn't need to know. Bethany pulled a key card out of a pocket in her bathing suit and the doors slid back. Inside a lava-rock foyer, a waterfall extended the full height of the room, and a skylight overhead bathed the water in pastels. The sun was setting on their first day aboard the *Sea Majesty*.

By then, Milano had caught up with them. Moving silently around the cluster, he disappeared down a hallway. Bethany said, "I'll go change," and left via another corridor.

"How big *is* this place?" Cat murmured to Vincent.

"I hope he doesn't say no," Vincent murmured back. "She'll probably burn the place down."

After a couple of minutes, a middle-aged man with a firm, tanned face and a physique to match returned to the foyer with Milano. He was wearing khaki trousers, a Hawaiian shirt, expensive-looking leather sandals, and a Rolex. His hair was salt-and-pepper gray and his eyes were blue. His smile was more practiced than genuine but he extended a hand to Catherine first and said, "Forrest Daugherty. I understand you had a run-in with my bodyguard."

Milano coughed into his fist and said, "I explained that I startled you on your way back from the pool. If you'll excuse me." He left the group in the foyer and walked down the same hall where Bethany had disappeared.

"Detective Catherine Chandler, NYPD, and this is my husband, Doctor Vincent Keller."

"N-Y-P-D, eh?" Daugherty gave her a once-over but made no other comment.

"Yes."

"And a doctor." He shook Vincent's hand.

"He used to be Special Forces," Cat interjected. "Afghanistan."

"This is your way of guaranteeing my daughter's safety," he drawled. "It's very kind of you to spend time with her. She's not the most social person."

"We'd be very happy to have her over tonight," Cat assured him. "We'll order some pizza or something—"

"No bother. Our chef has already begun dinner. I'll have it sent over."

"Oh. Well thank you," Cat said. "That'd be nice. And you don't mind if I go with her to see Sprinkles?"

He looked at the two of them as if trying to make some sort of decision. Then his demeanor changed, and he leaned forward slightly.

"Here's the deal," he said. "My ex-wife has been dating a very questionable individual. I think he's mobbed up but I haven't been able to prove it yet. Then about two weeks ago, someone tried to hack into one of my companies' databases. One week ago, my ex phoned and told me her home had been broken into and a lot of jewelry had been stolen. Milano reported that he'd been tailed picking Bethany up from school. And someone tripped the alarm system on *my* property. We didn't see anything on the security camera footage, but I decided to get Bethany out of there. It was very short notice, and her school is still in session but they have this end-of-year internship requirement. She has to shadow someone at their job and write up a report. I've set it up for her to hang around Captain Kilman. He's the captain of the *Sea Majesty*."

"Sounds perfect," Vincent ventured.

Daugherty's face fell. "You'd think. Well, she had arranged an interview with a veterinarian and she was furious with me for putting the kibosh on that. She blames me for the divorce and yeah, I'm gone a lot. And I know my ex talks a lot of trash about me. Absentee father, all that."

Cat nodded. "Father-daughter issues are tough. I have some." She slid a glance toward Vincent. Her late father, Bob Reynolds, had spearheaded Muirfield, the project that had turned Vincent into a beast. Reynolds had gotten her mother pregnant with her but they had broken up before they'd realized it. Cat had only learned of all of this when the man who had raised her lay dying and she had been unable to serve as a blood donor for him because they had no matching biological markers.

Daugherty beamed at Cat. "I figured there was some reason she let you in. She's a brick wall, that one. So Milano will walk you down to visit Sprinkles and then he'll stick around outside your suite. Don't tell Bethany. She hates having a bodyguard."

"Got it." Cat and Vincent nodded at each other and then at him. If that was the only stipulation required to make it possible for Bethany to spend the evening with them, they were all for it.

"I'm ready," Bethany announced. She appeared in a T-shirt advertising a heavy metal band and leggings. She had on black mary janes. Her hair hung in her face and she had reapplied her heavy eyeliner. Ignoring her father, she walked up to Cat and Vincent. "Let's go."

They walked out of the suite and headed for the stairs. She said, "Did you check the room service menu? Do they have vegetarian pizza? Because I don't eat meat."

Cat glanced at Vincent. "Well, your father said he would send your dinner over—"

She stopped walking. "No way!" she cried. "Does he have to mess up everything? *I just want pizza.*"

"Maybe he'll send over pizza," Vincent said reasonably.

"Maurice went to the Cordon Bleu, that stupid French cooking school," she said. "It'll be something unpronounceable and it will taste like gorgonzola cheese." She looked miserable.

"Tell you what," Cat began, "you and I will go see Sprinkles and Vincent will get some pizzas for us from the Italian restaurant they have on board. What's it called? Villa something?"

Her face shone. She looked so young and excited. Cat wondered if she was accustomed to pouting and throwing tantrums because that was the only way she knew to assert herself.

"Villa Capri," Vincent said. "I'll get a large vegetarian and a large meat-lovers." He eyed Bethany. "You look like a popcorn kind of person. And maybe... Twizzlers?"

"Yes!" she cried. "And Jolly Ranchers if they have them."

"Got it. You have a soda preference?"

"Diet root beer."

Vincent smiled. "Okay. See you guys in a bit." He gave Cat a peck on the cheek and headed off.

"This is going to be amazing," Bethany said, and Cat's heart broke a little for her. Then she remembered that this poor little rich girl had manipulated her into a showdown with her bodyguard. Better to tread carefully in case the path was planted with land mines.

Bethany showed Cat where the elevator was and they went straight down to the fourth deck. The girl's mouth curved into that same secretive smile and Cat pictured Milano racing down ten decks' worth of stairs to keep up with them. Barking and baying signaled that they had reached the ship's kennel. The air was stuffy and three dog crates seemed to have been wedged into a corner where nothing else would fit. Cat still didn't understand why the wealthy passengers couldn't keep their dogs in their rooms. Especially since one of them was a Shih Tzu dressed in a rainbow of satin bows.

Until she saw the other two dogs: a German shepherd and Sprinkles, who was an enormous Great Dane. So gigantic, in fact, that he didn't seem real.

"Hi, boy-boy, hi," Bethany said. She opened up his cage, pulled out a leash she unwound from her jeans pocket, and attached it. Then she eased him out. He studied Cat for a few seconds, and then he buried his face against her hand.

The gentle giant made a sweet chuffing noise.

"Hi, Sprinkles," Cat said.

They walked him together between two rows of stacked cartons, then out through a hatch to a nondescript metal deck. The air was fresh and clean and Sprinkles leaned against Bethany as she rubbed his head. The moon glittered on the water. It was a sweet moment.

"I hate my father. He's a total douchebag," Bethany said. Then she began to walk Sprinkles up and down the deck. Without comment, Cat walked beside her. Sometimes the best way to ask questions was just to remain silent.

"He can't just let things be normal. All we want is effing pizza."

Cat got that. When Bethany glanced over at her, she nodded. "It's like sometimes you just want vanilla ice cream. Without anything else. But someone wants you to be happy, so they make you a banana split," Cat said.

"Exactly. And they make the ice cream from milk flown in on a private jet from France."

"That'd be terrible," Cat agreed, smiling to herself.

"The worst," Bethany grumped.

Miguel's wife Barbara hadn't seen the humor in Rachael's birthday comment about what Daddy did with the other ladies who were not Mama. She was understanding up to a point, but after the last little party guest had left, she'd laid into him. What did she expect? He was a red-blooded man. And now *he* was pissed. So he called his people on the *Sea Majesty* to see how it was going. The reception was terrible even though they had satellite phones.

"*Anything?*" he barked.

"Not yet," came the reply.

"Then step it up. I don't care what you do, but get it done." He slammed down the phone.

* * *

Waiting for the pizzas, Vincent was watching a Las Vegas-style floorshow through a window in Villa Capri while he sat on a bar stool and drank a beer. An extremely well-endowed, heavily made-up but nevertheless very beautiful woman was singing a sad love song in Spanish. Tears ran down her cheeks and as she ended the song, she lowered her head and whispered the last words, "*Adios, mi amor.*" Applause rose up and Vincent made rings on the counter with the bottom of his beer bottle.

The pizzas were taking a long time; he might have gotten better service if he'd ordered from their room. He ducked out to snag the popcorn and candy from the Da Kine Sweet Shop across the hall. While he was browsing, trying to decide if Red Vines were an acceptable substitute for Twizzlers, he realized that the shopper beside him was the singer from the show. She had taken off her stage makeup but he would have recognized those, ah, eyes anywhere.

She must have noticed him looking at her. She smiled and said, "Hey, how ya doin'?" Her accent was pure New Jersey. The breathy Spanish accent was completely gone.

"Great. You?" he asked.

"So far so good," she said, and pantomimed knocking on wood. "You never know with a new venue."

"Oh, you're new?"

She nodded. "Got this booking last minute. That's why my name's not on the website."

There seem to be a lot of late additions to the crew, he thought. He wondered if that was normal. It happened at the hospital sometimes: A spate of docs or nurses called in sick and suddenly you were working with per diems you might never see again.

"Not bad, a free trip to Hawaii," he said.

She smiled at him. Looked him up and down. "Yeah. The scenery's great."

"So I hear. But we're in the middle of the ocean."

"But the scenery *is* great." That breathy voice was back, and Vincent chuckled. She was hitting on him. Not that he was tempted in the least, but it was flattering.

"Well, I'm sure I'll see you around," he said, taking his purchases to the counter. "Please put these on my room," he told the clerk. "Honeymoon suite."

"Yes, Mr. Keller," the clerk replied.

He turned back to say goodnight to the woman. She was holding up a cell phone. Was she taking a picture of him?

"*Buenas noches,*" she replied.

CHAPTER FOURTEEN

A blanket dropped on top of Heather as she dozed in her chair. She jerked awake with a shout. Svetlana was silhouetted by the camping lantern, the outline of her body fuzzy against the brilliant light.

"Be quiet," she said, and handed Heather a small container of yogurt, a sweet roll in a cellophane wrapper, and a water bottle. Heather's hands shook as she accepted the food and water. Then Svetlana gave her a plastic spoon.

"Thank you. Thank you so much," Heather murmured as she gobbled down the sweet roll.

The Russian woman said nothing as she walked out of the cell and pulled the door shut.

Only, the lock didn't click.

Heather stopped chewing. After Svetlana disappeared, she counted to ten. Then she jumped up out of the chair and took two silent giant steps to the door, grabbing one of the bars because there was no knob.

It hadn't shut.

Her heart hammered. She pushed on the door.

It swung open.

"Oh, my God," she whispered.

Her mind raced. She listened hard.

Did she do it on purpose? Is it some kind of test? I gave my word that I wouldn't try to escape and they said they would kill me if I did try. But they are going to kill me anyway. And they haven't used me to talk to Cat yet.

Maybe they don't need to. Maybe they already have the chip. Maybe my sister is dead.

The thought galvanized her. She tiptoed to the camping lantern and grabbed it up, shining it on the dark square Svetlana had glanced up at. It was smudged glass, so yes, maybe it was a window. And it looked like it might be the kind that slid open sideways.

Am I dreaming? Is this really happening?

Sweat beaded on her forehead. Heather set down the lantern and carried one of the two folding chairs to the wall and set it beneath the window. She was dizzy; she hadn't had any real rest and very little to eat. She could already see that the space between the chair and the window would be too high for her to reach.

She went back for the table, moved the chair, and put the table against the wall. She hefted the chair on top of it. Then she tried to climb up, but her little tower was too tippy. Adrenaline was charging through her system. Her body was quivering. She got the second chair and put it down beside the table to steady it, stepped up onto it, then hoisted first her right leg and then her left onto the chair on top of the table. *There! Yes!* Her fingers reached the edge of the window. Then the table made an ominous cracking noise and began to wobble. She dug her fingertips into the edge of the frame, unable to see what she was doing because she was blocking the lantern's beam with her body. Did the glass move sideways a fraction of an inch?

Fire then ice washed up and down her chest and spine as she fought to keep her balance. Her hands and arms shook.

Everything shook. Another cracking noise echoed through the darkness. The table was falling apart beneath her.

"C'mon, c'mon," she begged the window as she pulled with all her might. It was stuck. She had the presence of mind to realize that if she jerked too hard and the window suddenly opened all the way, the force of her momentum might send her flying off the table. She studied the darkness over her shoulder. No sign of Svetlana or worse, Ilya. So far, so good, except for the table.

Then she had an idea.

She climbed off the chair, down onto the table, and then onto the chair on the floor. Once she touched back down onto the cement, she pushed the chair underneath the tabletop. The back scraped the underside of the table and served as additional rickety support. Then, hesitating only to make sure that the cell door wouldn't swing shut, Heather dashed into the cell, grabbed her blanket, water bottle, and chair, and hurried back to her own leaning tower of rusted furniture and used the chair as her stepping stool. She put down the blanket and water bottle, intending to break the window if she couldn't get it open. She had forgotten to adjust the angle of the lantern; she still couldn't judge if she was making any progress.

Then a wisp of cool air passed over the knuckles of her left hand. She smelled diesel oil and sewer stink. The window was opening. She was doing it.

How am I going to raise myself up?

Don't get ahead of yourself.

Another quarter of an inch, then an inch. Another inch. Her progress was torturous. Getting closer. Closer still.

"Oh, please," she whispered aloud.

The window slid open with a tremendous racket. She almost fell off the table but she grabbed the sill and clung to it. She didn't know if there was a screen. In the dim light, she could manage to see that at least there were no bars.

She couldn't do a pull-up from a stationary stance. She wasn't strong enough. She needed to push off with as much force as she could muster. But if she came back down she would probably break the table. There'd be even more noise.

I can't do it. They'll come. I should figure out something else.

But she couldn't think of anything else. What could she do with the blanket?

Tie the water bottle around one end and throw it through the opening?

Again, she faced the problem of mustering enough force. And then she heard footsteps.

"No," she groaned under her breath. She looked at the cell, images of herself repositioning the furniture in their original locations and locking herself inside warring with a close-up of Cat's face as someone shot her. Heather had made a promise. She was going to do this.

One, two, three, she bent her knees and leaped upward. She threw her body forward—*There's no screen! Nothing's in my way!*—and grabbed the outside of the window. Her legs dangled; then she found her footing and started climbing up the wall.

The footsteps were louder. To Heather's ears, they rang like cannon shots.

She held on tight and tried to swing her leg upwards. The space was so small; what was she doing? She should go back, pretend nothing had happened—

"No way," she muttered.

She swung her leg up again. Her knee smacked into the glass panel on the right side of the window frame. The glass shattered. Suddenly the window was twice as large as before. Ignoring searing pain as the shards cut into her palm and the side of her knee, she put everything she had into getting out, getting free.

Shouting erupted behind her. Running. Heavy footfalls toward the window. Her right leg was almost out. Light blazed around her.

"Stop, stop now!" Svetlana bellowed.

Heather gritted her teeth. The muscles in her left arm spasmed as she pulled up as hard as she could.

A loud pop sounded. Then her butt felt as though someone had slapped it super-hard. She went limp and fell.

I've been shot.

With a cry, she collapsed onto the chair, and as she began to pass out, the table broke apart and she landed hard—way too hard—on the floor.

Everything hurt.

CHAPTER FIFTEEN

"Yeah, I seen your dog," the woman at JT's front door said. She was wearing a tattered turquoise housecoat and a pair of yellow slippers, smoking a cigarette and fanning herself with one of the dozens of MISSING DOG – REWARD posters he and Tess had blanketed the neighborhood with.

"Dead," she said. "In that alley back there."

Some people are heartless, JT thought. Tess had warned him to expect at least half a dozen false alarms because of the reward money. They might even get a few fake Princess Mochis offered to them.

"Do you have any evidence?" he asked.

For a moment his heart stopped when she held up a leash that resembled Mochi's. That was what she had probably found in the alley, not the dog.

"Nice try," he said, and shut the door in her face.

The phone rang, and he picked it up. It was Tess.

"You are not going to believe this," she said in a huff. "That kid with the drug charges? Chief Ward's friends? He's *walking*. Not even probation."

"Well, that's what your boss wanted, right? You did

everything by the book, Tess. You stood your ground. It's not your fault." He smiled faintly as he heard her huff again. "We should celebrate, in fact."

"Any Mochi action?" she asked him.

"No real leads." He decided not to tell her about Mrs. Housecoat.

"We find Mochi, *then* we celebrate."

"We'll find her."

"Hey, speaking of no action, I tried to call Heather a couple times, to see if she could help put up some posters, and she hasn't returned my calls," Tess said.

"She's probably kicking back and watching movies. She's got a new boyfriend, right? Ravi something? When the Cat's away…"

"Maybe when she was sixteen. Anyway, I gotta go."

"We'll find her," JT repeated. "No sweat."

He hung up and nervously devoured half a pound of gummi worms.

The rain was just the beginning, so Captain Kilman warned. Bethany told Vincent and Catherine that Captain Kilman was more worried about the impending storm than he was letting on.

"But mostly because the passengers will get bored and fussy. Like babies. I think a storm will be cool. So tonight, what are we gonna play? Because I am gonna kick your butt, Vincent."

It was their third night out and Catherine and Vincent had made a pact to tell Bethany that they needed a night off. But as Vincent took in the teenager's bouncy eagerness, he caught Cat blowing the air out of her cheeks. His wife's shoulders were rounded. Yeah, he didn't want to break it to Bethany either. But this was their honeymoon.

"You need to write up your internship report entry for

today, right?" Catherine said. "And feed Sprinkles."

"Yeah, but then…" Bethany trailed off. Her lips parted as she looked from Catherine to Vincent and back again. And in the span of five seconds, the hard, surly expression she had been wearing when they'd first met was back.

"I see," she said tightly.

Catherine pretended hard not to see. "After you get all that done, then you'll kick his butt."

"Never," Vincent put in. "You won't be able to touch me."

And from the way things were going, he'd never be able to touch Catherine. Now they were both going overboard—so to speak—to placate Bethany and break their pledge to spend the evening alone.

"You don't want me to come over tonight," Bethany said.

"Of course we do," Cat said. "But… well, we've been wondering if your dad misses you."

She narrowed her eyes at Catherine. "You don't need to *lie*."

Catherine reddened. For a cop, she was making a pretty big mess of this.

"Actually, we were thinking of asking him if we four could have dinner together sometime," Vincent said. "Like maybe tonight." Catherine nodded.

Bethany's eyes widened. "Are you *insane*?"

"We thought it might be interesting," she said. "Your dad's been to Hawaii before and we could use some pointers on what there is to do. We could invite him over tonight for a little while and then he could go back to your suite. You and Vincent could play and I-I'll read another book." Her smile was a bit on the strained side. "Or we could continue binge-watching *The Walking Dead*. Or both."

Bethany studied her. "You're sure," she said.

"Yes," Catherine promised. "So go do your report and feed Sprinkles, and we're going to look over the different tours for when we dock in Hilo so we can ask your dad about them."

"Don't you want to see Sprinkles with me?"

"I'd love to, but I've got to do some stuff and we need to figure this stuff out. So when you go home, ask your dad if he can come over, or we can phone him."

"He'll want to bring our stupid chef over here," she said.

Cat wrinkled her nose. "Let's let him. I mean, I love pizza and nachos as much as the next person, but I'm not going to be able to fit into my bathing suit if I don't eat something lighter."

"Yeah, same here," Vincent said, creating a united front.

Bethany didn't look thrilled. Vincent understood. But darn it, if he was going to spend the third night of this cruise babysitting, he was going to eat well.

"Okay," she said slowly. "I'll let you know what he says."

"Great." Catherine walked her to the door. "See you in a couple hours." As soon as she opened it, it started to rain. She held out her hand. "Oh, it's nice and warm. Run home quick so you don't get wet."

Bethany took off, and Catherine shut the door. Then without a moment's hesitation she kicked off her shoes and snaked her tank top over her head. She slithered out of her floral wrap-around skirt, and then her lacy bra and panties—two of the sexy purchases she had made with Tess and Heather. By then Vincent was naked too.

She pointed to their private lanai with its sinfully lush profusion of delicate ferns and brilliant flowers, the view of the open ocean. The rain was coming down harder. "It's so warm," she said. "It's like bath water." She looked at him coyly and added, "I've never done it in the rain."

Without another word, he scooped her up and carried her across the living room to the lanai door. He slid it open and stepped out in the gently falling water. It was very warm, and it slicked Catherine's hair away from her exquisite face as she gazed up at him hungrily. He spread his legs wide for balance and bent his head for a kiss. Her soft lips covered his;

then her tongue darted into his mouth. Oh, how he loved her. Wanted her.

This will be our year...

He set her down on her feet and she molded herself against him. Skin on skin; there was nothing between them now. Their love had been destined, and in the rain, on the immense, rolling sea, they reveled in it.

CHAPTER SIXTEEN

Miguel's primary operative met the secondary in the designated spot below decks on the *Sea Majesty*. They had never teamed up before, probably never would again, and neither knew the other's real name. It was part of an intricate system of cut outs that created dead ends for law enforcement and criminal organizations looking for retaliation, and left Miguel untraceable by either.

"The *jefe* is really pissed off at the delay," Two said. "I've only seen him this mad once before. Job got fouled up bad— target was wounded not killed, cops crawling everywhere. Blowback was considerable. The hitter who fouled it up never surfaced again."

"We have to do something, and we have to do it *now*," Number One said irritably.

Though they had individually made visual contact with their target and accessed the stateroom, neither had been able to get their hands or eyeballs on the jacket or what was supposed to be tucked away in the left-hand pocket. The original plan had been to pull a two-person bump-and-dip, and cleanly pick her pocket of its contents. No muss, no fuss. But so far the cop hadn't worn the thing in public. As luck would have it she didn't go out much on deck in the evenings, which was when she would be most likely to put it on.

"If he wants the merchandise by the time we land in Hilo," One added, "that only gives us two more nights to make it happen. I've heard that story about the hitter who messed up. If we run out of time and come up empty, we're never going to surface either. I say let's just kill them both now and grab the damned thing."

Two laughed out loud.

One scowled.

Two stopped laughing abruptly. "You can't be serious."

"We can throw the bodies overboard afterward. When the crew finally figures they're missing it will look like an unfortunate accident at sea. That happens a lot more than these cruise ship companies let on." One grinned. "Ask me how I know."

"One at a time, that's doable. But two..."

"I've done two before. No worries."

"I don't believe you. And when are we going to catch them alone long enough for a double hit? They're always hanging out with that kid and her bodyguard. And the guard is strapped; I know because I bumped him and felt the piece on his hip." Two made a face. "*Jefe* should have warned us about that."

"How could *he* know?" One snapped back. "*We're* the ones on board ship. It's up to us to tie up all the loose ends. If we have a problem we need to work around it, or flatten it. Even if that means the cop chickie and her brand-new hubby got to go."

"We still have forty-eight hours to get the jacket according to plan," Two countered.

"Face facts, the plan is in the crapper. Time to improvise."

Two said, "I contracted to do a simple B and E first. Or if the chance came up, maybe pick her pocket. That was the agreement. If we don't get what we came for it's going to go bad for us, no doubt, but you're jumping ahead to the last-ditch play. We're on a ship in the middle of the Pacific Ocean. We start dropping bodies all over the place and no matter how many go overboard there will be an investigation, guaranteed. The cops will quarantine the ship when it docks in Hilo. Our covers will be blown and there'll be no place to run."

"*Mine's* solid. It'll hold up. I'll be fine."

"Pul-eeease. A couple of forensic searches, they find and match your DNA or prints, and you're hung out to dry... for the next twenty years."

One did not seem convinced by this argument.

"We need to do some serious rethinking," Two said. "Come up with an alternative that's less risky. The cowboy option is always there if we have no other choice. Let's go over this later tonight, after you cool down a bit. We'd better get back now or we'll be missed."

As Two turned for the companionway, a shuffling noise came from the far end, just under the stairway. Someone was coming up or going down. Or had been listening to their conversation.

Without a word—or a thought, apparently—One pulled out the ugly plastic pistol that had been hidden in a carry-on duffle. Packed in pieces, graphite barrel concealed in a collapsible leg of a camera tripod, it had made it through the ship's metal detector and X-ray without being discovered.

Two held up both hands palms forward and mouthed the word, *Wait!*

But One paid no attention, digging into a side pocket, pulling out the pistol's short, fat silencer and quickly screwing it on.

Things were going south in a hurry. One seemed determined to off someone, and it didn't matter who. In desperation Two tried to grab the pistol away. One would have none of that, and shot a hard, quick elbow into Two's cheek. As Two staggered back, momentarily stunned by the blow, One bolted down the companionway, then wheeled around the staircase with pistol raised in a two-handed grip. Two's heart sank when the sound of three silenced shots—pfft, pfft, pfft—rolled down the narrow corridor. Two raced to see what had happened.

Rounding the stairwell Two looked down at the deck in disbelief. "Oh, my God, what have you done? What the hell have you done?"

"Shut up and help me get rid of the body," One said.

"No way. This wasn't part of the deal. No freaking way. This is on you, and only you."

With that, Two bounded up the stairway and disappeared, leaving One staring at the corpse. Livid at the desertion, One reared back and kicked the body so hard its arms limply jerked, then realized that taking frustrations out that way would only make the bleeding worse and probably smear it all over the deck. Having already done a thorough search of the ship's stores, One hurried down two flights of steps, entered a compartment and gathered up a plastic tarp and some bungee cords to wrap the body with. The bundling didn't take long for a practiced hand. Muttering curses, One hoisted the cocooned body firefighter style over a shoulder. One had to lock knees to keep from buckling beneath the dead weight. It was a good thing the dumping ground was close by.

The destination was a spot on the aft corner of this deck where the view from behind was obscured, the sea was accessible via a lifeboat bay, and there were no video cameras. In other words, a handy blind spot.

One left the body concealed under the lifeboat and returned to duty, waiting anxiously for night to fall.

It rained on and off all day, and the ocean grew rougher. Passengers spent more time at the rails, which was a problem. One stayed calm. Outwardly.

After dark, One hurried back and dumped the corpse unceremoniously over the side. No splash could be heard over the steady grind of the vessel's engines. With any luck, One thought, the body had been sucked down into the blades of the immense propeller and ground into so much fish food.

The unplanned murder had unavoidably delayed the main mission. There was no more time to waste. The person One had killed would be missed. Most definitely.

One marched to Two's stateroom and knocked on the door. Two immediately yanked it open, pointing a gun that was the twin of One's, right down to the fat silencer.

"Get out of here. Stay away from me. Or…"

One didn't believe Two had the stones to shoot. Brushing the gun aside, One pushed into the room and closed the door. The quarters were very close, and there was no porthole.

"What the hell were you thinking?" Two said, lowering the weapon but keeping it in hand.

"It seems to me we've had this conversation before," One said. "It goes nowhere. We have to move forward. The situation has escalated."

"*You* escalated the situation. *You* made this a crisis."

"We need a diversion. We're going to have to set the ship on fire."

Two's jaw dropped in astonishment. "We're *on* the ship, remember? We can't set it on fire."

"Just enough of a blaze to get everyone to the lifeboats. In all the confusion, one person will turn up missing. The person I killed. Presumed fallen overboard in the crush."

"The ship's fire suppression system will activate," Two protested. "They'll never lower the lifeboats."

"I know how to get around the system. And they don't have to get into the boats. They just have to muster at their evacuation stations on the main deck."

"You're out of your mind."

"No, listen to me. You wanted an alternative, and this is it. The cop and her new hubby will have to evacuate their luxury suite to answer the call to prepare to abandon ship. They'll leave the jacket behind. Easy pickings."

"What if they don't? What if she's finally wearing it under her life jacket, where we can't get at it? Wouldn't that be the cherry on top?"

"That's where you earn your pay. You wait in the stairwell for the fire alarm to go off. If the newlyweds step out of their stateroom with the coat, you shoot them both and then drag the bodies out of sight back inside."

"*Me?*" The color drained from Two's face.

"You're a pro, aren't you? This isn't your first dance."

"Of course... but ..."

"But nothing. Can you start a fire on a ship big enough to cause a full-blown panic?"

Two went silent.

"I figured as much," One said. "You don't like the way this worked out? Then come up with a better idea. And do it quick."

Two didn't say a word, just stared down at the plastic pistol.

"I'm in charge now, and you're gonna do what I say. No questions, no arguments."

When the gun came up again, One was caught by surprise. They were standing very close and there was no room to retreat. Looking down the barrel, One said tightly, "This is going nowhere good. You know that."

"Shut up," Two said. "When I step aside you're going to walk past me with your hands on your head. You're going to walk straight into the bathroom and I'm going to close and lock the door behind you."

"Whatever you're thinking, think again... hard," One said.

"I told you to shut up. Before you go through the door, put your right hand on top of your head and with your left slowly take out your piece and let it drop on the floor."

One used two fingers to pull the weapon from concealment. It clattered like a cheap toy when it hit the deck. "You can't seriously believe I'm going to give you a pass on this."

"No, but the *jefe* will if I bring back the goods," Two said, edging just a bit closer. "I think we both know what he's going to do to you."

One chose that moment to strike: left hand sweeping up in a blur, taking the silencer and pistol with it. The gun discharged with a *pfft!* The bullet slammed high into the door. One's fingers closed around the silencer and held the muzzle pointed at the ceiling. Two's finger was caught inside the trigger guard, wrist bent back at an awkward angle.

"Let go…"

One's right hand closed over Two's, covering it and the grip of the pistol. They struggled for control of the weapon, each grunting from the effort, glaring into each other's eyes. Then One moved a thumb inside the trigger guard, holding it against Two's trapped finger. Using the silencer for leverage One pushed the barrel closer to Two's chest, until the muzzle angled back under Two's chin.

"No… wait…"

"You lose," One said with a smile.

The thumb mashed down and the pistol discharged between them. One felt the heat of the blast. Two stiffened, head to foot, eyes clamped shut. Blood drooled out from between clenched teeth. One squeezed down again, making the trapped finger fire two more insurance rounds under the chin and up into the head.

The body slumped in One's grip, blood sheeting down over the chest from three wounds. One didn't let it fall to the floor, instead shifted it under an arm and dragged it into the tiny bathroom. Cracking back the shower door, One dropped the corpse's head and shoulders into the stall, right above the drain. Damn shower floor was maybe two by two. No way to get the whole body inside without folding it.

That accomplished, One took the hand sprayer from the wall and turned on the cold water, sluicing the steady flow of blood down the drain. It took about five minutes for the bleeding to stop. One felt no pity for Two, no remorse for the act. What had started out as a simple contract job had become a fight for survival. And One was a survivor.

Wiping the floor with a towel to remove any trace of footprints, One exited the bathroom and closed the door, making sure the latch clicked and held solidly. If the seas got rough they could make the corpse roll around inside and conceivably the momentum could knock the door open. With the bathroom door shut, any crew member looking into the room during the fire alarm would think it deserted and move along.

On hands and knees, One found all four shell casings and pocketed them. Standing on the room's lone chair, One extracted the slug from the door with a pen knife. The tidying up wasn't an attempt to conceal what had happened. There were three slugs still embedded in Two's brain. But it was a way to muddy the waters, introduce some confusion into the crime scene—which could add precious minutes to an escape plan.

One turned the stateroom's air conditioning and fan up to max, then gathered up Two's gun, unscrewed the silencer, and put it all in a pocket. The other gun went back into its hiding place under One's clothes. After doing a quick wipe down/smear of all surfaces that could hold a fingerprint with the towel, One took Two's room key from the little fold-down table, opened the door, hung up the DO NOT DISTURB sign, and backed out of the room, checking that the corridor was clear before locking the door.

The room key, shell casings, and pistol went down two of the corridor's widely spaced trash chutes.

After what seemed like an eternity, One was back on track and in control.

Time to light up the *Majesty*.

CHAPTER SEVENTEEN

Tess called to say she was working late. JT could hear the tiredness in her voice when she added that when she got home, they should walk the neighborhood again in search of Princess Mochi. None of the animal shelters could confirm the arrival of a chihuahua in the last twenty-four hours, which, when you considered the animal population of Manhattan, was both a lucky break and a disappointment. Ever since Hollywood celebrities had started carrying chihuahuas around like purses, the breed had become very popular. JT would have assumed any number of yipping little bulgy-eyed dogs would have been acquired in the day. But the lack of inventory also meant he had no false leads to waste time on tonight.

On the other hand, even though Mochi was chipped, there was always a chance that a shelter without working equipment would have picked her up, or that a rescue society was behind on their intake procedures and she was in gen pop, only the workers didn't yet know it.

Pacing like a father with a daughter out after curfew, JT decided he'd graded enough biochem projects for one night and done enough unproductive phoning and net-surfing. Tess liked to say that nothing beat a face-to-face interview when breaking a case. That meant going back out on the streets.

For mid-May, it was cooler tonight, so he put on his jacket and filled a plastic bag with doggie treats. Princess Mochi had a wide assortment of snacks (of course), all of it very high-end (of course). An image of Tess's encounter with the large street dog filled his mind and he decided to bring the ol' tranq gun. It had been a long time since he'd had to use it, but the familiar heft and shape of it were comforting. He and Tess had gone through a lot worse than finding a missing dog and come out the other end just fine. Just like Tess's black pump had so very *not*.

Still, he couldn't deny that his anxiety was threatening to blow off the charts. Princess Mochi might be a miniature Cujo—the rabid dog of Stephen King's inventive mind—but despite all the peeing, barfing, and shoe-destroying, and the endless, unceasing yipping—oh, dear *God*, the yipping—actually, because of that, he liked her. Why take such an annoying little creature to heart?

It didn't matter. He had. His worry extended past placating Tess's pissed-off cop brother. He wanted her to be okay. She was so little; if she ran into the streets, no car would ever see her. If she scampered off into Central Park, a squirrel would store her away in its acorn stash for the winter. Ever since Vincent had resumed a normal life—normal for him, anyway—and he, JT, had acquired a girlfriend who could drop him with one karate chop, his finely tuned protective instinct had had no target. No one to protect. Then Princess Mochi had whirred into his life like a bundle of joy dropped by a drone. He couldn't stop envisioning her hurt, or worse. On his watch.

In his workout satchel, he placed the tranq gun, her leash, copies of their reward poster, and some printed-out photos of her. He also had her pic—okay, twenty—on his phone.

He had more visual documentation of someone else's puppy than his own parents had of him.

He went outside. "Mochi," he called. "Princess Mochi."

A quartet of young guys in hoodies approached. "Mochi," one of them sang out. "Hey, man, we sellin' Mochi tonight. Get you higher than the Statue of Liberty." The four broke into laughter.

They didn't faze JT. He showed them a photograph of Mochi and said, "Have you seen this dog?"

"Is that your mama?" the tallest one said. "She must be a good cook, yo, because look at her and look at you!"

Another said, "Hey, there's a reward? Yeah, I seen her." Off JT's look, he nodded. "Swear it."

"If you *really* see her, email the address on the poster," JT said. No way did he want these comedians to call his cell at two in the morning just for kicks.

The shortest, youngest one looked at JT sweetly and said, "I hope you find her, mister."

The kid's sincerity triggered JT's vulnerability and he felt a little shaky. *There's hope for you*, he thought; aloud, he replied, "Thanks."

The four princes of the hood sauntered on. JT continued to walk the block, calling, "Mochi, Princess Mochi!"

"Yeah, Mochi, yeah," said a wizened old man who was sitting on a blanket beside a jelly jar with a few coins in it. He had a face like mahogany and was holding a sign that said US VETERAN GOD BLESS YOU. He raised a hand. "Her girl has her."

JT regarded the man with skepticism. "What girl?"

The man regarded JT with equal skepticism. "What's it worth to you?"

"If it's good information that leads to, well, a collar, it's worth a lot." JT cracked a smile at his own weak joke and showed the man the leash.

The man said, "Her name's Julia. Her nana lives in there."

He jabbed a thumb behind himself at a four-story brownstone. "Gives me coffee cake and we talk about *Star Wars*."

"You and Julia's nana?" He scrutinized the windows. "She lives in there?"

The man nodded. "I want my money now."

"I'll go talk to her." He scanned the building. No doorman. There were individual doors with porches, and the one the man indicated had a sign that said NO SOLICITORS. AND I ALREADY KNOW JESUS CHRIST.

It was dark out. She probably wouldn't open the door to a stranger. He knocked anyway. Through the closed door, he said, "I'm looking for my chihuahua. Hello? She's missing. A little dog. Julia may have seen—"

There was a lot of fumbling and lock-turning. JT remained composed. This was probably another dead end.

A stooped old lady with a kind smile and milky eyes peered up at him, or rather, in his direction. He had a suspicion that she was blind.

"Hi," he said. "We're dog-sitting and our dog went missing. It's a chihuahua named Princess Mochi and—"

"Yes," she said.

JT's lips parted. "*Yes?*"

"Julia took her. Her mother called me to let me know."

JT wanted to whoop for joy and hug her. He wanted to dance around in a circle with her. Instead, he said calmly, "May I have her phone number? Email? And possibly her street address?" When the woman hesitated, he said, "Or if you would get in touch with her and give her my contact information, I'd really appreciate it. We've been so worried." He held out one of his university business cards. She didn't see it in his hand.

"I think it would be all right if I gave you her work email," she said, taking the card without looking at it. "They live about two hours north of here."

JT didn't care if they lived in Bolivia. He wished she would give him Julia's mother's home contact information—it would be agony to have to wait a whole night—but he'd take what he could get. Besides, he was one of the world's foremost hackers and Tess was a cop. Between them, they could probably illegally obtain—

—*information that Julia's mom would know we had not been given.*

He had to cool his jets. Or charm this woman into giving him more information. "Thank you, Obi-Wan," he said warmly.

Her smile was tentative. "I'll be right back. I have her business card."

She left the chain on, leaving JT on the porch. The veteran on the blanket said, "Beam me up, Scotty."

"That's *Star Trek*," JT observed. "Is that what you talk about with her?"

The man replied, "It was the year everything changed."

"That's *Babylon Five*."

"Here you go," the old lady announced. She held JT's holy grail—the business card—between her thumb and forefinger. As politely as he could, he plucked it from her and stared down at the back of it, where she had written: *Esther Kupperman, Antiques of Florence*. There was a phone number and an email address.

"She's an antiques dealer?" JT asked.

"Their bookkeeper. Just call that number tomorrow and she can talk to you about the dog."

"Thank you. Thank you so much." He put it in his shirt pocket. "Here's another one of mine." Just in case.

"Stay shiny." She shut the door.

JT stared after her. "She's into *Firefly*? Huh."

"Render unto Caesar that which is Caesar's," the veteran said, and JT fished out his wallet.

"I have thirty-seven dollars," he told the old man. "I'll give you the rest after I pick up the dog."

"I can't make change." The man held out a hand. It was shaking.

JT gave him the bills. "Have you eaten lately?" He looked across the street at a deli. "Give me back the five. I'll get you a sandwich."

"No, it's my money," the man said, clinging to it. "Use your own."

"It's yours because I just gave it to you," JT huffed. "I'm good for the reward. I'll give it all to you later."

"Thief! Thief!" he shouted, cowering with the bills in his fists.

"Seriously, listen," JT began, then threw up his hands. "All right, it's your money. Just hang on."

He loped across the traffic to the deli and ordered a turkey and avocado sandwich with a big dill pickle and potato salad on the side. He bought the man a quart of milk and paid for it all on his debit card since he had twenty-nine cents left in his pocket. Then he sailed out of the deli and was waiting for a break in the stream of cars when someone grabbed the back of his jacket and yanked him into the alley.

"You steal that old man's money?" asked a voice as he was whirled around.

The four hoodie guys surrounded him, glaring.

"No. I gave him money. And I just bought him a sandwich, too." He held it out.

The tall one scowled at him. "You took his money to buy you a sandwich?"

"No, for him. And I didn't take—"

"Give it to us. We'll give it to him," the kid insisted.

Right. In a million years. JT scanned the quartet, his gaze landing on the short, sweet kid.

"I'm telling you the truth."

"And *I'm* tellin' *y'all* the truth, you don't give us that old man's money, you goin' to pay in another way, Grampa."

"*Grampa*?" JT's lips parted. "Do I look like… okay, okay." He held up his hands. "I'll get it. It's in my gym bag."

Tall Guy crossed his arms. Big mistake. Because JT was nobody's grandfather and he had a big, badass tranq gun in that bag.

When he straightened up with the gun in his hands, their eyes went wide.

Pftt, pftt, pftt—he shot the three biggest ones at point-blank range. They collapsed like marionettes. He spared the fourth one, the sweet one.

"What did you do?" the sweet one cried, dropping to his knees and grabbing onto Tall Guy. Then he cowered, covering his head. "Don't do it, don't! We was just hustling you!"

JT plucked out the tranq darts and showed them to the terrified boy. "I didn't kill them. I didn't even hurt them. These are tranquilizer darts. Like Tasers. They're just unconscious."

The kid bent close to Tall Guy's face. "He's still breathing. Call a ambulance, man."

"He's *fine*. I swear it." The last thing JT needed was to get mixed up in a street crime.

"How did you do that? Where do you get those?"

It would be a kinder, gentler world if New York street gangs used tranquilizer guns instead of regular guns. Kind of like the 1960s version of the *Batman* TV series, where everything was a joke. Speaking of Batman, Robin had just had his day.

"When they wake up, tell them if they steer clear of me, there's no problem."

The boy shook his head as he lifted up Tall Guy's arm and watched it fall back onto the ground.

"Mister, now there's *three* problems. Mean problems. There's no way they'll skip payback." He nudged one of the other guys, who didn't respond, either. They were all still out, and would be for some time. "Do you live around here? Because you should move, yo. Like, right now."

"Great, just great," JT muttered. Putting away the gun, the milk and the sandwich, he forced a car to screech to a halt as he jumped into its lane, then zigzagged across the traffic lanes like a frog in a video game and wound up in front of the old man.

"I did not rob you," JT said. He got the food and milk out of the gym bag and held them out. "Here's your sandwich."

The man was crying. "You took it. You took my money."

"Here." JT set down the food and the milk and stomped back toward his place. No. He couldn't go home. The kid would be watching him so he could report to his homies where JT lived.

He called Tess. It went to voicemail.

"I have good news and bad news," he said. "Call me back when you can."

CHAPTER EIGHTEEN

Pleased to be included in his daughter's dinner plans, Forrest Daugherty told Cat that he'd given his personal chef the night off, and suggested they dine at their scheduled dinner seating. There were two seatings per night in the formal dining room, and Cat and Vincent had yet to sample the cuisine. But Daugherty made up for that by offhandedly remarking that they'd all be eating at Captain Kilman's table.

Cat had read up on cruise ship etiquette and dinner at the captain's table was a singular honor. Time to dress up. She piled her hair on top of her head and accentuated her cheekbones with contouring blush. She added black jet chandelier earrings and a tassel necklace to match. Then she draped herself in a flowing, backless black raw silk gown and paired it with black silk heels and her new jacket. To her delight, Vincent had packed a tux, and they caused a stir when they walked into the dining room.

The space was filled with oval tables beneath crystal chandeliers shaped like enormous crowns; ice sculptures of dolphins and sea horses peered from oversized arrangements of orchids and bamboo. Large panorama windows framed the seemingly endless sea, which was filigreed with silver moonlight.

Forrest Daugherty rose from a table centered beneath a slightly larger crown chandelier and hailed them. As Cat and Vincent headed across the room in his direction, Vincent said, "Hmm."

"What?" Cat looked at him. Her husband was focused on Bethany's dad.

"His color's off," Vincent said.

"Maybe he's seasick. The boat is rocking."

Vincent narrowed his eyes as he studied Daugherty. "Not that much. Bethany told me about the stabilizers. She said it's common knowledge among ship doctors that lots of passengers talk themselves into feeling seasick."

"He looked really run-down the first time we met him," Cat ventured. She cocked her head as she watched Vincent's doctor-sense ratchet up a notch. "Do you think he's sick-sick?"

"I'd hazard a yes."

Heads turned speculatively as they wove among the tables. While this was the third night of the cruise, this was the first time they had shown up for their dinner seating. A heavily made-up woman was sitting on a white piano and singing in Spanish, and when she saw Vincent, she smiled and waved. He waved back and Cat arched a brow.

"One of my fans," he explained to her.

"Oh, I see," she said.

When they reached the table, they were formally introduced to the captain and the other officer present, Dr. Leslie Jones, a petite woman with bright red hair. To Vincent's left were Stephan Klein and Dre Morton, who were celebrating their engagement. The captain had agreed to marry them in a shipboard ceremony during the cruise.

"Champagne for the table!" Stephan told their steward. Bulked-up and sandy-haired, Stephan smiled at his fiancé, who was much trimmer, with black hair and salt-and-pepper eyebrows. "I feel like buying champagne for the whole dining room."

Dre smiled back, and Forrest Daugherty perked up and began to lift his hand. "No, Daddy. Don't," Bethany muttered. She rolled her eyes at Cat, who smiled at her and shrugged. *Rich parents, what are you going to do?*

"So these are our newlyweds," Dre said, leaning forward. He studied Cat's face intently, and then frowned. She touched her hair, wondering if something was out of place.

"Tell me, does it feel different?" Stephan asked. "When you say 'I do,' I mean. What's it like?"

"Perfect," Cat murmured, smiling at Vincent. "And yes, it feels different."

"Oh dear," Dre murmured, his voice catching. Cat wondered what was up with him. Did he not want to get married?

Vincent gave Cat a surreptitious nudge and tipped his head in Bethany's direction. Dejected, Bethany was staring down at her water glass. Cat felt a pang on her behalf. Maybe she was thinking about her parents. Even if it was the right thing to do, divorce was harder on some kids than others. Bethany *was* a poor little rich girl.

Then two bottles of Dom Pérignon arrived and the corks popped. The table steward and his assistant expertly filled seven glasses, presenting Bethany with what appeared to be ginger ale garnished with three maraschino cherries and a pineapple slice.

"Here's to love," Captain Kilman decreed, and everyone clinked glasses; even Bethany, who put on a game face.

"To love," Vincent said, and Cat smiled warmly as she sipped the bubbly champagne.

"So how did you two meet?" Stephan asked.

"Catherine was working on a case," Vincent replied. "She's a police officer."

"Oh my," Dre murmured again.

"Yes, it was a murder case," Vincent said. "I attempted to resuscitate the victim and Catherine found my fingerprints at the scene."

"And she thought you did it," Stephan said, chuckling. "A murder suspect and a cop. It's romantic, in its own way. Don't you think, Dre?"

"It wasn't romantic to us," Cat put in, but in all honesty, their first meeting had been supercharged with sexual attraction and the excitement that danger brought. And of course she figured out that he was the "beast" who had saved her all those years before in the forest, after the Muirfield agents had gunned down her mother. That had taken boy-meets-girl to a whole new level.

"It got romantic later." Vincent put his arm around the back of Cat's chair and she sipped more champagne. For a couple of pulse-pounding seconds, they were back in their own private world, despite the conversation and the people surrounding them.

Do other people have this? Cat wondered. *I never did before.*

Then she tucked the moment away like a handful of dried rose petals and turned her attention back to the table. To her surprise, Dre's face was a study in regret. Stephan murmured something in his ear and Dre nodded, peering up through his lashes at Cat. He appeared quite distressed.

Then another ship's officer, less formally dressed, appeared at the captain's elbow and spoke quietly to him. Captain Kilman turned to the table.

"I'm needed on the bridge," he declared. "I should be back in a few minutes. It's nothing to be alarmed about." He smiled at Bethany. "I'm sure my intern can fill in for me while I'm gone."

Indulging him, Bethany nodded. "I've got this, Captain."

She turned to the table and announced, "Storm's getting worse. We're all going to die."

Suddenly a flash of heat flared through Cat, beginning in the pit of her stomach, shooting up through her chest, and fanning out across her cheeks and forehead. She inhaled sharply. Had they turned down the air conditioning? Was that why the captain was leaving? She looked to see if anyone else at the table had had the same experience.

Another flash followed the first, and then a wave of dizziness. She lifted her glass for a sip of water, realized she had drunk from her champagne glass, and set it down.

"I'll be right back," she told Vincent. "I'm going to the restroom."

"Everything okay?"

She grimaced. "I think *I* may be a little seasick." She held up a hand as he began to scoot back his chair. "I'm fine. Mostly. Be back soon. Excuse me," she said to the table, as Vincent stood and pulled out her chair.

"The bathrooms are over there," Dr. Jones said, gesturing to the left.

"I need to go, too," Dre decreed, also standing.

He joined her as she headed for the restrooms. His smile was grim.

"Stephan and I just love that jacket," he said. "The fabric. We were just talking about how we wish we could have matching dinner jackets made for our wedding but of course we can't manage that, it's all so impromptu."

They were at the restroom doors by then. Before she could reply, he ran his fingers down the left front panel of the jacket. "Oh, there's a pocket. I didn't even see it. Lined? Wow, who made this? Perfect stitching."

What is his deal? Cat thought. He was practically manhandling her. Then he pressed a gentle arm around her shoulder.

"If you need somewhere to go, you can stay in our cabin," he whispered. "Take refuge."

"What?" Wobbly, she drew back, and he caught his lower lip between his teeth. Then he reached out his right hand; it hovered beside her eye.

"You did a good job with your makeup, but I can see it. He gave you a black eye, didn't he? That beast."

She blinked. *Beast?* Did they... know? Her vision blurred slightly. It was difficult to make sense of what he was saying. And then her mind caught up with his words and she laughed aloud.

"Oh, my *shiner*," she said. "No, no. Vincent didn't... Is that why you looked so sad at the table? You thought he did this?"

"You don't have to cover up for him. Even police officers can become enmeshed in abusive relationships. We want to help you. Do you want to speak to the captain?"

"No. Really. I-I'm fine." She didn't feel fine. So hot. And it was becoming difficult to string words together. "Except I think I'm getting seasick."

Just then, the woman who had been sitting on the piano approached them. She said, "Is the bathroom occupied?" When Cat shook her head, she added, "I'm Fidela Romero. I met your husband in the candy shop the other night. You're our newlyweds. Do you have a special song you'd like me to sing?"

"We do have a song," Cat said, remembering the first time they had danced together. And then in the bathtub, when they had thought they would have to part, but it had all come crashing down...

"He just got engaged." Cat pointed to Dre. "They're going to get married on the cruise."

"Ooh, do *you* have a song?" Fidela clapped her hands. "Did you alert the kitchen? They can make a wedding cake for you. What about a wedding dress for your bride?"

"I have a groom," Dre said. "We were eyeing Cat's jacket. Look at this fabric. Isn't it wonderful?"

"It is," Fidela said. "I just love this cut." Now *she* was caressing Cat's jacket. "My parents own a tailor shop in the garment district in Los Angeles. I used to help with the alterations and I can tell you that this is beautifully made."

"Thank you." Goosebumps danced along Cat's arms as the flush of heat transformed into an icy chill. She turned to Dre. "Will you tell my husband that I went to the cabin? I'm not feeling well."

Dre lightly touched her forearm. "But that thing we talked about…"

"Not an issue. Honest." Cat managed a smile. "This was acquired in the line of duty. Gangbanger," she added.

"Wow, *intense*." Dre's eyes were huge.

"Well, I'll see you both later." Cat lurched for the exit. "Please don't forget to tell Vincent."

"I won't," Dre said.

As she walked away, she heard him say to Fidela, "You don't suppose she's pregnant, do you?"

In the dining room, Bethany asked to take a look at the ice sculptures and her father accompanied her, much to her obvious annoyance. While the two were examining the shimmering dolphins poised above lacy coral, Vincent turned to Dr. Jones, who was seated on his left. Stephan was occupied, ordering a third bottle of champagne. Captain Kilman had not yet returned.

"I think Mr. Daugherty may be suffering from a significant medical condition," Vincent said quietly. "His circulation appears to be compromised. At the very least."

The *Sea Majesty*'s physician gazed at him coolly. "I'm not at liberty to discuss that. Mr. Daugherty and I have a confidential doctor–patient relationship."

So I'm right. Vincent picked up the champagne glass at his elbow and took a sip.

After a beat, the doctor said, "You and your wife are spending a lot of time with his daughter. I will tell you in strictest confidence that he hasn't shared the severity of his condition with her, and that she may be in for a shock."

He's going to die? Vincent frowned. "I'd assume that the *Sea Majesty* has a policy about permitting passengers who may require specialized medical intervention."

"Please don't trouble yourself, Dr. Keller." She took a drink of water. "I misspoke. Nothing will happen on the cruise."

I'm not sure she's being straight with me.

But there was nothing he could do about it at dinner. He took a sip of champagne; he realized it was Catherine's glass but drained it anyway. She could have his. Speaking of... He looked around for her. A wave of heat rushed up his chest and fanned over his cheeks.

Dre came hurrying toward him. "Your bride asked me to tell you that she's not feeling well. She went to your cabin."

Vincent got to his feet. Dre held up his hands. "I'm sure it's nothing," the man assured him. "She said she was a little seasick."

"I'm not feeling all that great, either," Vincent remarked.

Dre knit his brows. "I'd say it was something you ate, but we haven't eaten anything yet. You're looking a bit gray. Maybe Dr. Jones should check you both out."

Maybe Dr. Jones should stay with Forrest Daugherty, Vincent thought. As Dre turned to alert the physician, Vincent held up a hand. "If we need her, we'll call for her. I think I just need to lie down."

Dre nodded. "Well, I hope you get your sea legs soon."

"Thanks."

Vincent gave the man a nod and left the dining room. The stout sea breeze refreshed him as he walked up the stairway to their stateroom. Whatever had hit him had disappeared. Hopefully Catherine had recovered as well. But this gave them a perfect excuse to take a night off from Bethany, video games, and *The Walking Dead*. After he checked on Catherine he'd go back to the dining room and beg off.

Roberto was standing at the top of the stairs with his back to Vincent, almost as if he were studying their front door. It took Vincent a moment to place him as the man who had first escorted them to the honeymoon suite. He wondered what Roberto was doing there.

"Did Catherine ring for something?" Vincent asked him.

Roberto jerked, then turned around and moved his shoulders. "If she did, I'm sure your steward is handling her request, but I'd be more than glad to check on that." He began to walk away.

"No, no. It's fine." He moved past Roberto and swiped his key card. "Good night."

"Goodnight, Dr. Keller."

The birdsong trilled as Vincent entered the suite and shut the door behind himself. The foyer was dark; he tiptoed across the room and softly opened the door to their bedroom. There were no lights on, but he could make out Catherine's form lying on the mattress.

"Vincent?" she moaned. "The room is spinning."

"I wasn't feeling so hot, either, but I'm better now," he said. "Maybe we should have laid off the champagne until we had something to eat."

She curled toward him as he sat on the edge of the bed. She had taken off her jacket, gown, and bra and lay in nothing but her lacy panties. "I only had two sips of champagne."

"True. I finished your glass." He picked her clothes off the bed and carried them to the bureau. "I'm sorry this night was such a bust."

"Yeah, we finally *bust* out of video game prison and I'm

wilting like week-old roses." She rolled over on her side. "Dre thought you were beating me up. He saw my black eye beneath my makeup."

Vincent closed his eyes and shook his head. "He didn't say a word about it to me."

"And he and that singer were practically fondling my jacket. I mean, it is a beautiful jacket, Vincent, and I love it, but it was like they couldn't stop touching it."

"Weird. Listen, I'm going to tell Bethany that we're not feeling up to company. I'll be right back."

He left Catherine in the stateroom and closed the front door, tilting with the roll of the immense ship in the gathering seas. As he dashed toward the dining room, he caught a whiff of ozone just before the sky burst open and rain poured down, much harder this time. The storm was building. He covered his head with his hand.

"I think we're in for a bumpy ride," Vincent muttered.

CHAPTER NINETEEN

When Tess heard Heather's voicemail pick up yet again, she hung up the handset and glared at her office's landline.

No Heather.

No call back.

It wasn't like her.

Through the window of her office door she could see the chaos of the squad room; uniforms and plain clothes, everyone seemed to be in motion, but it barely registered in her brain.

Maybe like JT had said, Heather was off somewhere with that new boyfriend neither of them had met. But every time she had housesat for Cat before and was going to be away from the apartment, she had left word where she was headed and when she thought she'd be back. Heather could be impulsive, and she was always apologetic after she'd leapt the wrong way, but she was never distant or secretive. Dealing with Cat's little sister was frustrating at times but Tess couldn't ever stay mad for long. Heather brought out protective, maternal feelings.

Tess winced, remembering the pee test she still hadn't

taken, then pushed it to the back of her mind.

Why hadn't Heather returned her calls?

She was usually compulsive about that, along with texting and tweeting—a chatty person. Tess checked her cell again. No texts. No tweets. She realized that her attitude had gone from not at all concerned to irritated to more worried by the quarter hour. If something happened to Cat's sister on her watch she knew she would never forgive herself.

Tess looked at the piles of paperwork stacked on her desk, glanced over at the wall clock, and heaved a sigh. Nine p.m. She had already put in a thirteen-hour day with lunch—an apple and reheated coffee—at her desk. A captain's job was never done, and she was on duty twenty-four seven. She decided the paperwork wasn't going anywhere and could wait until tomorrow.

Tess took her weapon and badge from the desk drawer, grabbed her coat, purse and Cat's spare key, and headed out the door. She thought about calling JT back to tell him where she was going, but she didn't want to hear him tell her she was "just being silly."

She drove to VinCat's building in an unmarked "company car." As soon as she stepped inside the darkened apartment, a gross, piney odor hit her and made every muscle in her body tense. It reeked like someone had spilled a whole bottle of disinfectant.

"Heather?" she called as she flicked on the light.

No answer.

She immediately drew her weapon, quickly chambered the first round, and dropped the safety.

"Heather, it's Tess. Are you okay?" She advanced with the department issue automatic lowered, holding it in a two-handed defensive position that she could switch to gun-aimed and-blazing in a heartbeat.

When she reached the living room and hit the light switch,

Tess froze. She saw the signs of a struggle… and worse. Someone had splashed disinfectant all over the couch, but the darker blotches on the seat cushion and backrest looked like blood. And a lot of it. The sheer size of the stains told her that someone had most certainly died in Cat and Vincent's living room.

Oh no, not Heather. Please not Heather.

But as far as she knew there had been no one else in the apartment since Cat and Vincent left.

The horror of what might have already happened made her teeth clench and she let out a soft moan through her nose. A homicide so close to home, to someone dear, turned a seasoned murder cop into an instant civilian. Tess started to hyperventilate, but caught herself before she completely melted down.

Nothing is certain. Not yet. For Pete's sake, keep it together. Do this by the book.

Tess squeezed her eyes shut, took five deep, slow breaths, and let her inner cop kick in.

She moved quickly through the apartment, turning on all the lights, scanning it over the sights of the pistol, checking each room just long enough to verify it was empty. Satisfied that she was alone, she holstered her weapon, took out her Mini Maglite, and walked carefully back to the couch. The intense spotlight revealed two small, closely spaced holes in the seat cushion, pretty much in the center of the stain.

A double tap. From the hole diameter, a nine milli or .380 auto.

Tess leaned closer, avoiding touching or standing on anything. She saw a tiny crescent of white bone, the size of a fingernail clipping, clinging to the frayed edge of one of the holes, and down inside it something pale glistened in the bright light.

It looked like it could be brain matter.

Head shot.

There was nothing visible on the floor directly in front of the stain. Holding her breath, Tess knelt down and swept the flashlight under the couch. The beam lit up a scrap of white plastic about half an inch wide, a quarter inch long, and roundly pointed at one end. Tess could see the fine ribbing on the side facing up. She didn't have to fish it out to know what it was. A piece of zip-tie.

It had been an execution.

Oh God, Heather…

How was she going to tell Cat? What was she going to tell Cat?

Tess started crying and couldn't stop. The dam had burst. She jumped up and hurried away from the couch, not wanting to contaminate evidence. She found a tissue in her pocket and sobbed into it. When her shaking finally stopped, she put the tissue away and turned to look at the couch.

Procedure was crystal clear, but what if what had happened here was beast-related? With Cat gone, there was no one in the division she could trust to keep it under wraps. She had to call it in ASAP and notify CSU, no doubt about that, but first she needed to piece together some of the facts. And she had to hurry.

As Tess returned to the bedroom, she held the flashlight between her teeth and pulled on a pair of latex gloves. The duvet that she remembered as a gift from Cat's wedding shower was missing from their bed. She checked the closets and under the bed. It was definitely gone. The obvious conclusion—that it had been removed and used to conceal the body during transport—made Tess shudder.

Move on. Do the job.

The lacy edge of something black beneath one of the bed pillows caught her attention. She carefully lifted it by a corner. Vincent and Cat would never have left their underwear jammed under their pillow like that. Not in a million years. When her spotlight passed over the floor something scattered on it twinkled. Then she realized the picture frames on the dresser had lost their glass. She opened the drawers and found the clothes in a jumble. Someone had made a half-hearted effort to straighten the bedroom after it had been tossed.

Every room in the apartment had been gone through in the same fashion and hurriedly restored to order.

Tess had a lot of unanswered questions.

Was it a solo intruder or a team?

Who are they?

What were they looking for?

Did they find it before they left?

The more disturbing ones came last: *Whose brains had been blasted into the couch cushion? Where is Heather?*

Tess walked back to the apartment door and shined her light on it. It had not been forced; the locks and jamb were intact. She swept the light lower and noticed a symmetrical dent in the wood about six inches from the bottom and three inches from the facing edge. Some of the paint was missing and the flakes were on the floor below the wall molding and the thick metal doorstop that stuck out of it. Someone had slammed the door back hard. Like they had shouldered their way in after the locks had been opened. But Heather wouldn't unlock the door to a stranger.

Could it have been the new boyfriend? God, they knew nothing about him except that he came from India or Bangladesh and had some kind of elite job as a systems designer or programmer for a big New York firm. Heather didn't understand what he actually did for them so she couldn't explain it to Cat.

In a terrible way, that made sense. Heather had no luck with men, was always getting hurt—but never like this.

Tess stepped out into the hall, turned off the hall light, then checked the outside of the door. When she aimed the beam of her Maglite at a narrow angle to the surface, it revealed shiny mirror-image smears on the edges of the door and the jamb. Without touching either surface she moved her face into the gap. Whoever had deposited the smears was taller than she was, and they had left behind a cheek print. Not admissible identifying evidence unless DNA could be collected from it, but it helped Tess flesh out a timeline of events.

Someone—most likely Heather's boyfriend, but not confirmed—had forced his or her face between door and jamb and held it pressed there hard and long enough to leave a visible trace on both sides. Heather was not strong enough to have held the door partially open with someone larger pushing on the other side. Tess stepped back into the apartment and examined the safety chain. It looked fine, but when she shined her light on the slot that the chain tab fit into and leaned closer she saw the bottom of the slot bulged slightly—it had bent but it had held. A beast would not have been stopped by a little chain. A beast would have torn the door off its hinges and not bothered with zip-ties or a handgun.

Heather had known who was on the other side, and had unfastened the chain to let that person in. That and the intact door pretty much ruled out a beast-related crime. It was looking more and more like the new boyfriend was involved. That after Heather dropped the chain, he had shouldered the door open and broken into the apartment. The classic prelude to domestic violence.

Could it really be that simple? That horribly familiar?

Young female picks the wrong guy?

After the crime of passion, had the boyfriend ransacked the place looking to gather up any incriminating evidence? What could Heather have possibly brought with her that would incriminate him? Tess made a note to check Heather's apartment right after she made her calls. She started with the dispatcher and made the incident report, then phoned the head of CSU directly.

The third call was going to be the hardest, and Tess knew it would only become more difficult if she didn't jump in with both feet.

She took a deep breath and dialed.

CHAPTER TWENTY

In the *Sea Majesty*'s enormous laundry room, Number One smiled grimly at the ironies of life. The cop had finally worn the jacket but lifting the chip—if she still even had it—had proved impossible. It was a pity that Two had proven to be so myopic and difficult. Two had been the pickpocket, not One. But now Two was dead, the body wedged in the cabin bathroom. One had to assume that the corpse would be found. Successful assignments did not hinge on luck. It was time to step it up. Time to start the fire.

The unattended washers and dryers were running full blast. They were checked on the hour. One had twenty minutes to make the magic happen. Aware of the location of every security camera, One kept to the shadows, knocking back and forth against metal and wood as the ship rocked. Carrying a small case of supplies, One entered the room where the dry lint that had been gathered from the dryers was stored until docking at Hilo, where it would be taken off the ship and disposed of.

Lint was highly flammable.

The storage area was supposed to be airtight, but One had figured out how to secure several doors so that they would remain open in the roughest of seas—a wise precaution, since the storm was building.

The lint was kept in plastic bags. A simple twist tie was all that stood between One and the fuel required for the flames. Gloves on. Show time.

Eighteen minutes.

Luckily, there were no cameras in this room, and the cameras in the laundry room were easy to disable. No witnesses as One opened the plastic bags and sprinkled the floor of the storage room, the laundry, and the halls with the soft, powdery lint. However, One was armed, and had no hesitation about using the plastic weapon again if someone appeared unexpectedly.

Soon there was a blanket on the floors approximately three inches deep. One sneezed hard. It was a lot of lint, but not enough to create a fire big enough to send passengers and crew to the lifeboats—unless it spread. One unscrewed the sprinklers for the fire suppression system as well as the redundant backups and opened more doors along the passageway so that the fire could travel. Then One hurried to collect the secret weapon—cans of gas from the ship's stores for the outboard motors on the lifeboats, carefully gathered and placed in a locker as close to the lint room as possible—a Herculean effort considering the short amount of time One had had between hatching the plan and being forced to execute it. Hiding the bodyguard's corpse underneath the lifeboat had provided the spark—no pun intended—of inspiration for using the gas. One dumped gas all over the lint and the warm, clean sheets, towels, and passenger laundry, watching the pungent liquid spread.

Five minutes. Maybe this was too close. Maybe when the laundry attendants came to transfer the loads from the washers to the dryers, there would be some more deaths if One wasn't finished. Not that One cared.

Stay on target.

One stepped out of the room and pulled a can of hairspray and a lighter from the case. The lighter transformed the hairspray into a blow torch. The fine lint and gas ignited in a fireball. The blast pushed One backwards. The fire was much larger and hotter than anticipated.

Gasping, One raced ahead of the flames, lurching from side to side as the ship struggled in the storm. One nearly fell, grabbed the rail of the stairway, and took the steps two at a time as the fire pursued inches behind.

CHAPTER TWENTY-ONE

Heather woke up on her side, on a cold, damp concrete floor. When she rolled over onto her back, burning pain lanced through her butt cheek and she let out a little yelp. It wasn't the only place that hurt. Her head ached and there was a throbbing goose egg behind her ear. Both her right shoulder and elbow were bruised and she couldn't straighten out that arm without wincing. She had a dim memory of hanging from a high window, then losing her grip when the gun fired. The rickety table and chair had broken her fall, but it was still onto unforgiving concrete.

She blinked up at the ceiling through her tears, trying to force her eyes to focus.

The table and chairs were gone. She was not alone.

Svetlana stood by the open cell door, water bottle in one hand and the other hand open, palm up. "You take aspirin for pain."

There were three white tablets in her hand.

They *looked* like aspirin.

Her butt hurt. Her head and shoulder hurt. She didn't care if they were cyanide. She gulped them down.

"Thank you."

"Asshead shoot," Svetlana said. "I could not stop. You lucky he bad shot. He aim for head. You not hurt bad. Just little bruise."

Heather didn't feel lucky. And she wasn't reassured about the scale of her injury. Asshead had a big gun that shot a big bullet. She envisioned some gruesome Frankenstein scar on her otherwise perfect tush that she would have to explain to every future boyfriend. "Oh that? I got it when I was kidnapped by the Russian mob. He was aiming for my head…"

Heather struggled to her feet. It hurt to put weight on her left side; the pain radiated from her rear cheek up her back and down her leg. She tried to look over her shoulder at her behind, dreading what she would see. The stretching of her lower back made her butt hurt even worse and she gave up.

"Am I bleeding?" she asked the Russian. "Do I need stitches? Are you going to get me a doctor?"

"No. Bullet tear jeans back pocket. I look inside seat of pants, it nothing, just little scrape on skin. If you want, we find Band-Aid…"

It didn't feel like a scrape. It felt like she'd been kicked by a horse.

Svetlana reached out and softly patted the back of her hand. The caring, intimate gesture and the earnest look in the woman's eyes took Heather by surprise.

"You and me, we have to get out of here," Svetlana murmured.

"Yes, oh yes!" Then Heather caught herself. "Why? Why are you helping me now?"

"Because they will kill you soon. Doesn't matter if sister has coat or not. Uncle will order job and Ilya will do it. He already saying what he make you do before he kill you. You don't want to die that way."

She didn't want to die *any* way.

"But what about the risk for you?" Heather said, still

trying to understand the woman's motivation.

"Ilya want me dead too. Trick Uncle into doing it, or he do it by accident and lie. I am in same boat as you. Your sister with police?"

Heather nodded.

"Then maybe she get me witness protection if I bring you back to her?"

"Cat will, I know she will."

"Others here besides Ilya. Big warehouse building. Cars parked on alley at loading dock. You drive car?"

Heather told the unvarnished truth. "I have a license."

"You know city?"

Heather nodded, but with even less confidence. Once again she was being a people pleaser, telling the woman just what she wanted to hear. She did that because she wanted everyone to like her, no matter how much trouble it got her into. But Svetlana didn't seem to notice her hedging. The Russian was very worked up. Heather didn't want to give her a reason to abandon the escape plan. How hard could it be to find the precinct?

"Good. When time come you drive and I use this if they follow."

Svetlana took out her handgun. "I no shoot inside building unless have no choice. Too much noise. Others come. Trap us. You walk okay?"

"Yes, of course. I'm fine."

"Then come, we go. You carry light. Stay close."

No doubt about that, Heather assured herself, picking up the camping lantern by its wire handle.

Svetlana led her through the room that enclosed the prison cell. She opened the door a crack and said something to someone on the other side in terse Russian, then stepped well back. When the door swung inward, a large man with a wide, flattened nose rushed in. He looked like a heavyweight boxer or wrestler—thick neck, long, muscular, ape-like arms. Svetlana jumped forward to meet him, adding her momentum to his, and smashed the steel butt of her pistol into his chin.

The big guy's legs shot out from under him and he hit the floor on his back, head bouncing off the concrete. Except for the sizeable cut on his chin that was dripping blood over his stubbly jaw and down the side of his neck, he looked like he was sleeping peacefully.

"Is he dead? Did you kill him?" Heather asked in horror.

"No, he having glass jaw."

Heather didn't know beans about prize fighting, but she had heard that phrase before. It meant you were too easy to knock out.

Svetlana stepped over the man. "Come on," she said. "Before he wake up very mad."

It was harder to walk than Heather let on—or fully realized. The powerful impact of the gunshot, glancing to her butt or not, added to the fall from the window had caused her leg and hip to stiffen up. And the aspirin hadn't kicked in yet—if it ever was going to.

"Give me light," Svetlana said.

Heather handed it over.

Svetlana took it in her left hand, with the gun behind it in her right.

The swaying beam revealed a grim, gray, low-ceilinged corridor. Water puddled in places on the floor. The basement was airless and rank. Greasy-looking rats squealed and scampered out of their path.

The right-hand wall was lined with rows of dirty pipes, electrical conduits, and heating ducts. Heather couldn't see very far to the left; they were moving at a near jog, and the lantern's light didn't penetrate far into the gloom. Boilers? Furnaces? Electrical transformers? Heather couldn't tell. Svetlana seemed to know exactly where she was going.

Another light appeared ahead; they were headed right for it.

Her Russian protector slowed and said quietly over her shoulder, "You wait here. I let you know when okay."

Heather had no choice in the matter. She found a place where clustered pipes made a right angle, creating a little niche she could duck down behind. From that vantage point she watched Svetlana continue on under the low ceiling. When the two light sources joined it got much brighter, and Heather could see the cage door of a freight elevator, the light bulb over it, and two men sitting on cheap, white plastic chairs on either side. They didn't get up when Svetlana approached. She said something Heather couldn't make out—too soft and in Russian. Whatever she said, it made one of the men push up from his chair. The other guy just sat there with arms folded across his chest and grinned smugly up at her.

Not for long.

Heather had seen Cat do spinning sidekicks hundreds of times. Because she didn't weigh very much Cat needed the spin to put momentum behind the blow. Svetlana had thirty-five pounds on Cat and close to ten inches in height: no spin required. Her lightning sidekick caught the seated man full in the chest. The back of his head bounced off the wall and he slid onto the floor like something boneless, a squid or a jellyfish. While he was in mid-slide, the other man gained his feet, shoving the chair back out of the way, making the legs screech on the concrete floor.

Svetlana recovered from the sidekick with a precise little hop. Because of her angle of view Heather couldn't see the front snapkick, but she saw the man's face jerk up toward the ceiling when Svetlana connected the toe of her boot with his chin. And she also saw the follow through: The blonde's right leg and foot swung up high over her head. As if in slow motion, the man's arms opened wide, back arched, and he reverse swan dived into the floor with a soft thud.

"Come!" Svetlana called, urgently waving her forward.

Heather could see the unseated man was breathing. Swan Dive, she couldn't tell. Both his legs were doing a quivery dance that was very scary.

Svetlana pulled her into the elevator and yanked down the safety fence.

"Cars two floors up," Svetlana said. "More guarding loading dock."

The elevator started up with a jerk. There was a light inside, another single bare bulb.

"So far it's good," Svetlana said, putting down the lantern.

Heather watched her check her pistol, dropping the magazine into her palm, looking at the little slot in the side that showed the number of rounds it held. Satisfied, she slapped it back in place and lowered the safety with the ball of her thumb. Amazingly, her manicure had survived intact.

Heather felt goosebumps rise on her arms. Svetlana had said she didn't want to start shooting. Or maybe she meant she didn't want to *start* shooting before they got to the loading dock? What-ifs flooded Heather's brain. What if they couldn't reach the car? What if Svetlana got wounded or killed? What if Ilya captured her again?

She tried to think about something else—anything else. No doubt, things couldn't get much worse. Ravi had been killed before her eyes. She had been tied up, knocked out, kidnapped, put in a nasty cell with rats, and shot in the butt. Which still burned like she'd sat on a hot coal. But she had an ally now. An ally who had just beat up three men without chipping a true-red nail. She had to keep a clear head and not panic, no matter what happened, no matter what else she saw. She had to pretend she was Cat. Something she had done countless times growing up—and since—but this time her life depended on it. They were going to make it to a car and she was going to drive it away, and then when they were finally safe she was going to let go and melt into a shuddering puddle.

The elevator stopped with a lurch. There were bright lights beyond its barrier fence. Heather saw the inside of a hangar-like room. It was wide and had a high ceiling. The floor was divided into rows of stacked wooden crates and cardboard boxes on pallets. Unlike the basement, there would be no darkness for them to hide in.

"Get ready," Svetlana said, reaching for the gate. "Keep close behind… If I run, you run… This maybe little noisy…"

When the gate swung up, Heather reached out and touched Svetlana's back, keeping fingertip contact as the woman advanced.

A man challenged her in Russian. Heather couldn't see around Svetlana's back, but it was Ilya's voice, coming from the left.

Svetlana turned toward the sound. And when she did, Heather could see him. His face was scarlet as they stepped almost toe to toe.

"This cost you life, stupid woman," he said in English, no doubt for Heather's benefit.

She twisted out of the way as Svetlana's right elbow snapped back. Through her fingertips she could sense the uncoiling power as the blonde put legs and hips into the blow. As with the boxer guy downstairs, she slammed the gun butt square into Ilya's jutting chin. He staggered backwards, blood coursing from an ugly gash under his mouth.

But unlike the boxer, he did not go down like a sack of cement. He swung his own pistol up.

Svetlana bounded forward and hit him again with the gun butt, a straight right that landed under the nose. She grunted from the effort and there was an audible crunch on impact.

The second blow dropped Ilya to his knees on the concrete. Still not out.

He grimaced, showing broken, bloody teeth, and fired his pistol. The deafening blast of a near miss echoed through the warehouse.

Before Heather could think, Svetlana leaped away from her, putting two yards of distance between them. Clearly stunned, Ilya waved his gun around, trying to draw a bead on her. Svetlana stepped behind him and brought the muzzle of her weapon down behind his ear in a short, tight arc.

The gun discharged again as his eyes squeezed shut. He toppled forward onto his face and did not move. Svetlana quickly dipped a hand into his jacket pocket and came away with a set of keys attached to a black leather fob.

"Quick now," Svetlana said. "Cars."

Heather grabbed her hand and they ran down an aisle between stacked crates toward a double set of wide, pull-down metal doors. As they neared them, the door on the right started to rise with a clatter. Heather saw the feet and legs of the men on the other side.

Svetlana didn't slow down; she opened fire as she ran. The din hurt Heather's ears and made her flinch; bullets sparked off the concrete beneath the door. Someone screamed.

The door continued to roll up on its own as all but one of the men dove aside for cover. One was down on the platform, grabbing his ankle, thrashing, and yelling. Then he rolled off the edge of the loading dock, out of sight.

Svetlana cleared the doorway with Heather in lockstep, puffing hard to keep up. As she darted down a short flight of steps, she fired a couple of shots, presumably to keep the rest of the men's heads down.

Backed into parking spots in front of the dock was a trio of huge SUVs. Two were black, one white.

"White one," Svetlana said. "Here key. Get behind wheel."

Heather opened the driver door and climbed in. She felt like a little kid in a grown-up's armchair—barely able to see over the dash and the seat was set so far back she could just touch the pedals with her toes. Fumbling with the key Svetlana had given her, she managed to get it into the ignition.

"You say you drive car?" Svetlana said as she slammed the passenger door.

"A car yes, but this is a tank." When she turned the key, the engine started at once. It sounded very powerful.

Gunfire rattled from the loading dock. The SUV shuddered as bullets pocked the rear doors.

Heather found the parking brake and dropped the car into gear, jamming her toes down on the accelerator as hard as she could. With the tank's rear wheels squealing, she took off.

Into darkness.

"Lights!" Svetlana cried.

Heather found the controls embedded in the middle of the steering wheel and pushed the switch. Then she looked up. The headlight beams lit up the outer wall of another brick warehouse—she was heading straight for it!

She cut the wheel over hard. Too hard. The heavy SUV fish-tailed into the turn, rear quarter slamming into the wall with a jarring crash.

"Drive! Drive!" Svetlana shouted as she turned to look out the back window. "They are coming!"

Drive where?

Heather had no idea where she was, or even if she was still on Manhattan. She'd been unconscious when she'd been taken here.

The turn put them in a narrow alley bracketed by tall brick buildings. There were trashcans on either side of the alley. Accelerating, Heather plowed through them. She could speed up or slow down, but had no sense of control. The big car seemed to float between the towering walls, scraping noisily for a second against one side, then when she compensated, colliding momentarily with the other side. In the distance ahead she could see the black gap of the alley's mouth: It looked very small.

High beams from behind lit up the car's interior. Before she could look up into the rearview mirror, the back window imploded. Something smashed into the back of Heather's head rest, and then slapped the inside of the windshield. She stared in amazement at the oblong keyhole the bullet had cut through the glass.

"Faster! You go faster!"

Heather gripped the wheel tightly in both hands and straining her leg to reach, jammed the gas pedal to the floorboard. The sudden surge of power lifted up the front end of the SUV.

She didn't know what she was doing. She wanted to cry, but was too afraid to close her eyes.

Screeeeeeeeeech! The wall on the right exploded in a spray of sparks as the side of the SUV scraped hard against it.

The alley mouth loomed. There was a perpendicular street beyond it. And the headlights and tail lights of passing cars. Heather prayed for a gap in the cross traffic.

A scene from that movie that took place in Venice where the robbers drove MINI Coopers suddenly popped into her head. They had used the parking brake to make tight turns. The SUV didn't have that kind of old-fashioned lever brake. And she wasn't sure she would have been strong enough to use it and steer the car if it had. But she knew she had to brake or she would roll the car when she tried to make the turn out of the alley—there would be no wall to slam into to keep the vehicle upright.

The question for which she had no answer was: "When do I brake?"

It answered itself when she roared out of the alley doing ninety miles an hour.

ASAP.

Heather stomped both feet on the pedal, locking up the brakes. The rear of the SUV began a right-hand drift as she slid across two lanes of traffic. Instinctively she turned into the skid, which brought the front of the car around to the left.

Bright headlights blasted into her face. Wide-set, bright lights.

Its air horn blaring, the semi-tractor trailer bore down on her.

Momentum carried the rear of the SUV past the edge of the truck's front bumper. The car chasing them wasn't so lucky. From behind came a terrible crash. It had broadsided the trailer, but somehow, someway she had made it safely across the centerline. There were more lights and horns and squealing brakes as she barreled into both lanes of traffic headed left.

"You can drive," Svetlana said.

Heather flushed with pride and excitement.

High beams behind them flashed again, blinding Heather as she looked up into the rear view. It wasn't the Russians, though. It was just someone mad at her for cutting them off.

The SUV had drifted right before she realized it. The car slid against the cars parked along the curb with a screech and crash as side mirrors were shattered and ripped off. By the time she got them back on track she left half a block of destruction in their wake.

Heather cut a hard right at the next cross street. Frantically she made a series of left and right turns, zigzagging.

"We lose car," Svetlana said, "but new one follow. You take us to sister."

"Can I have your cell phone?"

"No phone. At warehouse."

Heather had no idea where they were.

CHAPTER TWENTY-TWO

*B*oom. *Boom. Boom.*

Thunder? Cat wondered as her eyelids fluttered and she tried to rouse herself. The ship was pitching, or else she was sicker than she thought, or maybe she was dreaming—

Was that a doorbell? Did they have a doorbell?

"Yes," she muttered. Then her eyes popped open. It was raining and that was a doorbell. Had Vincent forgotten his key?

She got up and slipped on the fluffy white *Sea Majesty* bathrobe, calling hoarsely, "Just a minute!" as she belted it and swayed left and right. Lightning flashed and she caught her own reflection in a mirror. She looked a sight. Her mascara had smeared, giving her hollows for eyes.

The doorbell rang again. She peered through the peephole but could see nothing—it was too dark—so against her better judgment, she opened the door. It was a man in a yellow raincoat over a ship's uniform holding what looked like a big cell phone about a foot long with an antenna.

Satellite phone, her brain supplied. *Emergency.*

"Come in." She stood aside to let the man in.

"I'm Tom Rourke, the purser," he said. "You have an

emergency call from Captain Tess Vargas of the NYPD." He held out the phone.

Cat went numb from head to toe. She wanted to panic but years on the job kicked in and clamped down every emotion in the book. She became a steady thread of action: *Do this, do that, do this next. Item one: take the phone. Item two: talk to Tess.*

"Please wait here," she said, and carried the phone back into her bedroom. Her heart thumped and turned over in her chest. This was bad news. Tess wouldn't place a satellite call for any other reason. An image of Heather and then of JT burst like fireworks in her soul. The numbness threatened to lift but she forced it to stay. She was under fire.

Officer down, the thunder rumbled.

"Tess." She took a breath, unsure if the phone was still connected.

There was a plink, static, and Tess. "Cat. Cat, listen, *I don't know*, okay? No one knows for sure."

"Knows..." She shuddered once, very hard, as if she had been dunked into ice water. "It's Heather. What's wrong with Heather?"

"I went to your apartment. Forced entry. Signs of a struggle. There's blood on the couch. Lots of it. I don't know if it's hers. What's her blood type?"

"What's her..." Cat was slipping into shock. "Oh, my God, oh, God," Cat gasped. "Tess, what-where is she?"

"We don't know. There was no one here. I need her blood type."

"Type A positive. Tess, describe the scene."

"I need to move fast, Cat. What's that guy's name? The new guy she was dating?"

"Ravi Suresh." She gripped the phone with both hands and fell onto the bed when she tried to sit down. This was not happening. Forced entry. "Tess, you need to fill me in."

"Tell me about Ravi Suresh."

Why? Cat closed her eyes. She didn't have the luxury of falling apart. That was for civilian victims. "Thirties maybe, works for Chrysalis, from India. I only met him once. But he lied to us. He said he had a text from work and he didn't." She concentrated hard. "He was nervous."

"But no animosity between them."

Tears welled. Cat wiped them away. Lightning flashed and the rain danced on the deck outside like shell casings.

"Cat," Tess prodded.

"She came over after he left the party early—we were at a dinner together—because Vincent told her he didn't get a text. She spent a ton of money on her dress…" And Cat broke down. She began to sob. "Tess, oh Tess…"

"Hold on, Cat. Just hold on. I need your help."

Cat steeled herself. "So she came over to spend the night because she was going to come in the morning anyway. She took that picture of us that I texted you." She shut her eyes as she imagined Tess taking notes: *Vic last seen alive by sister at approximately nine a.m.* "Do you have her phone?"

"Not so far. But her purse is here."

Cat bit her lip to keep from screaming. A bad sign. The worst.

"Damn it, run it down for me, Tess. The whole thing."

"The door was smashed into the door stop. Someone was shot on your couch. I have good DNA samples and CSU is on the way. We'll type the blood stat. Your place has been ransacked. Your stuff is everywhere. It looks like someone was looking for something."

The room was whirling. Cat kept a grip on the mattress with one hand and leaned her head forward. The phone weighed at least twenty pounds, or so it seemed.

"Looking for something," Cat echoed. A thought began to form. She tried to grab onto it.

Her mouth away from the phone, Tess said, "Okay." To Cat, she said, "Listen, CSU is here. As soon as I have more information I'll call back." There was a catch in her voice.

"What aren't you telling me?" Cat demanded.

Silence.

"Tess, it's me. Cat. Tell me."

"Remember that duvet you got as a shower gift? We could never figure out who gave it to you? Well, it's not on your bed."

It was used to wrap a body. A homicide cop's first thought.

"I'll fly home," Cat said. "We'll be there as soon as we can."

"Okay. Remember that we don't know anything yet. You know how this goes. You have to stay calm. You have to help me." Tess's voice caught. "Any information, thoughts, guesses, *anything.*"

Looking for something. What could someone have been looking for? The secrets of Vincent's DNA? The data on Julianna's experiments? Nothing to do with Heather, certainly.

"Have you got people where Heather's been staying?" she asked.

"Not yet. Is this correct?" Tess rattled off a Brooklyn address.

"Yes. What about Ravi Suresh's apartment?" Cat remembered that she'd just given Tess his name. They wouldn't be there yet.

"We'll get right on it. See if he's at work, if he has... answers."

An alibi, Cat filled in.

"Don't touch that," Tess said away from the phone. "Cat, I have to go."

No, please don't. "I know," Cat replied. "You need to do your job."

"You've got the best working on this." Tess did not speak from ego, just pure, simple knowledge.

"I'll see you soon," Cat promised.

The call disconnection was like a sock in her gut. She sat for a moment and then she lurched to her feet and staggered back to the foyer, where the purser was waiting.

"I have to get off the ship," she said. "Can I get a helicopter to transport me to the airport in Hilo?"

The purser made a moue of apology. "I'm afraid that's not possible. We're in a storm front and it would be too dangerous."

"You must have motorized craft aboard."

"We're two days from Hilo," he countered. "But once the storm dies down, we'll talk to the captain."

He's placating me. They're going to make me wait until we land.

"Can you radio ahead for plane reservations? I've got to get back to New York as soon as possible."

He took that in. "I'll make it happen," he promised. Then he added delicately, "Is this a bereavement situation?" She knew that airlines made special arrangements for customers who had a sudden death in the family, mostly boiling down to cheaper fares.

I don't know.

"No, but it is a crisis," she said.

"Would you care to speak to the chaplain?" He gave her a once-over. "Or our physician?"

"Not right now. But thank you." She herded him to the front door. She needed to think. She needed to pack.

Pack.

They were looking for something.

"If you need anything," he began, and she opened the door. The rain sheeted in, pelting her face like tiny slaps.

"I'll let you know. Thank you." She gave him a wave and shut the door. With the rain and the shock, her haziness decreased markedly, but she knew she still wasn't a hundred percent.

Still, she was fully dressed in a blue-and-white striped top and blue linen trousers and had her suitcases open and half-filled by the time Vincent returned. He was soaked to the bone.

"Oh, Vincent," she cried, and told him about the call. Like her, he struggled to remain calm. As he held her, she became aware of a hard object in the right pocket of his jacket. He pulled out a dinner napkin and unwrapped it. Inside lay a champagne glass.

"I think someone drugged us," he said. "No one else at the table was as out of it as us. I stuck around to check them out."

"Drugged? Did you tell Dr. Jones?"

He shook his head. Using the napkin, he set the glass down on their coffee table. "It was only a supposition. And we don't know enough to know who we can trust. For all we know, Dr. Jones herself slipped us a mickey. That said, Mr. Daugherty mentioned that he hasn't seen Terry Milano for a while. I haven't seen him. Have you?"

Cat shook her head.

It always boiled down to that. Whom they could trust. But that wasn't an issue solely for people like them, a couple who shared extraordinary secrets. Look at Heather.

Heather knows about Vincent. And Muirfield. And Liam. Someone was looking for something in our apartment. I know it's got something to do with packing for the trip. I can feel it. But what?

"Something I packed," she said, and then the light bulb went on. "Vincent, it's my black jacket. I wore my jacket to dinner tonight. It's the first time I've put it on since the cruise started. My champagne was drugged, and Fidela and Dre followed me to the bathroom. Then they pretended to admire the jacket so that they could touch it."

"And Heather wore it at the charity dinner," Vincent put in. "She had it on when Ravi showed up. They went to get drinks at the bar, and then he left right away."

"Our hotel room at Playa del Rey was tossed. Those other rooms were probably burgled to throw us off the scent." Cat touched his arm. "Speaking of scent, when you tracked the hotel perps, what did you get?"

He thought carefully. "Male, female. Specific mixtures of body odors, perfume, deodorant, shampoo. The female was older than the male. He's got arthritis. No one we've met on the ship yet, or at least I haven't caught their specific scents on the ship. But if they approached me, I would definitely recognize them." Cat's father had transformed Vincent into an apex predator, able to catalog a wealth of detail about his prey even if they were no longer in his immediate vicinity.

Cat parsed that. "Maybe they didn't come aboard. What if someone tried to get the jacket from our apartment, but failed because we had already left? Then word was given to toss our room in Los Angeles, but *that* failed because our luggage had been sent to the ship? So now there are people who were planted aboard the ship trying to get it? Vincent, this is all part of a plan." She shut her eyes for a moment, hating to speak the dreaded words. "A conspiracy."

He picked up the thread. "Roberto was surprised to find Paul already in our suite unpacking our clothes when we came aboard. Maybe Paul was looking for the jacket. But tonight I saw Roberto loitering around our suite the first time I came from the dining room tonight to check on you. So it could be Roberto."

"Or even Forrest Daugherty. He booked passage last minute. Maybe Terry Milano isn't MIA at all. Maybe Daugherty is just covering for him," Cat pointed out.

Vincent nodded thoughtfully.

"So someone is looking for something in my jacket," Cat concluded. "Maybe Roberto or Paul. Or Fidela. Or Dre."

"Maybe Dre and Stephan together," Vincent said. "Maybe

they only pretended to get engaged so they could sit with us at the captain's table."

"To get to the jacket," they said in unison.

Together they hurried back into the bedroom and the pile of clothing Cat had stripped off when she had lain down. She plucked up the jacket and they turned on the bedroom light. They spread the jacket on the bed and leaned over it, shoulder to shoulder, Vincent observing as Cat began a methodical examination. She inverted each pocket, right first, then left.

There.

It was a clear plastic box the size of a Mentos, half-inch by half-inch. Cat grabbed the end of the sheet to pick it up, shook her head, and used her bare fingers. Really, what was the point? She didn't have a print kit and they needed to move fast. Whoever had drugged them might be waiting outside right now, impatient to get this tiny cube.

If they think Heather knows anything about this, they'll keep her alive. It was not a statement of fact. It was a prayer.

As Vincent held his hands beneath the little box in case anything popped out, Cat caught her fingertip under the plastic flange and eased back the top. They both peered at it. Something metallic gleamed on a field of gray foam-like substance. A computer chip. They looked at each other. In their experience, computer chips were bad news.

"Only Ravi Suresh could've had access to this kind of tech and 'Heather's' jacket. He tracked her to our place so we need to assume he knows the jacket is here by now. We need to assume someone aboard is looking for it."

"We *know* someone aboard is looking for it," Cat corrected him

They locked gazes. Did Vincent's eyes begin to glow golden? She wasn't sure, but the moment served as a reminder that they weren't defenseless. Beast-Vincent was a terrifying creation brimming with fury, operating at super-speed, massively strong. He could tear the steel waterproof hatches of the *Sea Majesty* off their hinges, leap from one deck to another. When faced with one or two human assailants, there would be no contest.

But if Vincent beasted out on the ship in front of witnesses, that would blow their world wide open. However, to save their lives, he might have to do it.

"We can't let them find it." Cat began scanning the room for hiding places.

Every stateroom was equipped with a safe, but that would be too obvious. It had to be a place they could get to fairly easily to retrieve it without it being discovered if their room was tossed. Whoever was after it might not know that she and Vincent were onto them, and they also probably weren't sure if the box was still in her pocket. It was small and so lightweight that Cat hadn't even realized it had been there. Something that insubstantial could have fallen out on its own. But whoever was looking for it would want to verify that.

For a moment she considered lifting the tiny chip out of the plastic box and placing it in an envelope in order to hide it. Their suite came equipped with stationery. But she was afraid they would lose it during the transfer. For all she knew, it contained a tracking device that was beaming out its location right now. Maybe it could be used to trigger a bomb brought aboard the ship. Maybe whoever wanted it so badly was prepared to destroy thousands of innocent lives rather than allow it to fall into someone else's hands.

Maybe they will contact me to offer a trade: it for my sister.

She wouldn't, couldn't think about that now.

She went to the closet and slid the box into the toe of a pair of red flats she had yet to wear. Then she straightened out her row of shoes and did the same to his. Then she second-guessed herself, took it out of her shoe tip, and grabbed up the bag Vincent had received when he'd bought all the sweets for Bethany at the candy shop. They still had half a pound of Jolly Rancher hard candies. She untwisted a rectangle of sour apple, popped it into her mouth, concealed the plastic box in the wrapper, and put it inside the sack with the rest.

She knew from experience that their steward would leave the bag alone—unless he decided that the time had come to tear the place apart inch by inch.

Then she went to the bathroom, redid her face, tucked her hair back into her updo, and put on the jacket. Vincent grabbed two umbrellas that had come with the suite and together they went outside. The rain was still coming down hard. They made it to the railing as they headed for the dining room but their umbrellas were on the verge of inverting and within seconds, were useless.

At night, the *Sea Majesty* shone bright lights on the waves and tonight was no different. Cat wondered if it was wise to let the passengers see how rough the seas had become. The *Sea Majesty* was currently moving through a trough as waves crested to its right, forming a wall of water rising that seemed to barely miss the side of the ship as it crashed back down. They both darted back under the cover of the archway.

"I can see why Rourke nixed the helicopter and the watercraft," Cat said wanly. "We need to figure out how to play this. Let's assume that if we're right, and someone on board the ship is looking for the chip, they're an underling working for someone higher up."

"Right." Vincent raised his chin and frowned slightly.

She swallowed down deep terror. "If that person broke into our apartment in New York, and not Ravi…" She started to lose it. "If they were following Ravi, and Ravi was trying to get to the jacket because Heather was wearing it…" Her hands shook. "If we let them know that we have the chip, their operative will try to collect and we can buy Heather some time."

"Catherine," Vincent said, but she held up her hand. She refused to consider that Heather was dead.

She said, "If they're monitoring the ship, if they've planted bugs... or if they have someone on the payroll on the bridge, maybe even the captain... if I call Tess and tell her we have it, maybe the head of their operation will hear. They'll know."

"Catherine," he repeated.

"I know it's risky. But if they don't know you're a beast, they won't know what they're up against." She gazed up at him. But he wasn't looking at her. His faraway look and alert stance told her that he was sensing something that she could not.

"I smell a dead body," he informed her. "And smoke. Lots of smoke."

CHAPTER TWENTY-THREE

"JT," Tess said, as she picked up. She was moving through Cat and Vincent's apartment with an ear cocked for CSU's field test results on the blood type on the couch. They had already confirmed the presence of bullets and bone and brain tissue. Whoever had been shot on the couch, the bullets had passed clean through the skull. The room was filling with people. They had detectives from the sixth precinct here now. She was the captain of the 125th, and on top of that, she knew the potential vic. She should stand down.

No way.

She had searched through Heather's things for more clues as to what might have happened, and to whom. Because this could not be Heather smeared all over the couch. It could not. Heather's cell phone was missing, and there were no recent emails between Cat and Heather about anything. Like most people nowadays, they texted. There was no way for her to reconstruct what had happened here.

Yet.

"Oh, my God, it's been so crazy," JT said on the other end of the line. "So there was this old guy. Do you know what *Firefly* is? *Firefly*, how wild is that? I mean, no one knows what *Firefly* is."

"JT," she said again, her voice gravelly and tight.

"But I know where Mochi is! Or at least, I have a decent lead. I have to wait until morning. But uh, well, I'm not sure what to do. There were these street kids and…" He paused. "Tess? Are you there? What's wrong?"

"I'm at Cat and Vincent's." She told him why, running it down clearly, concisely. Now that she had walked through it with Cat, she could keep her feelings out of it. Sort of.

"So there's no body," she concluded. "I don't know what I'm looking at, exactly. But I know what I'm seeing."

Death.

"Tess," JT said after a long silence, as if her name was his mantra. "I'm on my way."

She was moved. There had been a time—a long time—when he would not have thought to rush to her side when things went south. He had not put her first. Now he was.

"Stay there," she said gently. "This is a crime scene now, and I may need to move fast. Wait until—"

Tess's heart stuttered as the CSU tech glanced up from the microscope Tess had told them to bring. "Results in. Type O, Captain," the tech announced. Tess sagged with relief.

"It's not Heather's blood," Tess told JT.

"Thank God," JT breathed. "Tess, what the *hell*—"

"Captain Vargas, there may be linkage between this and the jumper." That was Detective Kelly Goss. When the woman could see that Tess wasn't following, she said, "We had a jumper off the roof of this building earlier this week."

"*What?*" Tess's adrenaline spiked. "JT, gotta go."

"Wait, Tess, please," JT said.

Tess cut the call and put her phone in the pocket of her jacket. "What jumper?" she asked Goss.

"A John Doe," Goss said. "Assumed to be a suicide, so low priority."

"John. You're sure it was a John." That the victim had

been male, in other words.

"Yes. There were a couple of bad jokes about only being able to tell from the waist down. On account of no… well, *other* head," Goss replied.

"No head?"

"Well, there were parts of a head. It's a long way down."

"No ID? Prints?" Tess asked. It was incredible to her that she had not heard about this, but really, why should she have? If Heather had already been abducted—*that's how I'm going to see this,* she decided—and Cat and Vincent were gone, it would be a miracle if a suicide in precinct six caught any interest from anyone in the one-two-five.

"I'm not working it," Goss said, "but nothing popped when prints were run through IAFIS. We used the NYPD database, too. And nothing."

"Do you still have the body?"

"I'm sure we do. We're backed up and again, this looks like a straightforward suicide. The shoes were on the roof ledge. You know that's an MO for a jumper."

Or a cover-up for a homicide.

"Do you know any other details? Missing person reports? Was this apartment canvassed?" *Did anyone answer the door? If so, who?*

"I don't know, Captain."

"Kelly, footprint," the other detective called. Tess walked around the bloodstained couch with the detective. "A partial."

Tess bent over with Detective Goss. It appeared to belong to a woman's heeled boot, judging by the shape and size. And she was pretty sure it was bigger than either Cat's or Heather's.

"Hold on," she said, and went into Cat's bedroom. She retrieved a heeled boot and then went into Heather's old room, where a suitcase lay open. Heather was working for a temporary agency, which meant packing a number of different styles of outfits for various jobs. There were no boots, but she did have some heels. Tess selected a sampling and carried all of them back to the two detectives and the photographer, who was snapping pictures of the partial.

She gave each detective a shoe. As she had anticipated, Cat's boot and Heather's high heel were smaller than the partial. So another woman had been in the apartment during or after the shooting.

"I don't think you caught a suicide," Tess said. "I think it was a homicide." She ran down a mental list of precinct captains. "Is Devon Frost still your boss?"

Goss nodded. "Yes, ma'am."

"I need his home phone number."

Goss gave it to her. Tess placed the call. It was late but Frost picked up on the second ring, just as she would.

"Captain Frost, Captain Vargas, one-two-five," she said, and ran it down. Then she said, "This is personal. This is the apartment of one of my detectives, Catherine Chandler. She's on a cruise with her husband, and I've notified them. But her sister was housesitting, and she's missing."

"And you think the body we scraped up off the street was a guy named Ravi Suresh."

"I don't know. Suresh has no prints on file but we can get them at his apartment. He works at Chrysalis. If you can get us a warrant—"

"Of course. Let me call the judge. I'll call you as soon as the warrant's issued. Is Goss there? I'll send you with her. She's good. Has a little sister, too."

Heather is *like my little sister.* Again, tears threatened her professionalism. *I've got to stop being so emotional.*

"Detective Goss," Tess said, and put the detective on. Goss listened, slid her glance toward Tess, and nodded at her.

"Yes, sir," Goss finished, and hung up. "Captain Vargas, Chrysalis is close and we don't have Ravi Suresh's home address yet. My captain is calling the warrant in for Chrysalis. Let's take my car. If Suresh has any kind of security clearance—and we both know he must—he'll have prints on file there. We can get them." As Tess began to object, the detective raised a hand. "We can get his home address at Chrysalis too."

Tess said, "As soon as we have the address, Captain Frost will send detectives to his apartment?"

Goss shrugged apologetically. "Or you and me. The sixth is on a big case—*another* big case," she corrected herself. "So we're a little short on extra hands. But by the time Captain Frost calls with the warrant, we can be halfway to Chrysalis."

"We'll be at the front door if you let me drive," Tess said.

Goss inclined her head and fished the keys out of her pocket. She explained the situation to her partner, a guy with a haircut close to non-regulation, who replied, "Happy hunting. I'll keep you in the loop."

"Likewise, Steinberg," Goss replied.

On the way out of the apartment, Tess remembered to explain the situation to her own partner. She called JT and told him about the jumper.

"Sit tight," she told him. "Go look up everything you can find about Ravi Suresh and Chrysalis. I think he was the murder victim. See if you can connect him to anything. If there's a woman in the story somewhere. I mean a woman besides Heather."

"You want me to go look up everything," JT repeated. "On my computer. At my place."

Tess furrowed her brow. "That's where you can hack into the…" *Good stuff*, she was about to say, but Goss had just caught up to her. "Call me if you find anything."

"Okay, remember how I was talking about the street kids?" JT said.

Goss handed her the keys and they got into the elevator. "This call is probably going to get cut off," Tess told JT. "Are you okay?"

"Fine," JT said quickly. "I'm just fine. No worries. I'll go do my Robin thing."

"Good." Tess hung up.

We make a good team, she thought. Before she realized what she was doing, she pressed a protective hand over her abdomen.

She asked Goss, "Do you have any kids?"

Goss stared at her in horror. "Perish the thought." Then she twisted her face into an apology. "I'm sorry. Do you?"

"Not so much." Tess shifted. "I mean, we're dog-sitting and it's like having a kid."

"Except dogs don't need braces and prom dresses and college tuition. Dogs don't post pictures of you asleep on the couch with drool on your chin all over social media."

Yikes.

The elevator went down and Tess noted the assemblage of police vehicles. No press yet. She hated the idea of more publicity for Cat and Vincent. In his first attempt to rejoin society after eleven years in hiding, Vincent had been paraded in the media as a war hero with amnesia. Then the late, not-lamented Assistant District Attorney and former beast Gabe Lowan had manipulated the press to get Vincent labeled as a homicidal "vigilante" whom every red-blooded New Yorker tried to track down. After that, Liam, the ancient beast responsible for the death of Cat's ancestor Rebecca and the beast Rebecca had loved, attempted to frame Vincent for his own crimes. They had kept that one out of the limelight, but only barely. Through it all, Tess had lied and covered up and would again for her two friends, but she was sick of it all. Sick to death of how many innocents were harmed from the fallout caused by her own government's failed program to create super-soldiers. She included Cat and Vincent in that endless chain of near-demonic cause and tragic effect.

Suresh wasn't a link in that same chain, but if he had been

killed because of some high-tech program, it was more of the same. And Heather, that most innocent of souls…

Do not let Heather be dead.

"Here, Captain," Detective Goss said, indicating their ride, a nondescript sedan. They climbed in, Tess behind the wheel. The city was ablaze with lights and traffic. A couple strolled down the sidewalk arm in arm. The woman was carrying a bouquet of roses and she playfully bopped the man on the head with it. Tess gave one moment of mourning for Cat's aborted honeymoon before she put on her game face.

Goss's warrant came in.

"Good to go." Goss couldn't keep the excitement out of her voice and seemed to know it, as she became more subdued and added, "I know this is very personal, Captain Vargas. I'll do everything in my power to clear this case."

It's not a case, it's Heather, Tess thought, and a queasy roll of anxiety rumbled through her abdomen. Queasiness, or morning sickness?

She nodded at the woman. "Thanks."

"I've followed your career. I know you believe in adhering to procedure, same as I do," Goss went on. "Step by step, orderly procedure. Covering our bases as we go. That's why you had such a high clearance rate."

Is she reassuring me or warning me? Tess wondered. She replied, "You must know that my clearance rate took a huge dip for quite some time."

The detective hesitated, then said, "Permission to speak freely?"

What, are we on Star Trek? Tess thought. She nodded. "Please."

"Well, isn't that because you were partnered with Detective Chandler?"

Stunned, Tess pulled in her chin as she looked over at Goss. "Really? That's what people think?"

Goss nodded.

"But the years when my clearance rate was the highest were the same years when I was partnered with Detective Chandler."

Goss shifted in her seat. "Well, ma'am, the belief is that you did the work, and that you got it done in spite of her, not because of her. After all, she got called into IA at least twice." She grimaced. "This conversation has turned sideways, and I'm sorry about that, Captain. I know she's your best friend and this is not the right time to have this discussion."

Tess looked at her hard. "I don't think there *will* be a right time to have this discussion." She felt bad for Cat. If her fellow cops believed that Tess had carried her for all those years...

Maybe I did carry her later, when she was trying to protect Vincent. And I did put in for a new partner when I caught her destroying evidence. All that is trailing after her, Tess thought. *She's done stellar work since then, but a lot of it has been under the radar, for Homeland Security and ridding the world of Liam. But she'll never get credit for it.*

"I overstepped." Goss had gone a little pale. "I-I didn't realize you hadn't heard all this before."

Concentrate on the case, she thought. *On Heather.*

"Let's move on," Tess said.

Goss inclined her head. "Gladly."

"You realize we may be looking at a kidnapping in addition to a homicide," Tess ventured. The detective's lips parted but she said nothing, only nodded—reluctantly. The bead Tess drew was not comforting. *I think she's going to get in my way. I may have to peel off from her.*

It took twenty minutes and forever to arrive at Chrysalis, a towering octagonal structure illuminated with blue and purple lights. Badges got them into the private executive lot adjacent to the building, and into an elevator leading to the twenty-seventh floor, where Ravi Suresh's laboratory was located.

"Dude has a lab, wow," Detective Goss said. As they got out of the elevator, they flashed their warrant at a very nervous security guard, who understood that he had to let them in, but started punching in numbers on his station console phone right away.

Suresh's office and lab were both listed in the warrant. They had to call the guard over to unlock his office door. Tess braced herself for an argument, but there was no pushback. Then as the door was opened, she half-expected a toss, but it was pristine. A well-padded leather chair sat behind a mahogany desk covered with as many computers and monitors as JT's desk, only these were smaller and sleeker. The far wall was a curtain of glass that looked out over the city.

"I'll call in for some IT support," Goss said, taking out her cell phone.

We don't have time. We so don't have time, Tess thought but did not say. "Good idea." She did a visual scan of the desk for a plain old-fashioned notepad, a pile of receipts; something that could lead to additional warrants covering cell phone calls, credit card charges, anything that could create a trail. She felt like a runner waiting for the starting gun.

Then she saw that the top drawer to the desk was pulled slightly open. And inside lay the unmistakable shape of the lower third of a smartphone.

"I'm having trouble catching a signal," Goss said. She indicated the wall of glass. "I'll try over there."

The second Goss's back was turned, Tess darted her hand into the drawer and plucked up the cell phone. She glanced at Goss, who was facing the glass. Could she see Tess's reflection? She put her back to Goss and dropped the phone into her jacket pocket.

"It's Goss," the detective said into her phone. "Yeah, I'm

at Chrysalis, on my warrant. There's a whole lotta sci-fi stuff here and… yeah, exactly. Do you think it'll hold up? Okay, good. Yeah, we'll be here."

She hung up and turned to Tess. "Captain Frost is checking with the judge to make sure our warrant covers the computers."

Tess stared at her in disbelief. "Of course it does." *Unless they didn't word it correctly.* "May I read it?" she asked in a calmer tone.

Goss tapped her phone face and held it out to Tess. An attachment had opened. "Here, Captain."

Tess began to read. Everything looked fine to her. But she knew that until Captain Frost gave his detective the word, no one was powering on a single device.

I have the cell phone.

She said, "Okay, while we're waiting, I'm going to the bathroom. I'll be right back."

Ducking out of the office, she saw the security guard, who was on his phone, and asked him to unlock a bathroom. It was then that she saw the glow of an office window farther down the hall.

He said, "No need to unlock it, ma'am. These eggheads work around the clock." He pointed to the end of the hall, past the office light.

"Thanks," she said.

She walked down the hall and stopped at the door of the occupied room. She rapped once, then opened the door.

An attractive middle-aged woman looked up from a bank of computers similar to Suresh's. She smiled pleasantly at Tess. "Yes?"

I don't have jurisdiction, Tess reminded herself, but she flashed her badge anyway. The woman's lips parted.

"I'm Captain Vargas, NYPD," she said. "We're here investigating a case. May I ask you a few questions…"

She looked at the nameplate on the woman's desk "…Ms. Vanderberg?"

Startled, Anne Vanderberg lifted her hands off her keyboard and folded them against her chest. "Is it all right with Steven? Steven Lawrence, I mean. He's our CEO."

"This is a matter of urgency," Tess replied. "Do you know Ravi Suresh?"

"Yes, of course. We're on the project." She blanched. "I have a security clearance. I need to speak to legal before I talk to you."

The project.

"We have a warrant," Tess said smoothly. "But I just need to know a few basic questions. He's been gone from work for a few days."

"Yes. I figured he was ill. We've all been working so hard." Ms. Vanderberg reached for her phone. "I really should talk to legal first."

"So that leaves the rest of you holding the bag," Tess continued. "Makes for interruptions."

"Not really. Ravi's part was pretty much completed." She cocked her head. "Is he in some kind of trouble?"

"You must have strict protocols to safeguard your work—"

"May I help you?" a voice said from the door. Tess turned. A fifty-something man, quite handsome, stood in the doorway with her old friend the security guard.

"Steven." Ms. Vanderberg heaved a sigh of relief. "This is Captain…" She shrugged apologetically. "I'm sorry. I didn't catch your name."

"I'm Steven Lawrence," the man said. "The CEO of Chrysalis."

"I'm glad you're here," Tess replied. "We're investigating a possible homicide that may involve your employee, Ravi Suresh."

His brows shot up. "A *homicide*? The other detective told

me this was a suspected suicide."

Tess wanted to shoot Goss. Instead she plowed ahead. "Did Ravi Suresh have any enemies at work?"

"I need to call our attorney," Lawrence countered. "You understand. It's not that we have anything to hide. It's simply that we deal in projects at the highest level of secrecy and we must remain in compliance."

She could argue that he had to answer her questions. She could go back into Suresh's office and wait with Goss for verification of their warrant, or for the tech guys to show, whatever. But she had a feeling that the FBI, Homeland Security, and other government agencies were about to tie up this entire investigation with red tape.

And she had Suresh's cell phone.

She said, "Of course, sir. We understand completely and we'll do all we can to be of service. This portion of the investigation will be in the hands of Detective Goss. She's the lead on this case." She nodded at Anne Vanderberg. "I'll leave you to your work."

When she reached the door, Lawrence moved politely out of the way. As she walked back toward Suresh's office, the CEO and the security guard followed closely behind. The vibe she got off Lawrence was that while he was concerned about Ravi Suresh, he wasn't worried about anything else.

"Still waiting," Goss told Tess when Tess walked into the office. "I'm sure we'll have an answer soon."

"Right." Tess masked her own frustration and anger. "I'm going to move on. I'll catch a cab. Will you call me if you find anything?"

"Yes. I promise, Captain." Goss looked from her to Lawrence. "Have you heard back from your attorney yet, Mr. Lawrence?"

The man shook his head. Tess mouthed *Later* to Goss.

* * *

That used to be me, she thought as she hailed a cab and gave the driver Cat's address. *"By the Book" Vargas.* God, *I must have been so annoying.* She managed a plaintive smile. *Still, back in the day, Cat and I had the highest clearance rate in the precinct.*

Before she got in her car, she flashed her badge and went back up to the crime scene. Correction: Cat and Vincent's apartment. The cell phone felt heavy in her pocket.

"Anything?" she asked Detective Goss's partner, the haircut guy.

He rolled his eyes until the CSU who'd performed the blood test said, "Captain Vargas is Detective Chandler's best friend."

Whatever the detective was going to say next went left unsaid. Instead, he supplied, "We have two assailants. I talked to the ME's office and the autopsy is going to start on the John Doe in about an hour."

An hour. Tess was in agony but she didn't let it show. This guy was getting things done faster than Goss. Still, she remembered the lightning-fast results she'd become accustomed to when Evan Marks had still been alive. She'd had no idea at the time that he was hunting down the mysterious "human hybrid" whom Cat was protecting—that being Vincent, of course. Nor that Evan had laid down his life to save Vincent and Cat from Muirfield once he had learned the whole story.

Handing Haircut her card, she said, "I'd be grateful if you would call me personally with any updates."

She was making an end run, ignoring procedure and asking him to go outside his chain of command. So much for Goss's idol worship of her and her adherence to protocol. He nodded and looked at her card as if memorizing her number and put it in his wallet.

"Sure thing, ma'am," he said. Then he added kindly,

"We'll find Detective Chandler's sister."

So someone got it. Someone knew it was about more than Ravi Suresh and his "suicide."

"You ever want to move precincts, let's talk," she said.

"Name's Chuck Steinberg." They shared a look, sizing each other up, and then she was gone.

CHAPTER TWENTY-FOUR

When Tess pulled to the curb in front of JT's place, she found a quartet of guys in hoodies loitering around the front door. Was that a flash of metal? As in a *gun*?

"Hey," she said, showing her badge.

One of them swore and the four scattered. *What was that all about?*

She let herself in… and found JT on the other side of the door, baseball bat in one hand, tranq gun in the other. He leaped at her.

"Hey, whoa," she said, grabbing the bat and lowering JT's arm—much more considerately than she would have if her attacker had been one of those guys outside. "Were those dumbos harassing you?"

"You could say that," JT replied. "But you're here now, so it's time for Tums and Scotch instead of murder and mayhem. Good news, I hope?"

"Lifted Suresh's phone." She grabbed the cell out of her pocket and handed it to him. "Hopefully, a lead." She pointed to it. "Let's look at his phone calls. And? This is all off the books. I can't have our activity detected." She followed him as he carried the phone over to his Robin-cave, good feelings supplanting her ire at Detective Goss. JT would save this day.

I stole evidence, she thought. *Scratch that. I may have saved a life.*

"Hacking's what I do best," he said, sitting at his command center, and she bent over him and kissed the top of his head.

"That's debatable," she replied. Then she sobered. "This has got to break the case."

"It's not a case. It's Heather," JT replied, and she kissed the top of his head again and hugged him. He depressed the button on the side of the phone to activate the power.

"I didn't turn the phone on before because I didn't know if there was any kind of 'find my phone' app on it. I didn't want to lead anybody here."

"Well, you know what they say, 'All roads lead to Rome,'" he replied drily. She didn't respond, so he tried again. "I'm beginning to think my place is listed as a New York City must-see attraction." She still didn't quite get it. "Let's see what we've got."

She hovered over his shoulder while he plugged the phone into one of his electronic devices and brought up a screen. Lines of computer code pixilated into existence.

"No tracker app," he reported. "In fact, it's shielded from detection. Interesting." He studied the screen for a moment, then typed with his usual rapid-fire staccato style and sat back. "This is serious stuff." There was a lilt of admiration, even excitement, in his tone.

Yes it is, so please hurry, Tess thought, but held her peace. Exhaustion washed through her. She was drained, yet mounting anxiety fired off more packets of adrenaline into her system. Her hands trembled and she moved away, pacing, running her fingertips along the ridges beneath her eyebrows to keep a headache at bay.

I should call Cat to tell her it's not Heather's blood, she thought. *She's probably losing her mind.* But that was all she had so far. There were no guarantees that Heather was still alive. And if she called Cat right now, nothing would be resolved. It would be scant comfort that the blood on the couch belonged to someone else.

"I need to hack into the medical examiner's records, too," she said, thinking aloud. "Or maybe just go down there, see if I can ID Suresh as the jumper. There've got to be selfies of him on that phone."

"I don't think so, Tess," JT said. "This looks like an 'all work and no play' kind of phone. He's probably got... I'm in. Check it out." He pointed to his largest desktop display, where a string of ten numerals followed by a string of seemingly random letters began to crawl down the face of the monitor. "Ten numbers probably means phone numbers. And the letters might be encoded last names."

"Right." She nodded, hope a tiny spark flickering in her gray field of fear. "Which you can decode."

"Given enough time," he said under his breath.

They both knew that time was in short supply. Tess flipped open a laptop that he'd long ago configured for her to use—firewall-protected six ways to Sunday—and she looked up "Ravi Suresh" on Referenda. An article about the annual Chrysalis 5K for ALS research popped up, complete with a photograph of Team Chrysalis. Ravi Suresh was the second from the left in the first row. Steven Lawrence stood beside him and at his feet, a little French bulldog was dressed in a miniature version of their run T-shirt, featuring the Chrysalis logo of a cocoon superimposed over a chambered nautilus. Tess's gaze moved from the image to Princess Mochi's empty bed and she felt a tug.

"You said you found her," Tess ventured.

"*May* have," he corrected. "I have a work number for the mom of that little girl who wanted a dog. The one you met on the walk before Mochi peed on your head. Her grandmother says she took her. The girl, I mean." He grunted. "The nana is into *Firefly*. How about that?"

"Huh." Tess had no idea what that was. Maybe in happier times she could find out. If they ever had happier times again.

"Okay, here we go," JT said, leaning forward.

Each random string of letters reassembled into a word. And not just a word, but what appeared to be last names. And the name that came up the most was:

"Anatoly Vodanyov," JT read aloud.

Tess blinked. "Are you kidding? He's a Russian mobster. He's involved in all kinds of criminal activities. Everyone is after him. Homeland Security, Interpol, FBI. And us. As in NYPD. And also *us* as in you and me, apparently. Can you do anything with that phone number? Like, hack into *his* phone or anything?"

"Without a way in? Only late at night when you're watching James Bond," he countered. "If you could get a warrant—"

She paced again. "That ship has sailed."

JT kept skimming the list. Then he brightened. "Oh, hey, this is interesting. After, like, a dozen calls in a row to Vodanyov, Suresh hardly ever called him. He started trading calls with this number"—he pointed to the screen—"to someone named QQQQQQ." That's all I can get. It's so encrypted not even I can unencrypt it. Unless it's just a string of Qs."

Tess processed that. "So whatever he was doing, either Vodanyov passed him along to the next guy in the organization or he stopped dealing with Vodanyov in favor of this guy," Tess said. "Maybe he got a higher bidder."

"On what?" JT was thinking aloud. "Chrysalis is into some pretty woo-woo scary-level stuff. Weaponry, bionics, cloning… I wonder if they can clone a chihuahua yet."

"You said you found her," Tess retorted.

"I have a good lead on her," he answered. "Look. Here are more calls to Q. Is there someone bad named Q besides the Q on *Next Generation*? There was also a Q in James Bond, you know."

"It's like another language," Tess murmured.

Her phone rang. It was Detective Goss. "Captain Vargas, I'm still waiting for forensics. I did get a few things. Suresh is working on something very hush-hush. It's a weapon and it has something to do with computer chips. That's all Chrysalis is saying."

A chill tiptoed up Tess's backbone and knocked at the base of her skull. So this nightmare originated in high-level spooky stuff, as she had feared.

"Is anything missing? Let's see if this makes sense: Ravi doesn't show up at work, maybe he's stolen the prototype, tries to sell it." *To the Russian mob or somebody named Q.*

"It doesn't appear that anything like that has happened," the detective said. "A whole bunch of Chrysalis higher-ups are here with Lawrence but the vibe is concern for Suresh on a personal level only. They aren't acting like they've had a breach."

Maybe they're just really good actors. You were riding with one to Chrysalis just a little while ago. Tess said, "Did you catch Suresh's home address?"

There was a beat, and then Goss said, "Yes, ma'am. That's why I called you. Here it is." She rattled off an address in Brooklyn. Tess wrote it down.

"Can you meet me there? Is anyone else going there?" Tess asked.

Another pause. "Captain Frost is looking for more hands. There was a shooting on Houston that we think is unrelated to this case, but it's still in our jurisdiction. So we have to respond. He's on scene now. So no one *else* will be at Suresh's apartment anytime soon. No one on the books, I mean."

If Tess could have managed a smile, she would have. So much for worshipping "By the Book" Vargas. Goss was getting out of Tess's way all on her own. Maybe this was her way of apologizing for those things she had said about Cat.

"Thanks," Tess said. "I'll remember this."

She hung up. "JT, I have Suresh's home address. I'm going over there." When he began to push out his chair, she placed a hand on his shoulder. "You know you have to stay here."

"You're going with backup." He was not asking. He was demanding. Shaking her head, Tess headed for the old bank vault filled with safe deposit boxes that was part of JT's place. She opened the box she used to store extra weapons and ammo.

"*No?*" JT said as she returned. "You can't go alone. You may be running straight into the arms of the Russian mob."

"I have to do this, JT. By myself. Off the books. If Cat and Vincent were here—"

"*I'm* here," he tried again. She read the frustration in his eyes—and also the capitulation. He knew he would be more helpful by staying behind and serving as headquarters. "I'll pull up everything on Vodanyov and his people, see what I can put together. I'll start running facial recognition software on them. And Heather, and Suresh." Off her tight expression, he said, "Hey, we found Vincent, remember? Alive and well. Relatively well," he amended. "And now he's better than ever."

"Thanks, JT." Now she did manage a weak smile. "Cat may call in. Tell her everything we have. She may be able to put some things together on her end."

"On it." His body language said one thing; his features said another. His fear for her was warring with his desire to support his soldier as she entered the field of battle. Tess had always been about action, movement, heading into the fray. She had shaken JT's world upside down in so many ways.

What if I don't come back from this?

She gave one more thought to the pregnancy test kit, and the fact that she was even later than when she'd bought it, and put her arms around him for a real kiss. A real farewell.

No, no, no. I am not thinking that way. I am thinking Heather is back here with me safe and sound.

As for Suresh, Anatoly Vodanyov and the mysterious Q, Detective Goss could take care of them. They were her jurisdiction.

"Call me if *anything* pops." She took off her jacket, put on her shoulder holster, and slipped her jacket back on. She caught JT's green complexion and figured she should have gone Rambo out of his line of vision.

Then she was out the door. It was dark and she caught movement in the shadows. She pulled out her gun.

"This is the NYPD," she declared. "Step out."

There was a rustle in the bushes. Beneath moonlight and streetlight, a shadow spread across the sidewalk.

"I say again," Tess bellowed.

"Don't shoot me." Hands high in the air, a kid moved onto the sidewalk. He was wearing a hoodie—she guessed one of the four she had chased away a few minutes before. She didn't re-holster.

"Ma'am, if you know that man, you gotta help him," he said, looking over his shoulder. "My crew coming back for him soon as you gone."

"What? Why?"

"He shot them with some messed-up gun. Is he a animal trainer? Like for attack dogs and shit?"

Tess had to conceal a chuckle. She didn't suppose Vincent would appreciate being labeled an attack dog, but when he beasted out, he was more animal than human. For eleven years, JT had contained Vincent in a tiny world to keep him from harming himself—and others. It turned out that Cat's voice—Cat's love—was even more effective than a tranq gun. She could talk Vincent down so that he could reassert his humanity through sheer force of will. It was as Cat and Vincent said: They were better together. Stronger together. In so many ways.

"He's sort of an animal trainer," she said, "and trust me, you don't want to get into it with him. He is one nasty mother and that gun is just the beginning. Plus he's working for us. If anything happens to him, we'll know about it immediately and we will come for whoever did it." She pointed upward. "There's a bank of security cameras up there and the footage is fed directly into precinct headquarters. Every face they pick up is run through facial recognition software."

His eyes widened. He rattled off a few choice swear words. Tess knew he would repeat everything she had told him to his homeys, which was the point. But there was also a risk in what she was doing. Street kids had to prove they were the biggest, baddest, meanest dudes out there, or risk getting beaten up or worse by their rivals. It was an endless escalation that nearly always resulted in death. Prison was often their only refuge—and she could rattle off the names of dozens of perps she had put into prison, only to learn later that they had been killed in their cells or the exercise yard.

"If you ever want out, I can help you." She still didn't put her gun away, but she reached in a pocket with her left hand and grabbed a business card. "Can I give you this?"

"Lady, they find that on me, they beat me." She wasn't sure if he realized that he had taken a step toward her. And that he was staring at the card.

"Okay, if you change your mind, what you do is call the main number for the one-hundred-twenty-fifth precinct. You can get it off Referenda. Ask to speak to Captain Tess Vargas. That's me. Give me your name so I can tell them to let your call through." When he hesitated, she said, "You can make up a name. Like a code word."

"You a *captain*?" he asked. He took back the step and added two more toward the shadows. "Am I on the cameras? If they find out—"

"You're out of sight of the cameras. And I am a captain. Which means I can help you. I really can." She put her gun and the card back in her pocket. "These are tough streets."

"They're not so bad." He raised his chin. "Not for *me*."

This kid is still salvageable. And suddenly she found herself thinking about that spoiled white kid named Scott Daystrom and all the advantages he had. How he was so privileged he didn't even know his life was a bed of roses, except for the fertilizer he was busily dumping into it.

"You have any folks?"

He shrugged. "My dad's in gen pop. Mom... I don't know. Probably OD'd by now."

His dad was in jail, she translated. "Gen pop" meant "general population," where most of the incarcerated were housed. She sighed at this kid's brief summation of his childhood. Strikes against him, damage done. She'd been in the Big Sister-Little Sister program before. Sometimes you could help. Other times, the person who needed your help the most was too far gone to ask for it.

"Okay, listen, I have to go. But tell your friends about the cameras and leave that guy in there alone. *And call me.*"

She gave him a hard look but she couldn't gauge his reaction. He was hiding his face in the hood of his sweatshirt. She might have just turned the heat up under JT. She fervently hoped not.

She turned to go. He said, "I'm Robert. *If* I call."

Something loosened inside her chest. "I'll remember."

"But that's not my real name," he added.

"And I'll remember that, too," she said respectfully. She was willing to bet that it was, and a fleeting image of hopeful parents and a birth certificate gave her a fresh pang that was about expectations and outcomes. Maybe his parents had wanted him more than anything in the world and dreamed about getting him out of the neighborhood; maybe something had gone sideways to end all those dreams and they had spiraled downward. She was not a social worker.

But I am a human being.

He vanished into the night, but she knew he was still there. After she slid into her car and pulled away, she called JT and warned him to be careful around the windows and doors. Then she headed out, leaving everything in the rearview mirror, including, perhaps, the future of a boy whose best friends in the whole wide world would beat him up if they found out he'd talked to her.

She had to let him go. She had another life to save. Or so she fervently hoped and prayed with every fiber of her being.

She didn't know what lay ahead of her, but she was ready for it.

CHAPTER TWENTY-FIVE

"A dead body?" Cat said as Vincent went silent, shifting into predator mode. "What do you mean? Where?"

"The smoke is a bigger issue," he said ominously.

"I don't smell anything but rain."

"Yet."

He took her hand and hustled her toward the dining room. The ship was rocking more violently, and by the time they got inside, Cat saw light glinting off the ice sculptures as they teetered. Captain Kilman and Dr. Jones were conferring with several other *Sea Majesty* crew near the door. Vincent and she hurried toward them and Vincent gestured at the captain.

"Sir," he said, "I need to speak with you privately."

The captain regarded them both. He said, "Dr. Keller, in about five minutes, the ship's klaxons are going to sound and I'm going to order everyone to their lifeboat muster stations. There's a fire below deck. We're monitoring it and it's growing."

"You must have a fire suppression system," Vincent said.

The captain shook his head and lowered his voice. "It didn't go off. Something's wrong."

Cat looked over at their deserted table. Bethany, her father, and the engaged couple had left. Dr. Jones followed her line of sight.

"Dr. Keller, may I put you in charge of Mr. Daugherty? This is going to cause him a lot of stress. The Kuuipo and the Neptune Suites share the same muster station," the ship's physician said. "So they'll be there with their bodyguard soon. The stewards are going to begin knocking on doors to get the passengers out."

Cat turned to Vincent and mouthed, *Chip. I'll get it.*

He hesitated, then nodded. She said, "I'll see you at the muster station." She gave him a kiss and dashed out of the dining room.

The rain was a blinding sheet as she staggered from side to side. Taking refuge in a corridor, she figured that she still probably had about a couple of minutes before the klaxons began to shrill. Would they have to abandon ship into that rough, wild sea? What would the people who had Heather do then?

She decided to run down this passageway, then take the stairs up to her stateroom. The way was clear and she needed to hurry. About halfway down the passageway, she saw Paul, her steward, knocking on a door with a Do Not Disturb sign on it.

"Is there a problem?" she asked, and he whirled around with a cry. The expression on his face was a mixture of fear and guilt, and her cop senses went on full alert. She looked at the door and saw that he had a passkey in his hand.

"There's no problem," he said, but he could barely get the words out.

She took the key from him and swiped open the door. The air conditioning was on full blast, but even she could smell the coppery tang of blood, undercut with a slight tinge of decay. This must be the dead body Vincent had scented.

"Mr. Connors? He's not here," Paul announced querulously.

Ignoring him, she crossed to the bathroom door and tried the latch. The door swung open. There was a dark shadow at the base of the shower stall. When she opened the door, a bone-white corpse in a fetal position tumbled out on the floor. It was a man, and he had been shot in the head multiple times.

"Oh, man, oh, no way, I did not sign up for *this*," Paul groaned. He wheeled around and was almost back out into the passageway when Cat grabbed him by the arm and swung him to face her.

"What *did* you sign up for?" she asked him. But she knew the answer. "You were looking for it, weren't you? When you unpacked our things."

"I don't know what you—"

She hit him. Hard. He gasped. "Please, all Mr. Connors said was to find a little box and give it to him! That's all!"

"Did you kill him?"

"No way! I'm a steward!"

Cat believed him. That meant that someone else was in on this. And that someone had killed Connors.

At that instant, the klaxons began to scream. The fire. The lifeboats. She said to Paul, "Get everyone out. Do your job!"

Then she put everything she had into getting to her suite. It didn't take beast sense to pick up the stench of smoke, like burning tires. It must be filtering through the air-conditioning ducts.

When she grabbed the handle to their stateroom door she found it ajar. She pushed gently with the flat of her hand, opening it a crack. If the birdsong played, she couldn't hear it over the blaring ship's sirens.

The lights in the stateroom blazed. She hadn't left them that way. The ship's cabin lights could have been turned on in the emergency. One of the stewards could have used a master key to make sure the rooms were evacuated.

But there was another scenario, one with far worse consequences if she was right.

She entered the suite, bracing her legs as the floor rolled under her. The huge ocean liner didn't pound into the seas; it lumbered and wallowed like a huge drowning creature. Something to her right slid along the kitchen counter, then slid the other way as the ship righted itself. Vincent's morning coffee cup.

Against the wall she saw moving shadows, probably from the bedroom. She had no gun. But there was a ten-inch serrated bread knife next to the kitchen island's sink. For a moment she thought about grabbing it. But the knife had no point. All she could do was slash with it. That meant getting in very close and slashing effectively *a lot* before she could subdue her adversary. If it was the same person who killed the guy and shoved him in the bathroom, he or she was armed with a gun. Cat decided she was far better off with her hands free.

She peered around the open bedroom door. The drawers in the dresser were hanging open. Clothes were strewn everywhere. The bed had been stripped, and the mattress was overturned and pulled off the box springs. Everything that had been on the nightstand was on the floor, including the candy bag.

The bathroom door was cracked open. The intruder was in there. And if he or she was still looking, they hadn't found the chip.

Who are you? she thought. *What will it take to stop you?*

Through the gap she could see a man's back, and immediately recognized the coral flowered shirt and navy blue trousers. It was the substitute ship's photographer, Cecilio, the man who had taken their photograph when they had boarded the *Sea Majesty*.

He had the doors to the his-and-hers medicine cabinets

open and was hurriedly tipping items off the shelves and into the double sinks. Cat moved across the room, hoping to catch him from behind with his hands full of bottles of makeup remover and hair conditioner.

He didn't see her as she pushed the door inward. But when she crossed the bathroom threshold he looked up into the mirror and their eyes met. He let the containers fall onto the marble counter.

When he turned what looked like a plastic gun with a silencer swung up in his right hand. "Where is the chip?" he yelled.

"What chip? What are you talking about?" Cat said as she backed out of the doorway into the bedroom. "Why are you pointing that gun at me?" As she spoke she turned sideways to him, offering him a smaller target.

He followed her out. "Don't play stupid with me. It won't fly. You know what the chip is. And I know you have hidden it somewhere. It isn't in the jacket. I already checked."

He held the pistol steady despite the roll of the deck. Even so, Cat was pretty sure she could make him miss on the first and second shots, but there was no place to run after that. If he was any kind of marksman he would take her down from behind before she reached the stateroom door. With the silencer screwed on he could fire a dozen times and no one would hear.

"You killed Connors, didn't you," she said, changing the subject to buy herself some time.

His eyebrows lifted in surprise. "Oh, you found him."

"Yes. Did you do it with that pistol?"

Cecilio shrugged. "Not relevant." A cold smile failed to reach his eyes. "But I did kill that bodyguard with it."

Cat could not spare a second to mourn Terry Milano, but she did it anyway. She wondered if, in some even more twisted conspiracy than she had imagined, the chip was somehow connected to Forrest Daugherty, and that was really why he and Bethany were on the ship.

"Who sent you?" Cat asked. "Who do you work for?"

He motioned with the gun. "Stop stalling. Where is the chip? Where did you hide it?"

Cat decided it was time to press, even if it meant showing her hand. "Where is my sister?"

"Your sister?" Cecilio looked puzzled; then his eyes slowly brightened. "Don't worry, she's alive. But if I don't call to check in when I'm supposed to, she'll be killed. And it will be a very painful death. Give me the chip now, and I'll call to confirm that I have it, and my people will let her go."

Her heartbeat blasting into maximum overdrive, Cat debated. She wasn't convinced by his reaction that he knew anything about Heather. And if he did, and if he was telling the truth, his not having the chip yet was the only thing keeping Heather alive. Cat's stomach tightened. If Heather was still alive. And the missing chip was the only thing keeping the man with the gun from opening fire right now.

"Do you know I'm NYPD?" she said.

"Do you know I don't care?" He glanced at his watch. "Five minutes until I'm supposed to check in. You are wasting your sister's precious time. She knows the score. Imagine how scared she's getting about now... probably crying and begging for mercy."

"Okay," Cat said, waving her hands in surrender. "Okay, I'll get you the chip. Then you make the call."

But her mind was churning as she tried to figure out the most advantageous place to make her move. Her options were few. "This way," she said, beckoning for the man to follow. "It's on the lanai."

"I didn't look there yet."

Thank goodness for small favors, Cat thought.

She slid back the door to the lanai and a spray of rain hit

her in the face. Water stood in puddles on the stone deck; it sloshed back and forth as the ship rose and fell. The lights were on there too—romantic mood lights. Even with the extra-big chaise lounge, two tables and chairs, there was enough clear floor space to put up a fight.

Cat stepped around the chaise and lifted the nearest potted plant from its overflow dish. "Uhh, wait a minute," she said, rain soaking into her hair and the back and shoulders of her ill-fated jacket. "I think my husband must've moved these plants. I know I put it under the first one."

"Better hurry. Time is running out for your sister," Cecilio said from the doorway, keeping out of the downpour.

"It's got to be under one of these."

Perhaps growing anxious, Cecilio moved a bit closer, stepping out into the steady rain, but not close enough.

Cat lifted up the potted orchid, looked down at the dish, and exclaimed, "Oh, no! The rain! It's soaked through the pot… The little plastic box is full of water…"

"Get back, let me see it," Cecilio snarled, closing the distance between them.

He didn't wait for her to move out of the way, and when she did she planted her feet and pivoted from her hips. She slammed the clay pot against his forehead with everything she had. It shattered on impact, and the soggy potting soil flew over his face and into his eyes. Before he could recover, she grabbed his gun with her left hand, smoothly moving inside his reach. As she turned her back to his chest, she locked her right elbow over his forearm and trapped it against her hip. Both of them were suddenly pointing the gun in the same direction, fighting for control. Before he could push her away, she applied fingertip pressure to the nerves between his first two knuckles—a grappling hold. The effect was humbling and immediate—a red-hot poker from hand to armpit and unendurable pain. She felt his knees buckling. He had to open his fingers.

The plastic gun dropped to the deck with a soft clunk.

Cat swept it out of the way with the sole of her shoe. The man seized her by a shoulder. As he spun her around to face him, he drew back to head butt her, but before he could do that she got a claw hand up and raked him across both eyes, leaving matching red furrows down his cheeks.

He let out a scream and staggered backwards, clutching at his face.

Cat front kicked, aiming for center chest, his vagus nerve—and instant paralysis—but he blocked and deflected with an elbow and forearm. The force of the kick only pushed him further away from her.

Holding his arms up defensively, he shook his head to clear it. He circled the furniture in retreat.

Lightning flashed.

A second later thunder rolled. So close she could feel the rumble inside her chest.

When Cecilio brushed his face, pink, rain-diluted blood dripped from his fingers.

She tried another kick, but he kept out of reach.

He was looking around at the floor, obviously trying to locate the gun that had slid under the chaise lounge.

"Your sister will die," he said. "Even if I kill you and find the chip, I will not make the call."

It was a desperation ploy on his part. He was trying to force her to act in anger, and to make a mistake.

She feinted a drop-down move for the gun, but instead of reaching under the chaise, she jumped onto the elevated platform, complete with its own set of springs, and vaulted off, throwing everything she had into a flying kick. She had him dead to rights, but as she jumped the ship climbed a big swell. Cecilio lurched sideways, and she sailed past her target, hit the wet stone floor and skidded. She crashed into one of the chairs, slipping on the deck before she regained her feet.

Behind her, Cecilio had already overturned the chaise, bent over, and was wrapping his fingers around the gun.

CHAPTER TWENTY-SIX

The panicking passengers slowed Vincent's progress toward his designated muster station. As the ocean liner yawed sickeningly, he steadied himself on a handrail, out of the wind and spray. He couldn't see more than a dozen yards into the darkness. In his head he tried to calculate the height of a wave necessary to make a ship this big roll like that. The storm was intensifying. The bow slowly swung into the gale force wind, meeting the huge jumbled waves head on. Wind-driven rain, freezing cold, sheeted down the teak deck; it was like standing in a free-flowing creek. Vincent was soaked to the skin. People in hot orange life jackets huddled together at their lifeboat stations under rows of spotlights. Faces bloodlessly pale, they looked doomed. It was their worst nightmare come true.

His too.

He couldn't help but visualize the crew suited-up in their foul weather gear piling them all into the lifeboats and then lowering them into the churning maelstrom of the Pacific. As a physician—or a beast—he could do little about it, except to try his best to keep alive as many of his fellow passengers as possible, for as long as possible in the hope that sooner or later rescuers would arrive.

Finally he reached his destination but Bethany, her father, and the bodyguard were not there. He went up to the frightened crewman in charge of their station, who was holding tightly to a bullhorn and saying, "Please, do not panic! The situation is under control!"

"Have you seen Forrest Daugherty and his daughter?" Vincent shouted at him. "And their bodyguard?"

The man shook his head. "I'm sure they'll be along shortly, Mr…"

"Keller. I'm Dr. Keller," Vincent said.

"Oh, Dr. Keller." A stout woman wearing glasses raised her hand. "The girl told me to let you know that they went to get Sprinkles and they'll be right back."

He stared at her in horror. "Her father? Went down there?" He turned to the crewman. "Where the fire is?"

"Sir," the man said, "I'm sure they will be right back." But he lowered the bullhorn, at a complete loss.

"If my wife comes, tell her that I went after them, all right?" Vincent asked the woman. "Her name is Catherine."

"All right." The woman nodded. He could see that she was trying very hard not to panic.

"It's going to be all right," he said, and she gave him a weak little smile.

Vincent ducked under a steel arch, out of the screaming wind, and through a doorway to the nightclub where Fidela had sung. Under the still-turning glitter ball, rows of padded chairs were deserted. Wheeled beverage carts had been left overturned. Hawaiian hors d'oeuvres, serving trays, linen, and silverware were strewn over the plush carpet. The wait staff had disappeared.

The ship climbed another towering sea and he had to brace himself or slide across the carpet along with the dishes and glassware.

Then the heavy door to the stairwell on his left banged open. A crowd of men stumbled out—the ship's fire response team. He counted ten. They were wearing black Nomex suits with oxygen tanks, protective hoods, and full-face breathing masks. When they took their hoods off, their eyes looked exhausted, dulled by shock. He had seen the look more than once when he'd been a firefighter in New York and knew what it meant: The fire had the upper hand and it wasn't going to let go. As far as he was concerned, that changed nothing.

"There are three people missing," Vincent said as he stepped up to them. "One has a serious heart condition. I think they went down to the Deck Four hold to free their pet."

"Really dumb idea," one of the fire crew said.

The ship lifted and dropped and Vincent's stomach flew up into his throat. He frowned at the man, feeling a dangerous spark of anger, but stifled it. Although he had heard good things about the professionalism of cruise ship fire crews in general, he wondered about this one's training and experience level. A real fire on a real ship was a different sort of animal than a few days putting out staged fires on a classroom ship in dry dock—Vincent knew that from experience on the Hudson River. The confined spaces. The combustible and toxic materials. The walls of steel that could not be cut with an axe. This crew might be in way over their heads.

"Dumb or not," he said, "they need to be rescued. How do I reach them?"

The crewman who was in charge stepped forward. "These elevators are no longer functional. They automatically shut down during a fire. If you want to get down you'll have to take the stairs like we did."

Vincent turned for the stairwell door. A gloved hand on his arm stopped him. Stenciled lettering on the man's fire suit read CAPTAIN. He glowered into the crew chief's weather-seamed face.

"I don't see how they could have made it down to Deck Four using the stairway," the man said. "That's below the level of the fire, as far as we could tell."

Another crewman offered, "Unless they made it down before the elevator shut down, or detoured around the fire, used a different staircase…"

Vincent shrugged off the restraining hand.

"Is this the fastest way down?" he said. "That's what I need to know."

"You can't go down those stairs," the chief said emphatically. "You won't survive two minutes without a fire suit. The fire is out of control. We couldn't make a dent in it."

"Where is it centered?"

"Just aft of here. Somewhere on Decks Seven or Eight. Couldn't find the exact starting point. Couldn't get that close. Too hot, even for these suits."

"How do you know where it started if you didn't find it?" Vincent said.

"The ship still has engine and electrical power. If it started lower than that we'd already be dead in the water. In this kind of storm, trust me, no power means disaster."

The chief took a breath, then he swiped his forehead with a palm. "This shouldn't have happened. The fire suppression system totally failed. Which is impossible. It has built-in redundancies, duplicate automatic-sensing suppression systems. The fire should never have gotten this far out of control. I think someone tampered with the system."

"What do you mean 'tampered'?" Vincent said, his eyes narrowing.

"Some of the bulkhead doors were locked open, which allowed the fire to leapfrog. We couldn't close them to seal it off—they were too hot. I think it was arson. I think there's a terrorist on board, and he or she had the fire suppression weak points figured out. Unless there's a miracle this ship is going to burn to the water line, capsize, and sink."

"You'd better go back up top, sir," another crewman said. "Pray your friends are up there too and that you just missed them in the confusion."

"If someone was down on Deck Four they could still be alive," Vincent said. "They could close themselves off in an airtight room away from the fire and theoretically survive until their oxygen ran out."

"But that isn't going to do them any good when the hull breaches and the ship goes down," the chief shot back.

As if to punctuate the remark, the entire ship shuddered from the impact of a huge sea breaking over the bow.

Vincent made a decision. "Give me your suit," he said to the nearest firefighter. "And the O-two tank."

The crewman just stared at him.

"I was FDNY before nine-eleven. My brothers died in the Towers. Don't make me ask twice…"

"You're crazy," the other man said. "You don't know the layout of the ship. Going down there at this point is suicide."

"Do it," the chief barked. "Strip off your gear and hand it to him. The suit is no use to anyone now. How he wants to die is not our problem. We have to report to the captain."

Vincent kicked off his shoes and climbed into the suit and zipped it up to the chin. It had built-in boots and gauntlets. It felt familiar and reassuring, like putting on body armor. He shouldered the air tank and pulled on the hood, which had a headlamp. As he shoved past them for the stairwell door he also took a battery-powered lantern from one of the men.

"Fair warning," the chief told him, "you only have about twenty minutes of air left in that tank."

"Save four seats in a lifeboat for us," Vincent told him. "I'm not coming back empty-handed." He pulled down the breathing mask and sucked in a lungful of canned air.

The man who had donated his fire suit said, "Good luck."

Vincent didn't answer, not even with a wave of acknowledgment; he was already pushing through the doorway. The door automatically slammed shut behind him. Through the insulated fireproof fabric he sensed the sudden increase in temperature. Heat rose—it was a simple fact of nature. He knew the stairwell doors were shut on the decks below him or it would have been a thousand times more intense. If the doors had been open, the well would be acting like a blast furnace chimney, drawing masses of heat and smoke upward.

It was impossible to keep his feet as he climbed down the first flight of stairs. He bounced between the handrails, and as the ship suddenly rose under him his knees buckled and he found his backside unceremoniously planted on the steps. Inside the suit he was already sweating heavily from the exertion and the heat. Smoke noticeably thickened as he descended the next flight, a choking haze seeping through hairline cracks from below and flowing up to meet him. He was thankful for the bottled air.

Vincent kept steadily climbing downward. He was getting a better feel for the motion of the ship. He could anticipate which way it would lurch and how far it would drop, so he could brace himself.

Three decks down, the headlamp revealed blistering and smoking paint on the inner walls of the stairwell. Steam rose from the step treads under his boots, mixing with the smoke. It was getting more and more difficult to see anything below him. And it was getting hotter. Sweat peeled down his face, his arms, and his back. His toes squished in his socks. He thought about his brothers on nine-eleven, the long flights of stairs they had never made it down. Then he caught himself and put it out of his mind.

Focus, stay focused. Keep moving. Less than twenty minutes of oxygen left.

How was he going to find Bethany, her father, and the bodyguard? Beast out and track them? To do that he'd have to take off the mask; he'd have to breathe the scorching air to pick up the scent. If he did that he'd last no more than fifteen seconds before succumbing, either to heat or smoke, or both. And he wasn't sure his beast power would function as it usually did—could he even find a trail with so much signal clutter—heat, smoke, airborne debris—to filter through?

If Bethany, her father, and the bodyguard had three decks of insulation between them and the fire and had found a place to hide they were most likely still alive. If the fire had spread downward from Decks Eight and Seven, their chances of survival took a nosedive. If Deck Four was burning when he reached it, he couldn't remove the breathing mask to beast out. Which raised the possibility that he might never find them in time, not in the heat and smoke, and the unfamiliar landscape. He thought about Cat, and all the other people he could help if he abandoned the search. When to turn back/ who to try to save was a firefighter's most difficult decision. For Vincent it had always been a gut call made at the last possible second. He put that out of his mind, too.

He continued down, but more slowly and deliberately because of the low visibility. Another step. Then another. At the next landing his skin felt like it was going to burst into flames inside the suit. Vincent kept on going. The painted sign indicating Deck Eight had burned away—he only knew what deck it was because he was keeping count. Under its blistering paint the steel wall glowed a dull lavender-red. The roar of the fire mixed with the squealing and groaning of expanding metal. And there were strings of small explosions, like firecrackers. Probably rivets popping free of their welds as the walls flexed; the rivets that held the ship together.

Had the fire crew been right? That unprotected, no one could survive the inferno? Vincent's upper lip began to curl and a low rumble churned in the back of his throat. The urge to beast out became almost uncontrollable. He realized what was happening. The proximity of death was making the primal part of him want to fight back, to rampage against it with every ounce of fury he could muster. He knew how fast he could move in beast mode. Could he outrun fire? The heat of the fire? Could he cheat death?

The temperature seemed to diminish when he reached Deck Six. He wasn't sure at first because it was still broiling inside the protective suit. By the next landing, the change was obvious: The smoke had definitely thinned. Timing his bursts of movement between the ship's lurches and yaws, Vincent scrambled down the stairs and closed the distance to Deck Four.

On the landing, the stairwell walls were their normal color—no paint blistering. He unsealed the bulkhead door and opened it a crack. The lights were still on. He could see that the fire suppression system had worked here—and then some. White retardant foam and showers of water had been sprayed all over walls from nozzles in the ceiling, and the combination had made the floor a slippery mess. He carefully stepped inside and let the door shut behind him.

After turning off his oxygen, he removed the breathing mask and hood. Vincent took a deep breath. Under the cloying odor of the fire retardant, he caught a familiar scent. The molecular signature was Bethany's. No doubt about that. She had passed this way. And she was not alone. Vincent sensed the presence of her father. He could see her tugging him along behind, urging him to go faster. The man's breathing becoming more and more labored, his footsteps faltering.

Foam and water sloshed over the boots of the fire suit as the ship rose and fell. Vincent strained to hear over the moaning of the hull.

He could make out a shrill whimpering, not steam but a

dog. Then he sensed their heartbeats. There were only two human sets. One of the three hadn't made it. Concentrating harder, he separated the two rhythms. One was strong; the other thin, reedy, faltering. Bethany's father had either already suffered a heart attack, or was on the verge of having one.

Carrying the hood and mask and lantern, eyes blazing amber, Vincent sprinted through the puddled water and caps of white froth. Zeroed in and closing ground, he knew he was going to find them in time.

A fraction of an instant before the shock wave hit he sensed it coming, in a subliminal flash. As it bore down on him from three decks above he saw the sheer power of it: steel walls rupturing, girders bending, hunks of metal flying.

The explosion swept him off his feet, threw him backwards through the air, and slammed him into a bulkhead. His body slid limply to the deck. The beast light in his eyes glowed. Flickered. Then he passed out.

CHAPTER TWENTY-SEVEN

As Heather hung a sharp left into the post-apocalyptic blast-scape of abandoned warehouses and factories, the left rear wheel of the SUV began to bounce violently. Then the vehicle tilted hard, throwing Heather against the door, and a hideous scraping sound replaced the hideous scraping sounds the car had made earlier, when Heather had sideswiped the row of cars.

The SUV collapsed onto its side like a dying beast. Svetlana almost tumbled into Heather's lap. The Russian woman grabbed the wheel and cranked it hard while Heather was still holding onto it. The abrupt movement wrenched both Heather's wrists and she cried out in pain.

Svetlana yelled at her in Russian, gesturing to the door, and Heather forced it. Shooting pains skyrocketed up her wrists and down into her fingers from the effort. She clambered out and jumped to the ground.

More pain. She was a mass of cuts and sprains and bruises. Her wrists pulsated and she wondered if they were broken.

She gingerly straightened herself out. Svetlana jumped down after her, knocking her out of the way, and Heather smacked against the roof of the SUV. Heather wobbled back and forth, then craned her neck and looked down the street in the direction they had come. There appeared to be no one in pursuit. Incredible as it seemed, they had successfully outrun Anatoly Vodanyov's henchmen.

Heather's micro-second of celebration was cut short as Svetlana grabbed her by one throbbing wrist and took off like a shot.

"Ow," Heather groaned as Svetlana dragged her toward a dilapidated warehouse building. Watery moonlight revealed layers of graffiti, charred brick, and broken windows. Heather wondered why none of her misadventures had ever taken place in the nicer sections of New York. Or maybe even Hawaii.

The thought of Hawaii conjured an image of Cat and Vincent possibly running for their own lives through pineapple fields and stands of palm trees. She didn't know how long she had been kept prisoner. If Cat and Vincent were still at sea, they might still be safe. If NYPD could catch the bad guys, then her sister and her husband could still finish out their honeymoon safe and sound.

A glint in Svetlana's fist tore Heather from her reverie. Svetlana's gun was out. How many bullets did she have left?

They entered the building. Darkness engulfed them; their footfalls clattered and echoed. Heather's butt hurt.

"We need phone, we need phone," Svetlana said, stopping and bending over to catch her breath. Heather was so winded she didn't know if she could actually breathe any more.

"Yes, okay, a phone, where?" Heather cried. "Where do we get a phone?"

Svetlana forced herself back to a standing position and wagged the gun in front of Heather's face. "Shut up. No yelling. You yell, I shoot. Yelling tells bad guys where we are."

"Okay, sorry." Now Heather sucked in gobs of oxygen. "I always yell when I'm running for my life, you know?"

"Is bad habit."

Svetlana glommed onto her and swung her left, then right. Injured, exhausted, Heather dangled like a soggy, bleeding, seriously injured piece of rope. Svetlana seemed to have X-ray vision as she started up a flight of stairs Heather couldn't even see. Heather lifted her feet and put them down purely by rote; she was spent but she pushed on, not even pausing when they reached a landing and Svetlana kept going. She didn't understand what they were doing—why go up? If Vodanyov's minions figured out they were up here, all they had to do was block the stairway—but she was too breathless to ask.

They flew up more flights. Drenched in sweat, her knees and thighs aching as badly as her wrists, Heather fought to keep up with the Russian. Her butt was throbbing.

Then they were on the roof and the moonlight was shining down on them again. The rooftop was littered with beer cans, broken glass, and trash, which Heather gamely waded through as Svetlana yanked her toward the edge of the roof.

The edge of the roof?

Remembering what had happened to Ravi, Heather opened her mouth to scream for help. But that was stupid; the only people for miles around wanted to kill her. And if Svetlana had planned to kill her, she would have done it already. But images of Ravi's death and his hideous swan dive to the street whirled in her brain like a kaleidoscope. Her mouth filled with acid and her stomach clenched. She dug in her heels but Svetlana didn't notice as she reached the roof's edge.

She's been nice to me, Heather reminded herself, but she was moving into panic overdrive. For a couple of crazy seconds she thought about pushing Svetlana off the roof. *She's been really nice. She's already saved my life.*

Svetlana trotted down the edge of the roof to the corner, made a right, and kept going. She glanced over her shoulder at Heather, who debated what to do, filled her lungs with the fetid rooftop air, and caught up.

"Look." Svetlana pointed down. Incredibly, there was what looked like an occupied small industrial park amid the cityscape of dead factories and warehouses, and in it, an open mini-mart. Bright lights from the entrance coated the front of the store and the parking lot. There was one car in the space next to the front door.

"Come," Svetlana said.

Back toward the stairs they ran, just as in the distance SUV engines roared. Their footsteps clanged loudly as they crashed down the rungs and the notion seized Heather that the murderers could hear them and would know immediately to come into this building. The mini-mart was blocks away and whoever was inside probably wouldn't bother to call the police if someone was trespassing in this desolate landscape.

They left the building. Heather reflexively crouched over to make herself a smaller target as they ran down an alley. She tried to visualize where the mini-mart was and squeaked out a shout when Svetlana hung a sharp left at a T-intersection and made for open ground—a vacant lot.

"No! We have to stay hidden," Heather yelled, but if Svetlana heard and/or understood her, she completely ignored Heather and leaped over a truck tire. Glass, cans, half-opened foam containers draped with rotting fast food dotted the dirt like land mines. By then Heather had completely lost track of their location and could only trust that Svetlana was seeing the bigger picture.

They reached a stretch of chain link and Heather staggered backwards in despair. There was no way she could climb it. She was done in. Done for.

"Go, go, go!" Svetlana bellowed, smacking her on the arm.

"Ow! I can't!" Heather cried.

"Shut up! Up!" Svetlana smacked her on her butt. It hurt like the world's biggest bee sting. Then the woman bent down and positioned her shoulder under Heather's bottom and straightened. She locked her knees. "Up!" she ordered.

Sweat stung Heather's eyes. Her hair was in her face. She couldn't see what she was doing. But she hooked her fingers around the chain link and slid her toes into the diamond as if she was going horseback riding and the wire was a stirrup. She grunted from the pain but pulled herself up.

Svetlana said something in Russian. "Good, good, good, Heather. Good. More. Faster."

Heather almost retorted, "I'm trying." But *trying* would get them killed. She had to do this.

It took her a year, or so it seemed, but she was finally teetering at the top of the fence. The ground danced far below. She was afraid the drop would damage her ankles and was about to inch back down when Svetlana pushed her hard and she plummeted to the earth. Her cry of pain was masked by the sound of Svetlana's falling body as she joined her.

"I'm hurt, I'm hurt," Heather said. "I can't go on."

"Shut up."

Svetlana stood and pulled her to her feet. Heather rocked back and forth. Svetlana took off without looking to see if Heather was following her. Miraculously, Heather kept pace, moving through a white-hot curtain of fiery torture.

They hung a sharp left and it was like they had crossed the border into another country: There was a purple OPEN sign in the window of the blessed mini-mart and a clerk behind the counter, head down, probably texting.

And texting meant a phone.

Svetlana pushed open the door, gun in hand, and ran inside, Heather a few steps behind her. The clerk shouted, "Whoa!" and raised his hands in the air. His phone lay in front of him.

"*Nyet*, police!" Svetlana cried, pointing to his phone.

"Please, call the police," Heather translated. "Call them *now*. People are after us!"

"Call, call, call!" Svetlana said. She whirled around in a circle. "Where is buying phone?"

"Hey, so wait! *Wait!*" the clerk said.

Heather darted forward and grabbed the guy's phone. She showed it to Svetlana, who nodded. Heather punched in 911. The dispatcher answered.

"This is an emergency!" Heather cried. "I'm at—" She looked at the clerk, who just stood there, mouth opening and closing. "Oh, *God,* what is this address?" she demanded.

"You say or I'll kill you!" Svetlana shouted, aiming her gun directly at the poor, terrified man. He fell to his knees behind the counter and began to cry.

"Is there a robbery in progress, ma'am?" the dispatcher asked. Cool as a cucumber. Probably waiting for break time and telling the rest of the dispatchers how many robberies this made for the night.

"Yes!" Heather cried. "I mean no!" What if the cops rushed in and shot them? They wouldn't do that. Cops were not the foolhardy, trigger-happy mavericks people saw on TV. Except when they were.

She said into the phone, "I mean we need you! We need the police *now*! People are after us. Russian mobsters! In pursuit!" She tried to remember police codes. "My sister is Detective Catherine Chandler of the one-two-five precinct. Two females. We are in danger!" If she had been on a landline, the dispatcher would see where she was. Stupid, stupid cell phone.

Then she got an idea. Running down the aisles toward a bathroom sign, she caught sight of a bulletin board tacked with flyers about minimum wage, governmental regulations, and a business license for Marco's Cash & Carry. And on the license was the address. Same as on that roast beef sandwich.

"Is this a prank call?" the dispatcher demanded. "We are very busy here. There are severe penalties for tying up the emergency line for specious reasons—"

"Here, here is the address," Heather cried. She was halfway through it when Svetlana raced up behind her and grabbed her arm.

"Go!" Svetlana shouted. "Ilya is here! Out back way!"

"They're here!" Heather yelled. "Zip code! Here's the zip code!"

She ran. She couldn't hear anything and had no idea if the dispatcher was even still there.

A popping sound behind them drew her up short. Svetlana yanked on her, sending shooting pains up Heather's arm. She dropped the phone and picked it up. Pressed it against her ear as she stumbled for purchase.

"That is Ilya," Svetlana whispered. "Police are coming?"

"Hello? Hello?" Heather whispered into the phone. "Dispatcher, are you there?"

Dial tone.

"You-you bitch," Heather said, letting out a sob. Tears and sweat poured down her face. As she allowed Svetlana to herd her along, she punched in Tess's number.

"Vargas." Yes, yes, yes, it was Tess.

"Tess, oh, my God!" Heather whispered. "I was kidnapped. I got away. I'm with Svetlana. She has a gun. We just left Marco's Cash and Carry. Here's the address." She rattled it off. "We're heading…" She had no idea what direction they were going. "…away from the mini-mart. Out the back door. I don't see street signs. I don't see anything! Can you track us?"

"Call JT," Tess said. "Get on his grid. Right now. He's got the good stuff. Then download 'Find My Phone' if you can and invite me to follow you. If you can. Don't jeopardize your safety to do this. Get to JT first."

"Right, right," Heather said.

"I'm on my way. I'll call for backup. Call me back when you're done with JT. Help is coming." Tess was all business but Heather heard both the joy and the terror that Tess was clamping down. "Is Anatoly Vodanyov the man who kidnapped you?"

"Yes," Heather said as Svetlana pulled her into another alley and they ran the length. "Svetlana helped me escape, okay? She's a good guy." *She also throws dead people off roofs, but tonight, she is my guardian angel.*

"Okay. I'll pass that along. How many subjects are after you?" Tess asked. "What's your situation right now?"

"I don't know. Maybe a dozen guys. It seems like a dozen. We're running in an alley. There's a lot of alleys around here. We heard gunshots." She jerked, then stumbled over her own feet. Svetlana glared at her and she hurried to catch up. "The clerk! What if they hurt him? This is his cell phone. He can't call for help!"

"I'll send an ambulance," Tess assured her. "Stay out of sight. Don't go back there."

Angry men yelling in Russian punctured what little composure Heather had built up. She jerked hard and almost dropped the phone again. Svetlana duck-walked, head down low, and hissed at Heather to keep up.

"Tess!" Heather whispered. "They're almost here!"

"Call JT. Call me back. If I don't hear from you I'll call you in five minutes so get your phone on vibrate if you can. If you can't, tell JT. I don't want to get you shot."

"Okay. Don't forget the ambulance." Heather disconnected and ran after Svetlana.

Find us. Find us and save us. Please.

CHAPTER TWENTY-EIGHT

Vincent came to, the spinning in his head compounded by the erratic and violent oscillation of the huge ship as it forged ahead. Although its engines were still running, the tremendous explosion had killed the lights, at least in this section of Deck Four, and possibly throughout the rest of the vessel. A beast did not need lights to see in the dark, but the people he had come to rescue most certainly would. He fumbled around on the floor around him and found the lantern.

As he got to his feet, the roar of the blaze was considerably softer. At first he thought his eardrums had been overloaded by the concussion of the explosion, but there was no accompanying ringing in his head. Perhaps the blast's shock wave had suffocated some of the fires? Because of the drop in noise volume it was easy for him to relocate the two sets of human heartbeats, both of them trip-hammering. There were other heartbeats as well, same location, but not human, beating in a wild jumble. He picked up the breathing mask, as he knew stabilizing Bethany's father's condition might require oxygen.

As he hurried down the corridor, random details of

the aftermath of the explosion stuck in his consciousness. Though there was some buckling evident in the ceiling panels and signs of ruptured seams in the walls, there was no scorching or jagged edges or explosive pitting anywhere, which would have indicated close proximity to the event. It was clear the explosion had had its epicenter somewhere above him, and the intervening decks had cushioned its full deadly force. If the hull had been breached by it, things were going to go south in a hurry.

The Bethany trail ended at a closed storeroom door. The heartbeats he sensed, human and animal, were coming from the other side of it. A sense of relief swept over him—he had found two of them and they were still alive.

He quickly switched on the lantern. He hit the door once hard with his fist and announced, "Emergency rescue coming in!" Then he turned the latch.

As he opened the door, a yard-tall, four-legged whirlwind galloped out and shot past him. He turned and pinned the creature's backside with the light for a second before it disappeared down the hallway. A Great Dane. It had to be Bethany's dog. Where Sprinkles was headed, or thought he was headed, Vincent had no clue.

"We're in here!" Bethany shouted from the dark. "Please help us!"

Vincent turned the light beam into the small room. Bethany was kneeling over her father, who had collapsed onto the deck on his back. Tears streaked her face, and she looked panicked, desperate. Two smaller dogs—a German shepherd and a Shih Tzu—with their leashes tethered to the legs of a table started barking and growling at him. The German shepherd bared his fangs, snapped, and tried to take a hunk out of Vincent's leg. In the windowless steel room the noise they made was deafening. Vincent shined the light on his own face.

"It's me, Bethany. I'm here to get you out."

"Help my dad! Hurry, help him! He can't stand up."

"Have you seen Mr. Milano? Did he accompany you?"

"No! We don't know where he is!"

The dogs kept barking. Vincent turned to them and said, "Quiet." The smallest dog shut up, but the shepherd kept barking and trying to get at him. Then he said it again in German. It was like he had flipped a switch. The animal immediately sat and looked up at him with rapt attention. The shepherd was a guard dog, maybe police or military trained. Vincent had worked with similar K9s in Afghanistan.

"Bethany, can you hold this light for me so I can examine your dad?" he said.

She took the lantern from him. The beam veered wildly around the floor of the little room. The girl was shaking from head to foot.

"Can you please try to hold it steady?"

Vincent bent over Mr. Daugherty, first loosening his tie and collar, then reaching down to take his pulse at the wrist.

"He kind of passed out after we hid in here, before the explosion," Bethany said. "Is he going to be okay? Say he's going to be okay."

His pulse was irregular and weak.

"Of course, he's going to be fine," Vincent said, trying to be as calm and convincing as he could. He passed his hand between the light source and the man's eyes, making a shadow cross his face. The pupils were reactive. Good sign. But even in the harsh light, his skin and lips had an alarming bluish pallor to them. And the man appeared drowsy, like he was drifting in and out of consciousness. Whether it was from shock or trauma, Vincent knew his heart was not functioning normally.

He leaned closer to the man's ear. "Mr. Daugherty, Mr. Daugherty, can you hear me?"

Bethany's father opened his mouth as if to speak, but no

sound came out of his throat. After a moment he gave up and shut his eyes. The effort was too much for him.

"Is my dad okay?" Bethany asked shrilly. "This is all my fault. He tried to stop me from coming down to get Sprinkles, but I wouldn't listen. He wouldn't let me go by myself. I dragged him down here with me. I made him run." The light moved away from where Vincent was working, leaving him and his patient suddenly in the dark. The beam swept wildly around the windowless room.

"Oh, my God, where is Sprinkles?"

Vincent noted the question, but paid no attention to it. He slipped the oxygen tank from his shoulders and put the mask over the man's nose and mouth. "Breathe normally, Mr. Daugherty. Nice deep, even breaths. Everything's under control. Everything's going to be fine. We'll get you out of here in a minute or two."

"Where is Sprinkles?" Bethany practically screamed into his ear.

He didn't need this. Not now.

"I'm sorry," he said as he worked on her father, "but when I opened the door he brushed right past me. I couldn't stop him and I couldn't catch him. Why wasn't he tied up like the other dogs?"

"How could you do that?" Bethany raged. "How could you be so stupid?"

Vincent let her fury roll over him. "I didn't know your dog was loose in here."

"He wasn't loose. He was tied up. He got scared and broke the leash. We've got to find him!"

"I need to stabilize your father and get him up to the main deck where he can get proper treatment."

"I want my dog. I'm not going anywhere without him."

"Mr. Daugherty, are you feeling any better? Is the oxygen helping you get back some strength?"

The man nodded weakly.

"Do you know where Terry Milano is?"

He shook his head.

Okay, two humans and two dogs out of three each... for the moment. Time for triage and that gut call. Mr. Daugherty needed help now.

"There's enough air in the tank to make you comfortable while I carry you up to the lifeboats. Are you ready for me to do that?"

His eyes went wild, looking around the dark room for his daughter. He shook his head violently: *No. No.*

Vincent could see he had a big problem on his hands.

"Bethany, I need help getting the other two dogs up to safety while I carry your dad," he said evenly. "Can you help me do that? We'll come right back and find Sprinkles. I promise you."

"No, I'm not going to leave him down here alone and scared. I'll keep the two dogs with me until you come back."

Vincent wanted to explain the grave danger she was putting herself in, but he realized it would only make her position regarding Sprinkles more entrenched and she would be even less inclined to go with him. He decided to take another tack.

"Your father needs medical attention immediately. I can't give it to him down here. I don't have the supplies. He needs medication and he needs it now. I can't leave you here. You have to come with us."

"Don't let my father die!" she wailed.

"Look, Mr. Daugherty," he said, "I can have you topside in a couple of minutes..." He figured he could use a fireman's carry, and then with the guy draped over his shoulder he could safely beast out. Bethany's father wouldn't be able to see his face, teeth, and eyes change, and after he blurred up the stairs, Daugherty wouldn't remember what had happened or would think he had dreamed it.

The man gripped his arm and squeezed. He shook his head.

Vincent winced, not from the pressure of the man's hand, which was minimal, but from the predicament he found himself in. They were going around and around in ever smaller circles. Unless he found a way to break the impasse they were all going to die.

"Mr. Daugherty," he said gravely, "as a physician I have no choice but to get you out of here first. I promise you Bethany is going to be okay. I'll put you in the care of the ship's doctor and come right back for her. She'll be alone five minutes, tops. I'll leave the lantern here. And she has the shepherd…"

He untied the dog's leash from the table leg and handed the end of it to Bethany. Then he spoke three more words in clipped German. "The dog is police trained," he told her father. "He follows direct orders. I just told him to protect her. Are you okay with that, Bethany?"

"Yes, Vincent," she said.

Her father started to wave his hand in protest.

"I'm sorry but there's no time for that, Mr. Daugherty," Vincent said, smoothly pulling the man to his feet as he bent his own knees, then taking Daugherty's full weight across his shoulders as he straightened up. "Do not leave this room," he told Bethany. "I'll be right back."

CHAPTER TWENTY-NINE

When Cat saw the silenced plastic gun in Cecilio's hand she lowered her head and bull-charged him, digging in her toes and driving as hard as she could with her legs. In that split second she realized she had no choice but a go-for-broke frontal attack. The lanai was far too small for evasive maneuvers, and he was standing between her and the sliding door.

The business end of the gun swung around at her just as she jumped and kicked. When her right foot hit his center chest, the pistol went off with a hiss. She felt the heat of the near miss on her left shoulder. The impact of the running kick sent Cecilio flying backwards into the overturned chaise, and he fell over it hard onto his back. He made an "Ooooof!" noise as the wind was knocked from his lungs. She ended up with both feet flat on the ground, straddling his thighs. Cecilio fired the automatic erratically, straight up in the air. The muzzle belched yellow flame less than two feet from her face.

Before he could lower the point of aim and hit her, she grabbed his wrist with her left hand, pushing the gun away as she twisted and knee-dropped her full weight onto his throat. Cat was not pulling her punches or her kicks. If she had hit him cleanly her kneecap would have crushed his larynx, which would have swollen up in seconds and shut off his airway. He would have asphyxiated. But somehow he got his chin down and that took the brunt of the impact.

She still controlled his gun hand, but his other was free. They were wrestling on the rain-slick deck. He thrashed under her, trying to get a firm grip on the back of her neck. Cat had lost the advantage of surprise. Having learned his lesson, Cecilio kept twisting and turning his gun hand to keep her from nerve-pinching it. He got hold of her neck with his left hand, squeezed down hard, and started pulling her over backwards, trying to roll at the same time and get on top of her.

Hand-fighting a bigger, stronger opponent with longer arms in close quarters was a losing proposition. Fun and games were over. She used the edge of her forearm to knock his hand from her neck, then smashed the point of her elbow into his temple. One blow wasn't enough to stop the guy. He grabbed hold of the back of her top and pulled her backwards, again trying to flip her over. She hit him five times in the head with her elbow in rapid succession, and after the fifth strike he let go of the fabric.

Cat still couldn't get the gun out of his hand—he had a death grip on it—and she was done wrestling. She hit him once more for good measure with everything she had. If that didn't concuss him, nothing would. She watched his eyes roll back in his head, then jumped to her feet. Sidestepping the chaise lounge and rounding the little table and chairs, she bolted for the sliding door. Once through, she pulled it shut and locked it. She was shivering but she didn't pause. She raced for the bedroom, grabbed the bag of candy off the floor, and shoved it into her jacket pocket.

As she turned the handle to the stateroom door Cecilio rattled the slider from outside, trying to get it open. She was already running down the corridor when she heard the sound of breaking glass behind her. The ship climbed what had to be a giant swell and she had to steady herself at the stairwell entrance. Vaulting the stairs three at a time as the liner sickeningly dropped, she put distance between herself and Cecilio, scrambling out into the deserted main dining salon. She had found an alternate route, and she was grateful for shelter.

There was no shame in this retreat, she told herself. The killer wasn't going anywhere, she still had the chip, and when Vincent got hold of him...

Then the floor rocked in a different way.

From within.

And a terrible explosion slammed her ears.

The dishes and silverware on the rug jumped a foot in the air and the glitter ball detached from the ceiling and crashed to pieces.

The main salon's lights flickered and then they went dark. But there were still lights from above the stairwell leading to the lifeboat deck.

Cat scrambled across the littered floor and up the stairs.

Beyond the archway leading to the muster station, the rain was slanting sideways, driven by a steady howling wind. It was eerie. The deck was still brightly lit, looking almost normal, and beyond the rail, immense surges of white caps rode atop nightmare black seas. The up and down motion of the ocean liner was like an elevator—an elevator leaping up twenty feet, then falling the same distance. Cat's head spun, her stomach rebelled, and she had to focus on an imaginary horizon line to regain her equilibrium.

She pushed out onto the deck and used the rail to steady herself as she worked her way up towards the bow to their assigned station. The rain was freezing and she was drenched by the time she got there. She expected to see Vincent waiting there for her, a relieved expression on his face when she appeared. But Vincent was nowhere in sight. That realization froze her blood. Where was he? Why wasn't he there?

The other passengers looked positively green; they were clinging desperately to whatever they could—the rail, the lifeboat, the cradle that held the lifeboat.

A crewman stepped up and tried to get her into a life jacket.

"No!" She pushed him away and shouted into his ear over the gale, "Where is my husband? Where is Vincent? I left him here."

"Sorry, ma'am, but you have to put on your jacket," he shouted back. "I don't know who your husband is."

"He's a doctor," she cried. "He should be here, helping these people..."

"Please put on your life jacket."

"Mrs. Keller?" said a woman with misted glasses and dripping shoulder-length hair.

"Yes, yes, that's me."

"Dr. Keller was here. But a little girl and her father went to get their dog. He left to go find them."

Sprinkles.

Bethany wouldn't get in a lifeboat without him. The addition of a one-hundred-fifty-pound canine might be a problem for the crew and the other passengers, but that was a bridge they would have to cross later.

"There was an explosion," Cat said, her heart clenching.

"He left before that," the woman said.

"You can't go down there," the crewman said. "You have to be ready to abandon ship."

"Give me that damned flashlight," Cat shouted at the crewman. She didn't wait for him to hand it over. She ripped it out of his hand. "We will be back. All of us. Do not let the last lifeboat leave without us!"

"If the captain says launch, we launch," the man said.

Cat stuck a finger in his face. "You don't launch until I say you launch. Got that?"

The crewman nodded. "Yes, ma'am," he said tightly.

Cat half-skied, half-ran down the deck, catching hold of the archway's edge and pulling herself under its protection. When the ship leveled out in a wave trough, she headed down the steps to the main salon with flashlight in hand, dreading what she might find in the dark. Vincent was not invulnerable. He could be hurt, or even killed. If they had moved far from the hold where the pets were kept there was a good chance she would never find them. Or she could run into Cecilio again. Or somehow get trapped or lost below deck herself. She pushed those happy thoughts out of her mind—she had a job to do, lives depended on it. She was in her element.

She beelined for one of the stairways that led to the lower decks, the elevator wouldn't be safe right now.

The flashlight beam wobbled wildly in her hand as the ship's swaying bounced her around in the stairwell. Over the screeching and moaning of the hull, the klaxon bleated insistently, infuriatingly. There was smoke in the stairwell, but it didn't smell like an explosion. It rasped in the back of her throat. She wished she'd grabbed a linen napkin to cover her nose and mouth. Too late to worry about that now.

In the confusion of being slammed and stumbling to keep her feet she lost count of the landings she'd passed. The flash beam dead-ended in a cloud of curling smoke not five feet ahead of her.

Then she heard a different sound coming from below. Bellowing. Like a crazed wild animal. Not a beast, though. It wasn't Vincent. The noise grew louder and closer. When she looked back the way she had come she realized she couldn't run from it. She leaned against the stairwell wall. It was warm against her back. And braced herself to meet a frontal attack.

Eyes wild, jaws trailing slobber, a familiar face burst

through the smoke and rampaged up the stairs.

Sprinkles charged right at her and for a second Cat was caught flatfooted. The huge dog lowered his head and stuck it between her legs, cowering like a baby, his entire body trembling with fear.

"It's okay, boy," Cat said, shifting to free herself. "You're fine. Nobody's going to hurt you." She stroked the dog's head and ears as she found the broken end of his lead. Sprinkles licked her hand gratefully, then nosed the pocket with the candy in it.

"We're going to go find Bethany. Come on, you know the way."

Sprinkles happily followed when she started back down the stairs again.

They had only descended one flight when the dog froze. He looked up at her pleadingly then tried to run back up the stairs. Cat had to dig in her heels to hold him. When Sprinkles again tried to bury his head, Cat twisted away. The dog let out a baleful howl.

From out of the smoke burst a different sort of animal, the beast Cat loved. He had what looked like a corpse slung over his shoulder and an oxygen tank in one hand.

"Vincent! Thank God!"

His eyes lost their amber glow and his face changed back to his human appearance.

Sprinkles woofed and wagged his tail at him.

"You found Bethany's dog," Vincent said.

"More like he found me." The man in the fireman's carry was Forrest Daugherty. She couldn't see his face because of the breathing mask but he wasn't moving and appeared to be unconscious. "Is he alive?"

"Mr. Daugherty is in a bad way," Vincent said. "Bethany is still on Deck Four with the other two dogs."

When Cat started to protest he held up his free hand.

"She wouldn't leave without Sprinkles. Her father's critical. Catherine, I had no choice."

"I get it," Cat said. "You did the right thing, the only thing. You do what you have to do to help Daugherty. I'll go get Bethany." She hesitated. "Terry Milano is dead. I know who it is, Vincent. Cecilio the photographer. I found him in our stateroom."

His lips parted. "Are you all right?"

She nodded. "And the answer is no. He doesn't have it."

He took that in. "We'll meet you back at the lifeboats."

"Hurry."

"Of course."

"I think the explosion put out some of the fires," he said. "The heat in the stairwell has tapered off. After you get below Deck Seven the smoke pretty much disappears."

"How far down is that?"

"One and a half flights. I'll see you up top. I love you."

"Me too," Cat said.

Vincent's eyes flashed and when he snarled it made Sprinkles whimper. With Daugherty on his back, he blurred up the stairs out of sight.

Sure enough, the smoke diminished after Deck Seven. She and Sprinkles lurched and stumbled their way down to Deck Four. The Dane really perked up as soon as they passed through the doorway, and began pulling her along, harder and harder, oblivious to the sickening rise and fall of the ship.

"Easy, Sprinkles. Easy, boy."

The dog let out a joyful bark.

Then ahead of them, the other dogs started barking back.

A beam of light shot out from an open doorway on the right.

"Sprinkles?" Bethany cried.

The big dog broke loose of Cat's grip and crashed into his mistress. Jumping up on his hind legs, putting forelegs on

Bethany's shoulders and slurping gleefully at her face.

"Are you hurt anywhere?" Cat said, playing the flashlight beam over the girl.

"I'm fine. So are the dogs. Thank you so much for saving Sprinkles."

Seeing the Dane, the shepherd and the Shih Tzu wagged and wiggled.

"What about my dad?"

"I saw Vincent carrying him up when I was coming down to get you," Cat told her, purposefully withholding any details on his condition. "By now he's with the ship's doctor. You and I need to get topside ASAP. They won't hold the lifeboat for us forever. Can you handle Sprinkles going up the stairs?"

"Sure. But I'd better take Schmutzie, too."

"Schmutzie?"

"That's what I call the shepherd. And I think he's really German. Vincent talked to him in German. I don't know what his real name is. Vincent kind of gave him to me, so I think I should hold his leash."

"Fine. No problem. I'll take the Shih Tzu."

"Archer," Bethany said. "That's her name for real."

Going up was a lot harder than going down. When the ship climbed the waves it froze Cat's legs. No way could she overcome that kind of G-force. The dogs, however, thought it was some kind of race, barking at each other as they scrambled up the steps.

There was more awful-smelling smoke at Decks Seven and Eight. The stairwell felt hotter, too, like the fires on those levels had blossomed again. As they ascended the stairs to Deck Nine, Cat saw a pair of legs on the landing above them. Her flashlight beam revealed a smirking face she never wanted to see again.

Cecilio was holding his gun in one hand and bracing himself on the rail with the other.

"Better stop right there," he said.

"Who is he?" Bethany said. "Why does he have a gun?"

Schmutzie lowered his powerful body into a crouch and bared his teeth at Cecilio. The hair on the dog's back bristled from neck to tail.

"He's a creep," Cat said. "I kicked his butt a few minutes ago, but apparently it didn't stay kicked."

"Give me the chip," Cecilio said. "Or your sister dies."

"I don't have a sister, you moron," Cat said, sneering. It was a feint.

Cecilio seemed taken aback for an instant; then he grinned. "You have a little friend, though." He took aim at Bethany's head. It was a sloppy aim because of the wallowing of the ship. "Give me the chip or I blow out her brains."

"Remember this candy?" Cat said, taking the bag out of her pocket. "It was on the bedside table in our stateroom…"

"Yeah, so…"

"The chip's in here, wrapped up to look like a Jolly Rancher."

"A what?"

Cat reached into the bag and held up a candy in a twist of cellophane. "Jolly Rancher. What planet are you from?"

"Give me the chip."

"I don't know which one it is," she said, dropping the candy back in the bag and giving it a shake, "but it's in here."

"Find it."

"No," Cat said, "that's your job." Without another word she inverted the sack, dumping its contents on the landing. The candies scattered across it and tumbled down the steps.

Cecilio looked down in astonishment at the dozens of brightly wrapped sweets. When he started to take aim at Bethany again, Cat launched herself at him.

But the shepherd was already in motion. A brown and black blur shot from the edge of the stairs and hit Cecilio square in the chest, slamming his back against the handrail. Before Cecilio could recover, Schmutzie had his gun hand between powerful jaws and was snarling and twisting his head and body. Cecilio let out a shrill scream. He dropped the gun and it slid down the stairs, but the shepherd did not let go.

Sprinkles wanted in on the fun, and so did the Shih Tzu.

"Come on, Bethany!" Cat said, scooping up the little dog. "Let's go!"

They raced past Cecilio and the dog that had now pulled him to his knees, and dashed up two flights of stairs to the next landing. Then Bethany turned and shouted over the blare of the klaxon, "Schmutzie! Schmutzie!"

Cat was about to hurry them on when the shepherd appeared, a happy smile on his face. Bethany picked up his leash. They staggered up the steps, towed by the eager dogs.

Vincent was waiting for them in the ruins of the nightclub. Her heart leapt to see him alive and well in the flashlight beam, but the look on his face made it instantly sink. She was sure Mr. Daugherty had died.

"Where's my dad?" Bethany said.

"Your father is stabilized," Vincent said.

Much to Cat's relief.

"But there is a problem..."

He furrowed his brow in that way he had. He was soft-selling something, maybe because Bethany was there, working up to tell her something really bad.

The ship rolled heavily under them. Was it Cat's imagination or did it not fully recover from the wallow? Was the deck now permanently sloping? She shined her light around the big room. No, it was not her imagination. The ocean liner was taking on seawater, lower decks flooding.

"What problem?" she asked.

"Our lifeboat has already left. It was gone when I got here."

CHAPTER THIRTY

Gummi worms and Tums were JT's midnight supper. Being Robin sucked. He was worried about the woman he loved and yet here he sat like Wash, the pilot character on *Firefly* who always stayed behind on the spaceship while everyone else committed derring-do. He ate another gummi worm and stewed in his own juices, then punched up two more articles he had just opened on Vodanyov and Chrysalis—two very scary organizations, no matter which side of the law you were on, simply because they were so powerful—when one of the headlines crawling across his screen on his feed caught his eye:

Cruise ship bound for Hawaii ablaze.

"What?" he cried, craning his neck toward the screen.

Storm thwarts rescue.

"What's the ship's name?" he yelled at the screen.

JT's phone rang.

"Tess," he said without looking at the ID. "More bad news. I think Cat and Vincent are in trouble."

"A cat?" said the woman on the other end. "I thought you were looking for a chihuahua?"

"What? *Oh.* Yes." JT punched the keyboard and brought

up a satellite image of the mother of all storms, located midway between the West Coast and Hilo, Hawaii. If their ship was riding *that*—

"…I didn't even know Julia had taken your dog. When my mother called and said you'd spoken to her, I asked Juli about it and it turns out she and her best friend Megan have been hiding Princess Wookie in Megan's garden shed. I'm so very, very sorry," the woman was saying. JT made himself listen. Except—

—in the center of the satellite image a triangle appeared. It read *Sea Majesty*. The name of Vincent and Cat's cruise ship. It was on fire and in the middle of a storm? When had all this happened?

"Holy crap," JT blurted.

"Excuse me?"

Another call was coming in. Maybe it was them. Or Tess. JT said, "I'm sorry, it's just… I'm in the middle of something. I'm really glad you have Mookie. I mean Moochie. Mochi. I can come pick her up." *Once all this is over. If I don't die of a heart attack first. If we're not all dead.*

"Well, we live hours north of you. If we could arrange a time and perhaps we could meet you halfway—"

"That sounds great. Really great. Hold on. I need to grab this other call."

But the caller on line two had given up. JT checked the number on Caller ID. It was no one he recognized. A phone solicitor, probably.

Then *another* call came in, and he recognized this one. It was Tess. JT said to the woman, "I'm sorry to do this, but may I call you back?"

"Sure. Of course. I know it's very late. I figured you would be worried about your dog."

"I am. A lot. Bye."

He took Tess's call.

"Oh, my God, Tess," he said, "I think Cat and Vincent are in serious—"

But Tess was speaking over him. She said, "So did you start tracking her?"

JT was bewildered. "Do you mean Princess Mochi?" he asked her.

"What?" Tess asked, sounding equally bewildered. "JT? Didn't Heather just call you?"

"*What?*" He leaped out of his chair. It fell backwards with a crash. *That call was from Heather?*

"She should've just called you. Vodanyov is after her. She got free and she has a cell phone. I told her to call you so you can track her with your Homeland Security-level software. You can guide me, right? Just in case, I asked her to download—"

"Oh, my God, oh, my God, Tess," he cut in. "She *did* call me. I've been on the phone and I didn't recognize the number. Who… what… never mind. I understand. I'll call her back."

"Good. She may be hiding," Tess said. "I told her to put the phone on vibrate but she may not have had the chance. It might ring when you call her." She paused. "I may regret telling you to do this for the rest of my life, but call her *now*."

Tess sent two units and an ambulance toward the mini-mart while she waited for word on Heather from JT. Judging from the chatter on her radio and the GPS readout, her units had engaged seven armed and dangerous adversaries. Heather had put the number of her pursuers at a dozen. So it was likely that some of them had left the scene of the confrontation and were still after Cat's little sister.

Tess was driving blind past row after row of abandoned structures punctuated by occupied office suites and warehouses that reminded her of junkyard strays scavenging for scraps. JT still hadn't gotten back to her with a location for Heather and Svetlana and as Tess rolled on, she listened to the reports on the firefight. Two subjects down. Then an officer down. She listened for a name. Miller. She mentally crossed her fingers that the big burly cop had been caught somewhere on his Kevlar vest and that he'd come out fine.

A second officer down. Dispatch was sending another ambo. Tess clenched her jaw and fought down her impulse to drive to the scene and lend aid. Heather needed her more. She was an innocent. Tess's guys were performing the job they had sworn to do. But she was their captain, and they were her people.

Sweat beaded on her forehead and her stomach rolled. "Not now," she gritted, and her thoughts veered momentarily to the pregnancy test that she still had not taken. What if she got shot tonight, and it made her lose the baby?

Her phone rang and she connected. "Vargas."

"I have them on voice-to-voice and I can see them on my grid. I can also see you," JT said. "Follow my directions. Go west at the next corner."

"West," Tess confirmed. She put on the turbo and fishtailed around a corner. Her tires squealed. The stench of burning rubber seeped into the car.

"West again," JT said.

"West."

She forced herself to slow down. If she could have cut diagonally across the grid of buildings to save some time, she would have aimed the vehicle and pressed the pedal to the metal. But to her surprise, the blocks of rusted rebar and crumbling concrete began to give way to waist-high weeds, then to bushes, and finally to trees. The asphalt lost its regularity and the tires bounced into and out of potholes.

"Hey, I'm seeing a forest or something," she told JT.

"Okay, good. You're going into a greenbelt. Heather and Svetlana have just run in there and they heard gunfire close behind them. You may have to go in on foot." He didn't sound any happier about it than she was. "They're arguing about climbing a tree. Heather's hurt."

"Hurt how? How bad?" Tess cried, alarmed.

"Keep going straight."

She gunned it. Reminded herself that she couldn't do Heather any good if she wrapped herself around a tree trunk. Leafy oaks crowded the sides of her vehicle as the road disappeared and she negotiated what appeared to be a hiking trail.

"The trees are growing too closely together. I'm going to radio for backup and then I have to get out. How is Heather?"

There was a pause. Then JT said, "I've lost voice."

"Lost, as in…?" She stopped the car and opened her radio. "This is Captain Vargas." She gave her badge number and requested backup. Then she went back to JT. "What's going on?" she asked him.

"I don't know. Their cell phone is on and I'm still tracking them. But I can't hear them."

"That doesn't necessarily indicate that they're incapacitated," Tess theorized. "It could mean that their pursuers are close and they don't want them to hear you talking on the other end."

"Right. Okay, I have them about a quarter mile to your three o'clock. I can give you longitude and latitude." He did so.

"Got it." She turned off the car, grabbed her ear buds and her police radio, and put a loaded magazine in her service weapon. She racked the slide, putting the first round in the chamber. Locked, loaded.

She got out. She put one bud in her right ear and kept her radio off in her pocket, then shielded her phone with her hand as she pressed on the illumination and walked toward the coordinates JT had given her. It was eerily silent. She kept her gun out.

After at least a minute, JT's voice crackled. "They're on

the move but they're going very slowly. If you progress farther east, you'll eventually come up behind them."

"Understood," Tess murmured. "JT, can you multitask? Get on the scanner and see how we're doing at the mini-mart? I don't want to turn my radio on. But please don't lose Heather."

"Sure. Hold on." Another stretch while she aged twenty years, and then JT came back. "It's not going well. Two more Russians just left the scene. I assume they're on their way to Heather."

The news chilled her. "What about my backup?"

"Also on the way."

"Good." *Hang on, Heather.*

As she kept walking, she heard the most beautiful sound in the world—police sirens—when the *pop pop pop* of gunfire ricocheted through the trees. She hit the dirt, flattening herself against the ground. Then she elbow-crawled toward the nearest tree—a pine—and rolled beneath the branches.

"JT, talk to me," she whispered.

"Tess, the Russians who split off from the mini-mart are shooting at your backup as they arrive," JT reported. "From what I can tell, both sides have found your car. Your guys think the Russians have alerted their people that you're on foot so be extra careful. Heather's still on silent running," he added. "They're talking about sending in a chopper."

"Have the Russians called in? Made demands?"

"Nothing that I've heard."

"So maybe not a hostage situation at this point." Tess kept her voice even but they both knew what that meant: Heather and Svetlana might be worth more to Anatoly Vodanyov dead than alive. They were witnesses and Svetlana must know damning information about Vodanyov's dealings.

"Will the chopper help? Do you want me to let them know I'm in contact with you?"

"There are too many trees. And this is going down too

fast. Heather and Svetlana could get caught in the crossfire," Tess said. "Let me think about what to do. Am I still heading toward them?"

"Yes. They're pretty much stationary."

Maybe they climbed that tree after all. Or maybe they're hurt. Or maybe they've been captured.

The first scenario was the best, but it wasn't very good. She crawled from beneath the branches and pushed herself up to a crouch.

Suddenly she got the feeling that she was being watched. The back of her neck prickled. A branch cracked.

"Tess?" JT said. "Tell me what you want me to do."

His voice felt loud against her quivering eardrum. Besides, she needed to concentrate. She grimaced, put him on mute, and pulled the ear bud out of her ear.

There was a thud. It was barely audible. She triangulated. It was to her west. The feeling of being watched grew stronger. She remained where she was, alert for more sirens and/or gunfire. Heard neither.

One thing civilians didn't realize about police work was how much of it consisted of hurrying up and waiting. It took everything in Tess not to dash forward with her gun blazing. But she was one person with one gun.

Pop pop pop! More gunfire. Behind her. She clenched her fists. *You are here to serve and protect,* she reminded herself. *Stay cool. Don't rush in until you know what you're getting into.*

Crab-walking forward, she was on the move, heading for the last location JT had indicated for Heather. She clenched her teeth as her thighs began to protest way too soon. There was nothing else to be done. She had to keep her head down and she had to hurry. She swore that she would take the stairs from now on every chance she could, and kept going.

Then she came to a clearing. Hovering on the perimeter,

she wished she could ask JT for an update but the forest shifted and creaked around her as if it was busy, and full.

Go east? Forward?

There was another sound close behind her. Too close. Footfall? She held her breath and focused. Her heart roared in her eardrums and pounded against her ribcage, demanding to be let out.

This must be what Vincent feels before he beasts out, she thought. *Or this times about a million.*

She held that thought and exhaled slowly. Waited, waited, waited. If someone was coming up behind her and they were wearing night-vision goggles, they could see her. They could put her in their crosshatches.

What if I'm pregnant?

I am in the field. I am trying to save two innocent lives.

She licked her lips and tasted salt. She was still sweating. And thirsty. And her thighs were screaming.

She pushed on, keeping to the edge of the clearing, until finally she had to straighten up. Her quads seized and she leaned back slightly, stretching them out. The lack of activity told her that JT must have decided not to alert the one-two-five to her location. She had to assume she was alone in this.

She had heard no sounds for quite some time, and she was about to put her ear bud in and take JT off mute, when a shadow roared up right in front of her, startling her so badly she almost fell on her butt. She made out the silhouette of a man armed with an Uzi submachine gun. His back was to her. It was evident that he didn't realize she was there because he put a cell phone to his ear and murmured a few words in Russian, then hung up. Cigarette smoke wafted like an aura around him as he inhaled, creating a scarlet glow for her to see by. He remained where he was, a sentry.

Waiting for me? she wondered.

She didn't know if his phone was on or off. If on, whoever

was on the other end might hear if she attacked him. If she shot him, they wouldn't need a phone. They'd be able to hear it naturally. She didn't have a knife. She wasn't a Special Forces operative, she was a police captain. She knew martial arts, but he was so much bigger and he was armed. It was harder to knock someone out with the butt of a gun than it was portrayed on TV. It might take several attempts, and if his gun went off—

She was going to have to do something soon. Her luck couldn't hold out forever. Sooner or later he was going to become aware of her.

His phone rang. That meant no one was currently on the line with him. The best news Tess had had all day. Except, of course, for the fact that Heather had still been alive.

What the hell.

She jabbed her gun into the back of his neck.

"Don't move or I'll blow your head off," she said.

As she anticipated, he immediately dropped his right shoulder, attempting to slam into her with his left as he grabbed for her weapon. She threw herself backwards out of his reach—if he'd added in a jump kick, she might have been too close. The cigarette tumbled into the underbrush and a few dry leaves ignited. She could see him.

And here was the point where she had to shoot because he opened his mouth to yell. The report of the discharge was going to change everything but so was one dead bad guy. Except that he clipped her with a knife-hand thrust; not badly enough to prevent her from firing, simply delaying her—

—when suddenly something plummeted from above them and crashed into his head. He grunted. His knees buckled and he collapsed into a kneeling position, then fell forward on his face. Another projectile slammed against his skull. It was a large rock.

Tess looked up before she stamped out the fire. Two faces beamed down at her.

Heather and Svetlana.

"Tess!" Heather hissed. "Tess, thank God you came!"

"Ssh," Tess said. "Quiet."

She put out the fire. In the darkness, someone scrabbled down the tree and stood beside her. Svetlana.

"Glad," she whispered. Then, "Heather hurt. Cannot climb down."

Tess said, "Sit tight." If Heather wouldn't be able to keep up with them, then remaining in the tree until they could safely get her out might be their best choice.

Svetlana pushed the inert man over on his back. She crouched over him and shined a cell phone light on his face. His sandy brown hair was closely shaved to his skull.

"Ilya. You must shoot," Svetlana said. "He wake up, he kill us. Never give up. Or I crush." She picked up the rock and held it above her head with both hands, preparing to bring it down on the man's face.

With a strangled cry, the man bolted upright. A split-second later, Heather dropped from the tree with the tiniest squeal and landed on top of him. Fists doubled, she battered his head and face with rapid punches while Svetlana hit him with the rock.

Svetlana clamped her hand over Heather's mouth and said, "Good, good." Heather was crying hysterically.

Together Svetlana and Tess eased Heather to her feet. Heather lurched to the right, favoring her right foot. Svetlana wrapped her arms around her and Heather sobbed against her chest.

"Shut up, shut up," Svetlana cooed, patting her. "Is good." She looked at Tess. "He is dead?"

Tess pushed the rock off his face. The moonlight concealed whatever damage Svetlana had done, which was probably for the best given Heather's emotional condition. Tess felt for a pulse. There was none. Tess remembered her first kill in the line of duty—mandatory therapy, nightmares for months— and got to her feet.

"He's still breathing." It was a lie, and she let Svetlana know that with a quick squeeze of the other woman's forearm.

"Oh, too bad," Svetlana replied, and the odd note in her voice told Tess that she had gotten the message.

"He's not going to be able to warn the others," Tess said in an undervoice. "He's out of the game. Does he have information on Anatoly?"

"*Da*, much," Svetlana said. "He is nephew Anatoly."

"Then we'll leave him here. Maybe he'll get lucky and pull through. Heather," Tess said gently, changing course, "you need to stop crying. Can you walk?"

Heather wiped her eyes with her free hand. Before she could answer, Svetlana crouched down and hoisted her over her shoulder like a big sack of laundry. She straightened.

"Let's go," she said.

"Put me down. I can walk," Heather protested.

"Can't. And I am strong Russian woman." Svetlana turned to Tess. "I want witness protection."

"Okay," Tess said, having no idea if she could make it happen, but needing Svetlana's help if they were to survive. "I'll do everything I can." Possibly her second lie in the last five minutes. "How many are out here? Are they trying to recapture you or...?"

"I think 'or.' There are five more," Svetlana said. "They go ahead. Ilya stay here. Wait. Like cat and mouse." Hatred dripped from every syllable. "Anatoly say he love me, then tell Ilya he boss."

"Office politics can be tough," Tess drawled. She moved in front of Svetlana. "I'll go first, since I'm armed."

"We had a gun but we lost it in the crash," Heather said.

"Was good gun," Svetlana murmured.

"No talking now," Tess ordered.

They moved out, Svetlana behind Tess, keeping as before to the shelter of the trees. They crept through the darkness for a few minutes, until the crash of running feet made Tess halt and Svetlana softly bumped into her. Neither spoke. Then Tess tapped Heather on the thigh and passed her gun up to her. Heather took it. Tess gave Heather a pat: *You can do this.*

Whatever "this" turned out to be.

A brilliant light flashed on, blinding Tess. She lifted her forearm to shield her eyes; as they adjusted, she counted three figures in front of her. One was holding a Maglite. As she recovered from staring into the white nimbus, she made out shapes and sizes: three large men. On either side of the corona, a mean, victorious face grinned at her.

The one on the left marched up to Svetlana and slapped her across the cheek. Svetlana staggered backward and Heather grunted in protest. The rightmost one patted Tess down, enjoying it way too much, and Tess thanked her lucky stars that she had given Heather her weapon—and hoped that Heather could either keep it concealed or pass it back to her before it was discovered.

The man who had slapped Svetlana spoke to the woman in a barrage of Russian. She answered back, then quickly said in English, "One other besides Ilya is missing."

The man raised his hand again but Tess jumped between Svetlana and him, and the thug holding the flashlight laughed.

"Brave American cop woman," he said, "don't worry about Svetlana. She'd turn on you in two seconds to save her life. Just keep watching." Of all four Russians they had thus far encountered, he spoke the best English. Tess wondered if he was Anatoly Vodanyov himself. But everything she had read about the crime lord said that he left others to do his dirty work.

He spoke to Svetlana in Russian, and Svetlana set Heather on her feet. The same man who had searched Tess patted down Svetlana, taking even more time. Tess watched Heather hop on one foot with her hands against her chest. She was concealing the gun. As the man finished with Svetlana and moved on to Heather, Tess caught the quick exchange of hands; Heather had just given Svetlana the weapon.

Tess's stomach clenched. Svetlana was armed and she knew Tess was not. This was her moment of truth. It could be that she would step back across the line and shoot her and Heather both to prove her loyalty. She might see it as her only way to survive.

I can try to take her, Tess thought, but that was too risky. *Maybe Heather and I together.*

Still too risky. She had to assume all three men were armed in addition to Svetlana, and that they had at least one unaccounted-for backup. Just because Svetlana had counted five didn't mean there were only five.

But a surprise attack of Tess's people might be their only hope; as Tess watched, the man on the left pulled a gun from his bomber jacket. The mood shifted. No more fun and games. Heather gasped and looked over at Tess, but in the fuzzy light, Tess knew she could never hope to communicate a plan to Cat's little sister.

Then Svetlana said in English, "If two only…"

Flashlight barked at her in Russian. And Tess knew Svetlana was still on her side, trying to orchestrate a way out of this.

Except, it wasn't "two only." It was three. Tess thought, *Could I distract them long enough to change the odds? Start running? At least one would go after me. Then if she was quick enough, Svetlana could shoot the other two. When I got my badge, I was fully prepared to die in the line of duty. But if I'm pregnant…*

I don't know that I am. And these two need me right here and right now.

She took a breath. An image of JT formed in her mind. And then one of Cat.

She got ready to run.

The man on the right side of Flashlight pulled a gun as well. Glock. Probably hollow-point bullets that would do a lot of damage. Cause a lot of pain.

Heather cried out, "Stop! We won't say anything! None of us! *Ever!*"

Here goes, Tess thought. She prayed Svetlana was on her game—and fast on the trigger.

But just as she bolted, Glock fell forward soundlessly onto his face. Then a gun went off. As Tess whirled around, a second shot was fired. The second blast, at least, had come from Svetlana's weapon.

Flashlight's gun went off, wide, before he tumbled backwards onto the ground.

And then Bomber Jacket collapsed. But Svetlana had not fired again.

Heather ran screaming toward Tess as Svetlana ran to the inert bodies and kicked their weapons away.

"Get down, get down, get down!" Tess shouted at Heather. Svetlana kept her gun aimed at their attackers, then swiveled it toward the black forest.

"Tess! Tess! It's me!" a voice shouted. It was JT.

"Don't shoot!" Tess yelled at Svetlana. "It's a friend."

Svetlana grabbed up the flashlight and aimed it instead of the gun.

JT Forbes strode out of the forest. He was wearing Tess's bullet-proof vest, and he was holding the tranq gun diagonally across his chest. He was the most badass biochem expert Tess had ever seen. He must have shot Glock and Bomber Jacket. Svetlana had taken out Flashlight.

Heather ran to JT and threw her arms around him. She kissed his cheek and cried, "Thank you, thank you, thank you!"

"Hey, Batman," he said proudly to Tess as he gave Heather a hug. "There's another one out there I tranq'ed. And someone else I think is dead. His face is, anyway."

Heather caught her breath but did not say anything. Svetlana patted her butt.

"Ow," Heather grunted.

"Thank you, Superman," Tess said. "Let's get these civilians the hell out of here."

CHAPTER THIRTY-ONE

Archer, the bedraggled Shih Tzu, trembled in Cat's arms as Cat, Vincent, and Bethany herded the three dogs up the steep stairway that led to the wheelhouse. The poor little creature's many satin bows hung in filthy disarray and she reeked of smoke. She was so traumatized that she made no effort to protest as Vincent took her from Cat and cuddled her against his chest.

In front of Cat, Bethany urged the two larger dogs upward with an air of determined if shaky control. From somewhere deep inside herself, the teen had found a well of strength and she was using it to stay focused. Cat was impressed. For all Bethany knew, her father was dead, and the raging storm prevented any hope of rescue. Cat remembered her own trauma at nineteen when her mother had been gunned down, and the havoc it had wreaked on her psyche. Bethany appeared to be made of stronger stuff—or maybe she had back-burnered all her emotions, as Cat had done for years afterwards. Cat pledged then and there that she and Vincent would stay in Bethany's life if she wanted and needed them.

Emergency lights flashed red and white, red and white, and Cat could hear their shoes ringing on the metal steps between bleats of the klaxon. She looked behind herself to check for flames or—God forbid—onrushing seawater. Bethany had explained that a series of watertight doors could be activated either electronically or manually to protect the bridge and thereby retain control of propulsion and navigation. She had learned how to close the hatches during her brief internship with Captain Kilman. If anything happened, Cat knew Vincent would push her, Bethany, and the dogs through the hatches first.

Weariness weighed her down. She'd been drugged, fought for her life, and run all over the ship. She forced herself not to spin what-if scenarios that would demoralize her or otherwise sap what energy she had left and instead concentrated on the progress they had made: The Daughertys and the pups had been rescued from the fire. With any luck, the chip was history.

At the top of the last flight, they stepped over a large metal lip at the bottom of the entryway—the last watertight door—and into a sort of white anteroom fitted with a wooden desk that had smashed against a wall and photographs of the ship in dark wood frames, many of which had crashed to the floor. There was broken glass everywhere. Vincent leaned forward and grabbed one end of a Hawaiian-motif rug. Glass glittered as he turned it over and experimentally walked over it.

"No glass to cut the dogs' feet," he told Bethany. Then he opened the wooden door to the bridge and everyone entered.

It looked like the set of a science fiction movie and much less Captain Nemo-esque than Cat had pictured it: screens, joysticks, and keyboards, and not a wooden wheel in sight. Heads raised from a bank of seats—four valiant crew who had stayed behind. Cat caught sight of the captain, who was slumped in a chair with his head drooping downward. The grimace he gave her was a mixture of pain and relief. His eyelids fluttered shut.

"Daddy," Bethany said to her father, who lay on the deck

on a stretcher, covered up to his chin with a blanket. "I'm sorry for everything. I'm sorry, I'm sorry."

Dr. Jones approached Vincent. Archer yipped and pressed her nose into Vincent's armpit. "Mr. Daugherty is stable, Dr. Keller, but we can't do anything else for him unless we go to sick bay." She smiled sourly. "And I don't think that's a good idea. Captain Kilman was on the stairs when the explosion happened. He took a very bad fall, is showing signs of concussion."

"The lifeboats are gone," Cat said. "I assume you know that."

"We have one more option," said a tall man in an officer's uniform as he came up beside the captain's chair. His nameplate read: MR. O'BRIEN. "There's an escape pod at the stern. It's held in place by explosive bolts, and there's an inflatable ramp to soften entry into the water. If we can reach it, there's more than enough room for everyone."

"Including the dogs," Bethany insisted.

O'Brien opened his mouth and Cat said over him, "Right. Including the dogs." For now, that was a possibility.

"That German shepherd will probably need to be muzzled," he said.

"Schmutzie saved my life," Bethany retorted. "I can give him commands and he'll obey me."

Cat gave the man a hard look—*Please don't argue*—and he got it. Nodding, he said, "We have the ship on autopilot now. Our computerized system is doing a better job of keeping her afloat than we could." He cleared his throat. "We have three unaccounted for: their bodyguard, Terence Milano, a passenger named Wes Connors, and our photographer, Cecilio Kamuki."

"Terry Milano is dead," Cat said. "And Connors is dead, too. I found his body in his stateroom. It had three bullet holes in the head. Then I caught Cecilio going through our suite…"

Vincent shot her a concerned look. She knew she had to keep it vague. "Because he was holding me at gunpoint, he thought he could brag about what he'd done. He and this passenger Connors were working together, and Cecilio admitted he had killed him with his own gun. He also said he murdered Terry Milano, for reasons undisclosed. Cecilio is the one who started the fire."

The crewmen all stared at her, stunned, no one more so than the captain.

The captain roused himself with obvious effort. "But *why*?"

"It was a heist gone wrong, sir," Cat replied. "He wanted to divert everyone to the lifeboat muster stations so he could steal something of great value out of a passenger cabin." Then she fudged the truth, big time. "I don't know why he was in our cabin. I don't know what he was looking for. He didn't tell me."

"Prob'ly after something of mine," Daugherty said, slurring his words. "I packed a few things for safekeeping an' brought 'em with me. No idea if they're still in my stateroom."

"We can't check," Cat cut in.

"Course not. I have my mos' val'able possession here any..." Daugherty trailed off.

"Daddy?" Bethany said shrilly. "Daddy? Vincent? Dr. Jones?"

Vincent handed Archer to Cat and together with the ship's doctor bent over Bethany's father.

"So he blew up my ship to steal something?" The captain was incredulous.

"He only meant to start a fire big enough to send us to our muster stations," Cat elaborated. "It got out of control." She stayed on subject. "So that means that everyone still aboard is accounted for, and we can all leave." She added an emphatic, "*Now.*"

"No," the captain rasped. "I *won't*."

O'Brien leaned over Captain Kilman. "Sir, please give the order for us to abandon ship. At this point there is no saving her."

The captain remained defiant. "Do as you wish, O'Brien, but I'm staying aboard my ship."

O'Brien shook his head. He looked at Dr. Jones. "I never thought I'd be asking you this question, ma'am," he said. He cleared his throat. "In your medical opinion, is the captain able to fulfill his duty as commanding officer in this crisis?"

"I'm *staying*," the captain repeated.

Dr. Jones rose and said, "Mr. O'Brien, as ship's physician, I certify that the captain is unfit to remain in command because of the extent of injuries suffered in the line of duty. As you are the executive officer and next in line in the chain of command, the *Sea Majesty* is yours."

"All hands abandon ship," Mr. O'Brien said.

The ship was listing even more to starboard as the ten humans and three dogs descended the same tight stairway they had come up. Two of the crew carried the stretcher bearing Mr. Daugherty between them. Acting Captain O'Brien and another crewman slung the captain's arms over their shoulders and helped him navigate the steps. He had fallen silent.

Vincent and Cat carried powerful lanterns that revealed a gaping hole in the sloping top deck. Inside the ship the room lights visible through the stacked rows of windows erratically flickered on and off. The driving cold rain that plastered Cat's hair to her head and her clothes to her skin did nothing to extinguish the flames leaping high into the black sky. The wind flattened the billowing dark smoke into a caustic, smothering blanket as she held onto Bethany, who was trying to maintain control of the dogs' leashes. Vincent, who had gone slightly ahead with O'Brien to scout out the best way to get to the stern, carried Archer under his arm like a bag of potato chips.

They hurried along the high side of the slanted deck, using the superstructure for one-handed support as heavy seas lifted and battered the wounded ship. It was a desperate and miserable trek. A blaze of floodlights above the stern deck illuminated the entrance hatch to the escape pod, which hung suspended, bow downward in a cradle of heavy pipe. The steel boat was painted bright orange. With angled slits for forward windows it looked like a Stealth Bomber without wings. As the ship rose and fell in the waves, the pod remained stationary, held fast to the railed ramp by a massive stern bracket.

O'Brien climbed onto the frame, un-dogged the hatch, and opened it. Getting Daugherty and the stretcher through the hatch was easier than convincing the two big dogs that they should follow, but the crewmen handled it with aplomb and precise application of muscle.

As Cat climbed onto the skeletal frame, she made the mistake of looking down. An angry sea summited and valleyed a hundred feet beneath her, and the ship's motion made her feel like a yo-yo. She had to close her eyes for an instant.

Then she felt Vincent's firm touch on her arm.

"Here, let me help you," he said, guiding her through the opening.

Inside, in the red glow of the boat's emergency lights, everything was perpendicular—the high-backed rows of seat all faced straight down. Forrest's stretcher had been strapped flat on the ribbed deck with his feet pointed towards the bow. The dogs had their own seats and seat harnesses—all except for Archer, who was still tucked under Vincent's arm.

Cat used her hands to pull herself into the nearest available seat, then braced with her legs so she could fasten the shoulder harness. By the time Vincent climbed in beside her, the blood had begun to rush to her head. That coupled with the yawing and pitching motion of the ship made her stomach rebel.

She focused her attention on O'Brien in the pilot's seat. He was unlocking something on the control panel. He swung back a hinged cover, exposing a fat button.

"Is everyone securely belted in?" he said over his shoulder.

The response was affirmative on all sides.

Though her head was spinning, Cat was elated. They were actually going to survive this nightmare.

"I'm going to blow the explosive bolts," O'Brien said. "There will be a long drop, then a hard impact. Our momentum should carry us away from the *Sea Majesty's* stern. When we are clear I'll start the engines and move well off. Brace yourselves. Firing in three, two, one…"

Cat waited. And waited. Nothing happened.

"Firing in three, two, one…"

Again she clenched every muscle, anticipating a roller coaster ride to end all.

Again, nothing happened.

"Is something wrong?" Vincent asked.

"We seem to have a problem," O'Brien said. "The explosive bolts did not fire. We've got plenty of battery power in the pod, certainly enough to detonate the charges, so it's probably a wiring or circuitry issue. Maybe the pod's umbilical has partially disconnected or been damaged. Or it could be something mechanical. No way to tell without checking the bracket and the winch. I'll go do that now…"

"No," Vincent said. "I'm closer to the hatch and you need to stay at the helm in case the pod accidently releases. You have to run the boat."

"Dr. Keller," O'Brien said, "it really should be a member of the crew…"

"Not debating this," Vincent said as he handed a squirming Archer to Cat. "If I can't fix it, you can send someone else."

"Be careful," Cat said. "Please..."

"Piece of cake, Catherine." He smiled.

Torrential rain pounded Vincent's face as he opened the rear hatch. It was coming down with such force it was hard to breathe. Groaning softly he pulled himself out of the pod and, gripping a steel handhold, swung the hatch shut and dogged it. He had to admit it was way more comfortable standing in the wind and rain on a heaving ship than hanging upside down inside one like a bat.

He climbed the cradle and stepped onto the stern deck.

At least there was plenty of light to work by. He located the pod's umbilical—a cluster of wires and cables sheathed in thick plastic and held together at intervals with zip-ties. The end of it was hidden by the winch's housing. It took him a minute or two to figure out how to remove the housing. He couldn't go beast and just rip it off. Not without jeopardizing his ultimate mission.

With the housing off, the winch hook, stern bracket, female end of the umbilical, and explosive bolts were all in plain view. The winch hook was not attached—the pod was being held in place solely by the massive bolts. There didn't seem to be any mechanical reason for the failure to detonate—nothing looked bent or broken. The wire connections to the tops of the explosive bolts appeared to be intact. But appearances could be deceiving.

Vincent glared at them, wiping the rain from his face. If there was an electrical short, a minute break in the wiring between the umbilical and the bolts, and he re-established the connection, he wasn't sure what the result would be.

Had the explosion already been triggered from inside the pod? Had the circuit already been opened? Would reconnection instantly make everything go boom? If that were the case, he'd have no time to reach the boat before it dropped from the cradle. No time as a human, anyway.

But if he could beast out just as the bolts blew he could blur-jump onto the rear of the pod and ride it down the ramp. He couldn't warn Catherine and O'Brien and the others what might happen next.

Vincent took hold of the plastic sheathed cable, standing as far back from the bolts as he could and bracing his feet for the leap. As he lowered his control and let himself start to transform he sensed something behind him. His right arm was already in motion. He couldn't stop it from giving the umbilical a sharp snap downward.

Three things happened almost simultaneously.

The bolts exploded with puffs of gray smoke.

Someone slammed into his back, driving him to a knee.

And the pod dropped from the cradle.

In full beast mode, Vincent gazed down the ramp. A lightning flash revealed a human figure clinging to the rear of the falling pod, legs flailing. Vincent threw back his head and snarled into the wind and rain. Around him, the *Sea Majesty* seemed to bellow in reply—wounded, abandoned, enraged at her fate.

If a great wave shall fall...

She saw him fall.

And then she didn't see him at all. For a second she couldn't breathe. The pod started to move away from the cruise ship.

"Wait, where are you going? What are you doing?" she cried. "He's in the water!"

"I'm so sorry, Mrs. Keller, but your husband could not have survived that drop," O'Brien said.

"You don't know my husband. Open the hatch!" Cat yelled. "We're not leaving without my husband!"

O'Brien hesitated, then nodded at the crewman closest to the hatch. The man unbuckled his restraints and pushed it open. Wind, rain, and water blasted into the pod.

Cat shouldered the crewman out of the way and scrambled out onto the short aft deck. A wave crashed over her and swept into the cabin. She was knocked off her feet but she grabbed onto the handhold and held fast.

"We can't keep it open much longer," O'Brien shouted. "We'll be swamped."

"Vincent!" she screamed into the storm. The crewman joined her, scanning the heaving black ocean with the pod searchlight.

"There," the crewman said, pointing.

Beneath the glare of the searchlight, a face-down body rode the cresting swell. The ocean began to carry the body away and she almost dived in after it. As her heartbeat chorused Bethany's shouts and the dogs' barks, the crewman reached out with a grappling hook and snagged it. Cat lent an assist and together they drew the body toward the pod.

Cat didn't know she'd been holding her breath until the crewman dragged a limp arm onto the platform and lifted the man from the water. She and the crewman flopped him onto his back, and she exhaled, hands flattening on the man's chest.

It was Cecilio. He was most certainly dead. And there was something in his jacket pocket. She pulled it out: the candy bag. And in it, the plastic box.

"Catherine," Vincent said, as his head broke the surface beside the pod and he extended his arm.

"Vincent!" she cried.

When she gave her husband her hand, the box dropped into the water. The pod searchlight glinted off it as it sank, and then it was lost to the ocean.

And Vincent was found.

CHAPTER THIRTY-TWO

Miguel Escalante lay in bed beside his wife Barbara, who was fondling the diamond bracelet he had given her earlier that evening, along with a dozen roses, an abject apology, and his vow never, ever to cheat on her again. She had forgiven him everything. Who wouldn't, for half a mil in stones?

The TV was blaring and the ladies on *The View* were jabbering away. Some two-bit singer named Fidela was describing her harrowing escape from death aboard the *Sea Majesty*. Miguel wanted to throw his glass of champagne at the plasma screen. Two good operatives dead. The mission a failure. No one in the whole wide world would have placed blame at Miguel's door—except for Anatoly Vodanyov. Anatoly had threatened reprisals. Miguel had told him to go to hell.

"That sounds just horrible," Barbara said, as Fidela talked about her descent into the lifeboat, followed by many terrifying hours on the stormy sea. "What if that had been us?"

The show cut to some footage labeled HEROES OF THE HOUR! Miguel had seen the clip before and it made him crazy. He narrowed his eyes as the recording showed the cop and her husband climbing out of a rescue chopper that had just landed in Hilo. The cop was carrying a little dog in her arms. No black jacket. A reporter had rushed forward with a mic in her hand. Miguel had memorized Detective Catherine Chandler's responses to the reporter's questions. The last one drove him the craziest:

"No, all our belongings were burned in the fire." Then Chandler turned and faced the screen and said directly to it, "We took nothing with us when we left the ship."

It was obvious she was sending a message: *We don't have it. Leave us alone.* He wondered exactly how much she knew.

She was kind of hot.

"Do you want to go to Mexico City for a while?" he asked Barbara. "Go shopping?"

At JT's place, Tess and JT held each other tightly. Both were nearly on the verge of tears.

"You can buy mouse ears for dogs. Who knew?" JT ground out as Tess's brother Jamie displayed the tiny monogrammed hat for them. Between the two iconic black circles sat a miniature silver plastic crown atop a trailing rectangle of white lace. On the back was embroidered *Princess Mochi* in delicate gold thread. There was a strap to hold it under the most delicate of chihuahua chins.

"Look, Mochi, this is for you," Jamie told Princess Mochi. He held the hat out toward her.

"Grrr, grrr, grrr," Mochi replied, jaws snapping, teeth flashing. She pawed at the air, struggling to get at it. JT sighed. It was time to hand her over to Jamie.

Before she peed on him and Tess.

"So she was no trouble," Jamie said, accepting PM from JT and holding her, also at arm's length. She flailed and growled. When he tried to place the hat on her round head, she yipped uncontrollably. JT gave it five minutes. Then she'd chew it up or throw up on it.

"No trouble at all," Tess said.

JT's eyes widened at the LOST DOG – REWARD flyer sitting on his desk and positioned his body between it and Jamie. All was well that ended well: Julia's theft of Mochi had alerted her mom to just how badly she wanted a dog. They had gone to their local rescue shelter and were now proud owners of not one, but two chihuahua mixes—little sisters the shelter had not wanted to separate. Julia had renamed them Kaylee and Zoe, after two characters on *Firefly*. Julia told Tess and JT they could come visit any time they wanted.

Tomorrow was Tess's day off. It was only a five-hour drive.

"Connie will call you about dinner," Jamie said. "We'll fill you in on the trip then. You can't even believe how many pictures we took."

"Wow, can't wait," Tess said, and JT knew she was sincere. The sooner they agreed to sit through three hundred shots of Mickey, Minnie, and the Vargas clan, the sooner they would be reunited—if only briefly—with their little cutie.

"Thanks again, sis." Jamie kissed her on the cheek and shook hands with JT. He managed to leash Mochi without losing a finger, and then they were out the door.

"It's so hard to let go," JT murmured, and a tear slid down Tess's cheek. "Hey, big day, though. Happy day." He kissed the tear away. "Go get 'em, Wonder Woman."

She smiled bravely. "Roger that."

One of the downsides of becoming precinct captain was a decrease in action and an increase in paperwork. Captains assigned cases and rotations, attended meetings, and gave press conferences.

Except for today.

Tess felt like the quarterback coming in off the field as she stood with the group of FBI and Homeland Security agents at the bottom of the jetway. An air marshal was leading Anatoly Vodanyov down the stairs at JFK. The mayor smiled at Tess. Even the never-cheerful Chief Ward managed to look pleased. Svetlana Barishnova had flipped on Tess's watch, and had already provided the people with so much damning evidence that Vodanyov could be put away for life on three continents.

"I know your name. I set colleagues after you," Vodanyov said as he passed Tess.

"Yeah, yeah, yeah," Tess said. "That's what they all say."

The press conference was heady and so was the standing ovation when she got back to the precinct house. One of the secretaries had run out and gotten a huge cake and there would be drinking at Rosie's after shift. It was a good day to be one of New York's finest.

But it became an even better day when she shut the door to her office, sat down to bask, and got a buzz on her intercom:

A certain "Robert" was on the line. No last name, just Robert. The caller had said that "Captain Vargas will know who I am, yo." She did a little seated tap dance on the floor with her nicely stretched out new black pumps. It was the street kid she had tried to give her card to.

She picked up and said, "May I help you?"

"You said you could," Robert shot back.

"It was so kind of you to meet with us," Mrs. Suresh told Heather in their suite at the Ritz-Carlton. Despite the ravages of grief, she and Mr. Suresh were both very attractive people. Heather could see where Ravi had gotten his good looks.

Her throat tightened. She didn't want to be here, drinking tea and lying.

"Yes, well now you know. He died trying to protect me," she said. "He died instantly. He didn't suffer."

They were so grateful to hear that. Since Ilya was dead and Svetlana was being granted immunity in return for her testimony, no one would ever hear a different story.

"Good children are a blessing. Oh, Ravi, my angel," Mrs. Suresh murmured, touching Heather's cheek. Then she and her husband rose. It was time for them to go to the airport, to escort their son's body home to India.

CHAPTER THIRTY-THREE

Had it really been only two weeks since they had nearly died aboard the *Sea Majesty*? It must be true, because Cat and Vincent had still not used up their vacation days. Forrest Daugherty had put them up in the presidential suite at the Four Seasons in Manhattan and he was arranging them a fall vacation with him and Bethany in Tuscany. His security people were about to bust his ex-wife's mobbed-up boyfriend and he was overjoyed.

Now they were home, sweet, sweet home, which had been professionally cleaned and redecorated—also courtesy of Mr. Daugherty. They had not quite come to terms with the fact that Ravi Suresh had been killed in their living room, but since they hadn't been there, or ever directly seen the aftermath, it was easier to keep it in the abstract. Heather had more issues, but nevertheless, she had insisted on meeting Vincent and Cat at the apartment when they returned from the Four Seasons just ten minutes before.

"It's really not very safe to walk up a fire escape with a blindfold on," Cat said as Heather tied a scarf over her eyes and placed Cat's right hand on the handrail. Heather took her other hand.

"Just the last few steps," Heather insisted, "so you can't see the surprise."

"We've had a lot of surprises lately," Vincent said. Also blindfolded, he was close behind Cat and Heather on the stairs. Tess was guiding him up.

Cat and Heather reached the roof; Cat heard her sister take a deep breath and let it slowly out. Was she thinking of Ravi Suresh?

Languid Hawaiian slack-key guitar music began to play through speakers and for a moment, Cat was back on the *Sea Majesty*. The violence of their last hours aboard washed over her like a tsunami. The long flight home, the reunion with her sister, Tess, and JT... so much had happened.

But we made it through. Together.

Then as her blindfold was removed, she laughed and clapped her hands in delight. The rooftop had been transformed into an island paradise. Half a dozen potted palms were strung with strings of lights shaped like surfboards and ukuleles. Six folding chairs and a large oval table were covered with Hawaiian fabrics in a rainbow of hues. A paper honeycomb pineapple sat in the center of the table surrounded by a rainbow of plastic cocktail glasses garnished with colored tiki picks. Six places were set with red plastic tableware, hula girl-themed paper party plates, and matching napkins.

"Aloha," Heather said, draping a fragrant lei of purple plumeria blossoms over Cat's head and kissing her on the cheek.

"Aloha," Tess said, placing a rope of knotted leaves around Vincent's neck, then hesitating a moment before brushing her lips against his cheek. She herself wore a crown of white ginger.

"Aloha," JT said from behind a portable bamboo bar. He was wearing a Hawaiian shirt, a straw hat, and a brown grass skirt over a pair of jeans. He pressed a button on Cat's kitchen blender and it whirred to life. "Mai tai? Blue Hawaiian? One of each?"

"What is all this?" Cat cried.

"You never got to see Hawaii, so we're bringing Hawaii to you," Heather said. She and Tess were wrapping cellophane grass skirts over their pants, Heather in purple, Tess in red. Also draped in a grass skirt—hers was pink—Svetlana trotted up the fire escape carrying a large platter of miniature egg rolls and sushi.

"Aloha," she said. It was clear she did not include herself among these old friends, but that she was making an effort to join in the celebration. "There is much food coming."

As Svetlana came onto the roof, Tess went back down the stairs. "I'm getting the teriyaki chicken and the pasta salad," she announced.

"We have coconut cream pie and chocolate-covered macadamia nuts for dessert," Heather added. Her face was shining, and Cat was seized with another sharp, hard fear, just as when she had heard the Hawaiian music. She had almost lost her sister. Heather had almost *died*. Bad things did happen to people she loved, and loved deeply. There was no safety in this world.

Standing at the bar as JT poured frothy drinks into two of the plastic glasses and garnished them with maraschino cherries, Vincent caught Cat's eye and held it. She could see strength in his firm jaw, courage in his steady gaze. And the love. So much love.

Calm began to seep into her anxiety. Warmth diminished the chill that had swept up her spine. Tonight he would lie down beside her and hold her. In the morning, he would be the first thing she saw. His body, the first thing she touched. And whatever that day brought, he would be there to take it on with her.

Every morning that she woke up beside Vincent, she would

re-learn the most important lesson there was: that love really did conquer all.

We are always, always better together.

Vincent carried the drinks to her and held one out. She took it and they tapped the rims together, then sipped. Vincent peered through his lashes at her; she slid her arms around him and rested her head on his chest. Rest. Here she could rest. She sighed contentedly and listened to his heartbeat, the most wonderful sound she had ever heard.

Below them, on the streets, a siren wailed and horns honked. The gritty city was grinding through another day. Men like Anatoly Vodanyov were wreaking havoc. And tomorrow she would wade back into it and do what she could to protect the innocent and make the world a little more just. But for now, she was *here*.

"Penny for your thoughts," he murmured.

"You are my paradise." She nestled her head under his chin.

"That's what I was thinking, too."

They swayed as one under the neon moon in a glittering sea of asphalt, Beauty and her Beast.

It amazed Svetlana that despite her many documented and confessed crimes, she was allowed so much freedom—and to have a cell phone. In Russia, she would be rotting in a prison by now. In Russia, there would be no hope of witness protection. She was too small of a fish to be treated well.

As she watched the Americans, she smiled faintly at their childlike happiness. She was especially glad for Heather, who had put this party together. What a little fighter she had turned out to be. Most impressive. Her talents could be put to such good use.

However...

She walked a ways away and pulled out her phone. Dialed a number.

The connection was made, but no one spoke. She knew who was on the other end, and that he was waiting for her to speak first.

"Mr. Q, I have bad news. Chip two-six-two-b has been lost," she said in Russian.

There was a pause. "You're certain." Also in Russian.

"Absolutely. It was destroyed on the ship."

A longer pause. Then: "Where there is one undetected copy made and smuggled out, there can be another. There is a new possibility. A woman named Anne Vanderberg could be approached. A colleague of Suresh's."

"*Da*, so I've heard," Svetlana said. "She seems malleable. But you would need a man for that, Mr. Q. And besides, I'm afraid that I'm retiring."

"Really."

"*Da*. But you know that you are safe with me. Always." She could provide no useful information about him, and frankly would not want to. He had always been very good to her. He had treated her with the respect Vodanyov had never given her. The pig.

"Indeed I do know that I am safe. And as my thanks, I will give you what you want most. Anatoly Vodanyov will not see another sunrise."

"Thank you, sir."

"Thank *you*, Svetlana, for your years of service. When you hang up, we shall be done. I shall miss you."

"And I you, sir." Although they had never met, and never would.

She hung up, and rejoined the party.

When Tess came out of Cat and Vincent's bathroom, her face was streaked with tears. JT, who had gone into the kitchen to get more Kahlúa, set down the chocolate-colored bottle. They were alone in the apartment, and when she spotted him, she wiped her face and dropped her hand to her side.

"Hey," she said. He had seen stiffer smiles—on corpses—and she sniffled, then turned her head.

"Tess, what's wrong?" He came over to her and put his hand on her shoulder.

The floodgates opened. Tess began to cry, great hiccupping sobs that pushed out of her and made her shoulders heave. His heart thundered as he led her to the sofa and sat her down. This was a party, the happy ending, but something was very, very wrong.

"Please tell me why you're crying," he said, taking her hands in his. "Whatever it is, we can handle it together."

"JT, it's just, for *weeks* I've been worried about something… that something… that I was…"

He wasn't following, but he gave her his full attention. Was she sick? Dying?

"And we were so bad at taking care of Princess Mochi. That made it worse. We couldn't even take care of a chihuahua. And we were fighting all the time. So how could we… if I was… it was a disaster waiting to happen."

"But we found Mochi," he said. "Everything's okay."

She sobbed. "I know. I know, which is why I finally did it. Just now. I-I took a pregnancy test."

"*What?*" He was thunderstruck. He'd had no idea. "And?"

"And I'm not." She leaned her head against his shoulder. "I'm not pregnant."

She kept crying, and to his amazement, JT felt like crying, too. Having a baby *them* would have been pretty wonderful. It would have been *amazing*.

"It's okay, Tess," he said, patting her. "We'll have another scare. Soon. I promise."

"Thanks." She lifted her head and smiled weakly at him. "You always know how to cheer me up."

He took the compliment and brightened a little. "In the meantime, we could get a dog."

"Not happening."

He sighed. "Didn't think so."

Dr. Vincent Keller moved in a slow circle with his wife in his arms. JT and Tess were feeding each other chocolate-covered macadamia nuts and laughing. Heather was trying to teach Svetlana the hula. And he was falling more deeply in love with Catherine second by miraculous second.

I was so alone. I was at sea. Until she came. Then she brought me back to life.

We have gone through so much to be together, but she put it all on the line first to be with me. When I said no, she stood in the light. When I gave up, she said "forever."

Wildfire…

Catherine has walked through fire for me. She's stared death in the face. She has saved my life, and my heart.

She is the other half of my soul.

My destiny is to love her, and not just in this life. For all eternity. I know that. It will take that long to give her everything I have to give her, to love her as she deserves to be loved.

Catherine raised her head from his chest. Her velvety eyes glistened. Her face was wreathed with a smile.

"We're always better together," she murmured.

And he replied, "Always."

From the moment we met, we knew our lives would never be the same.

Vincent and Catherine danced on.

They danced on.

For more fantastic fiction, author events, exclusive
excerpts, competitions, limited editions and more

VISIT OUR WEBSITE
titanbooks.com

LIKE US ON FACEBOOK
facebook.com/titanbooks

FOLLOW US ON TWITTER
@TitanBooks

EMAIL US
readerfeedback@titanemail.com

Nancy Holder is a multiple award-winning, *New York Times* bestselling author (the Wicked Series). Her two new young adult dark fantasy series are Crusade and Wolf Springs Chronicles. She has won five Bram Stoker Awards from the Horror Writers Association, as well as a Scribe Award for Best Novel (*Saving Grace: Tough Love.*) Nancy has sold over eighty novels and one hundred short stories, many of them based on such shows as *Highlander*, *Buffy the Vampire Slayer*, *Angel*, and others. She lives in San Diego with her daughter, Belle, two corgis, and three cats. You can visit Nancy online at www.nancyholder.com.